RETRIBUTION

RETRIBUTION

Guild Tales Book 1

CONNOR KIMBLEY

Printed in the United States of America
First Printing, 2023.

Cover Art by Rashed AlAkroka
Edited by Shaun Baines

Published by Slum Affair
www.SlumAffair.com

ISBN: 979-8-9875684-0-8

To Gracie, the greatest dog one could ever have.

For the twelve amazing years of memories,
all the joy and comfort you gave to me in my darkest days,
and for helping me grow into the person I am today.

From the bottom of my heart,
Thank you.

Age of Gods

0 — AOG — THE DIVINE BIRTH

The divine entities are born, upon where they spend the next few imperceivable millennia together in a hollow void, bereft of color or perishable life.

~3200 — AOG — THE BEGINNING

Having spent millenia togehter sharing already known knowledge, the divine entities craft their realms, creating mortal life to alleviate their immortal boredom.

~4100 — AOG — THE FORGES OF LIGHT

O'deus, the god of light, finishes crafting the divine realm of Lyth'wa. With his mighty hammer, he forges a realm full of demi-gods, creating perfection in all things, hand-crafting each resident to be without flaw.

~5200 — AOG — THE JEALOUSY OF DEATH

Zeichfer, the god of death, rules Sol'tel, the realm of all dead souls. While proud of what he has created, death harbors nothing but other dead, becoming envious of the ability to create that the other gods possess, living off the scraps of what they leave for him in the form of their decaying creations. In his rage, he wages war on the other divine entities.

Age of Strife

~0-2000 — AOS — THE REAPER'S GRIP

With great success, Zeichfer wages his war, destroying many of the other divine entities, scattering them and their collective energy to the void.
His greatest achievement during this time is the entrapment of Lei'Vania, the goddess of life. Trapped in a cage of the undead, she is prodded and taunted by the remnants of life that she created.

Age of Heroes

0 AOH — THE GIFT OF GODS

With the energy of gods scattered freely amidst the mortal realms, the gods' creations develop powers beyond their limits, later known to the realms as magic.

~200 AOH — THE GOD-BORNE

A human possessing incredible martial skill and magical powers leads an army against Zeichfer, wielding a powerful sword crafted by O'deus himself.

With army and blade in tow, this warrior faces off against the god of death, striking a lethal wound against him and forcing him to return to his own realm.

Lei'Vania freed, the goddess of life cleanses the undead invading the other divine realms, bestowing the life and power of their souls to this great warrior, extending his life until he is almost immortal himself.
This human becomes known as the Eternal King.

~350 AOH — THE REALMS REFORGED

O'deus reforges the many divine realms that were sacked and destroyed by Zeichfer into a singular world, to forever be known as Gaea, after Lei'Vania's original creation. The three realms are separated, keeping only the smallest connection between Gaea and Sol'tel, so that souls may still move onto the land beyond, but never allowing Zeichfer to invade again.

The Guilded Age

0-10,000 TGA — MAY HE REIGN ETERNAL

Zeichfer banished and Gaea left to the mortals, the Eternal King creates his kingdom on the continent of Udrela, conquering and ruling the land so that he may reign over and protect the mortal souls he cherishes.

My life may be my own, but for a silver or even gold,
I can take another's and trouble you shall no longer face.
So speak quickly, oh troubled one, oh pitiful one,
For my time is valuable and shall not be wasted,
And there are other deeds that may fill my purse.

- Opening excerpt from *The Guide to Understanding*
Adventurers, Mercenaries, and Scoundrels Alike
by Dolan Urias

"Though one may wonder at his Eternalness' decision to grant
special privileges to all guilds, honourable or not, one cannot
deny their effectiveness in the dispatching of nightmares and
inconveniences."

- Duke Sebastian Euphrain to Father Nathaniel,
two days before the Duke's murder

PROLOGUE

Black Hollow was on fire.

The dour fortress, its stone walls having repelled countless attacks over the centuries, was blanketed in smoke. Wooden supports crackled and burned, watch towers collapsing under their own weight, crashing into buildings and blocking roads. Fires spread rapidly, tendrils of orange and yellow licking out, lighting up the evening sky.

Guards gathered in the streets, shouting out orders, directing the chaos even as it ate away at the foundation of the fort-town. Civilians rushed past falling buildings, carrying their children and possessions in a mad dash for the western gate. Only two ran into the flames, their steps knocking up cinder and dust from their hurried chase.

Ragged, black robes swayed through the tumbling structures, the heavy trunk strapped to the mage's back vibrating against the faded cloth swaddling his wiry muscles. Fireballs shot from his fingertips as he ran, spreading the flames.

A hooded figure slid under a leaning beam before vaulting over a bonfire, half of a nearby roof used for kindling. The rogue's cloak, mottled shades of brown and gray, billowed against his leather cuirass, flashes of steel flickering from the shadows of his mantle as throwing knives darted out, biting into the squirming trunk's surface.

The impacts threw the already precarious weight of

the trunk out of balance, sending the black-robed mage into a stumbling run, the next flurry of fireballs flying off kilter. One flew up into the stars; the other whizzed behind him, exploding around the hooded man, throwing him from his feet.

Crashing into the side of a burning shack, the weakened boards crumbled against the hooded man's weight, the cavernous inside eating the unlucky assassin. The building collapsed around him, the rogue disappearing from sight.

The man in black kept running, laughing manically, his burden in tow.

Pain wracked Talon's body, lungs burning as he sucked in the smouldering air. His leather burned, the crackling debris laying atop him leaving streaks of black across the armour's natural brown. With no shortage of huffing and grunting, Talon pushed against the debris pinning his chest, shifting the precarious bundle with cramping fingers. Given no small effort, he slid out, kicking away the remaining boards that clung to his breeches, the thick hide catching splinters from the rough oak.

Bundling his cloak in one hand and covering his face, Talon crouched below the gathering smoke, creeping towards the front door, passing chairs and shelves that acted as nothing more than fuel for the growing inferno. The combination of heat and compounding weight warped the door's frame on one side, jamming the latch. Taking a moment to gather his strength, Talon leapt, kicking out. The door rattled and cracked under his boot, but stayed shut. A second kick shattered the wood around the latch and the door buckled, swinging out on its hinges.

The building shuddered, and Talon jumped out as it collapsed around him, its supports eaten away by the flames. Rolling as he hit the ground, Talon heard more than saw the debris that flew from the tumbling structure. Groaning, Talon pushed himself back to his feet, the aching in his limbs subsiding as he regained his senses. "Gah! Where'd that bastard go?"

As if in response to Talon's question, an explosion bloomed in the distance, a stone's throw from the eastern gate. Without wasting a heartbeat, he rushed off towards the loud eruption, his approach slowed by his keeping to the main roads. Safety first, he thought drily, another house collapsing in on itself nearby.

Fighting against the tide of fleeing citizens and shouting guards trying to turn him around, Talon found his progress hard-earned. The smokestack leading him seemed to stand still even as he finally broke through the crowds, making a mad dash up a set of stone steps bringing him closer to his goal.

Clanging metal caught Talon's attention as he neared the top of the staircase, the roaring sounds of combat pushing him to move faster and jump steps. Striding past the final step, Talon came up into a wide clearing, the dancing inferno bordering the path to the eastern gate, the gargantuan defense standing tall in the background.

Black Hollow's guards, each a distinguished knight befitting their titles, clashed against lithe figures dressed in blacks and purples, steel swords clashing against barbed daggers cast in iron.

Dancing along to the fire's flickering rhythm, the rogues punched their daggers past swords and armour, puncturing veins and dyeing the roads crimson. Men collapsed, gurgling blood as it filled their lungs, the men and women dressed in shadows cackling as they tore away at flesh and muscle. Even as they themselves were cut down, flashing steel cutting through ramshackle gear, their glee continued. The hooded assailants were there for the slaughter, not victory.

Skirting the carnage, Talon watched from his peripheral as bodies piled in the clearing, the chaos left by the wildfire leaving the men of Black Hollow unprepared for the concentrated invasion. Gritting his teeth, he forced himself not to rush, muscles tight and aching to let loose. The scuffing of leather on stone stopped Talon's creeping, backing away as a barbed dagger thrust through the air, passing where his head had been a moment prior.

A *tennim* – known to the layman as a dark elf – crouched low to the ground, his dark leathers warbling against the shadows. Hectic steps led them in a rough circle around Talon, razor-sharp teeth sneering beneath pitiless eyes, their yellow glow like candles in the abyss cast from their frayed hood. With animalistic speed, he charged, dagger lashing out with quick, shallow stabs.

Talon drew his own dagger, sliding the blade from his belt with barely a whisper, the dull steel flicking away the jagged iron. Thrown into the defensive, Talon backed away, deflecting each hurried blow before striking out with his own, desperately clinging to every meter of ground lost. Driven back towards the flames with each step, Talon lunged, tossing his dagger at the shadowed face.

Twisting their neck with preternatural speed, they dodged the blade before lunging themselves, stabbing at Talon's face.

Talon kicked out, slamming the toe of his boot into their shin, knocking his crazed attacker off balance. With both hands, Talon grabbed and twisted their wrist, throwing them over his shoulder as he spun around. Slamming them onto their back, Talon drew one of his throwing knives, punching it down like a nail through the elf's neck. Pinned to the ground, they scrabbled at the small knife embedded in their throat, their twisted face grinning as the colour faded from demented eyes. Talon smacked the knife down to the base, giving them no purchase as black blood drained from the wound.

Ripping his knife from the leathery neck, Talon took a step back, out of breath.

The dark elf's gray, ashy complexion stared back at him, skin covered in scars pulled taut against bruised, purple lips. Jet-black hair wrapped haphazardly around pointed ears, the whites of their eyes dark as night. Twisted supplicants of the dark goddess,

4

Domitras, created to parody the purer forms of other elves, the *tennim* lived off spreading pain and death. Where other elves survived by protecting and coexisting with nature, their malicious counterparts required no such connection.

"Disgusting," he growled. Having caught his breath, Talon made a renewed dash for the eastern gate, picking up his dagger on the way and sheathing it.

His prey was escaping, and he had wasted enough time.

The eastern gate creaked open, a dozen dark elves pushing it from within, letting a new wave of the twisted creatures flood into the ocean of flames. Snarling faces pushed past one another, some killing their own allies to get ahead, while others immolated themselves in the city-made pyres, sating their desire for blood and death in whatever form they deemed fitting.

Talon kept his distance, moving slow as he crept around the edge of the intruders' awareness. Finding cover in shadow was impossible, so he stayed crouched behind stalls, crates, and wagons, using the blinding light of the flames to keep himself hidden. He watched as the waves of dark elves climbing over the walls slowed, most now filing through the open gate for an easier kill. Any sign of Black Hollow's impenetrable defenses had been scorched away, its walls acting as nothing more than a slaughter pen.

This, however, wasn't Talon's problem.

Scanning the walls, the pock-marked stone giving plenty of handholds, Talon came to a decision. From beneath his cloak, he slipped out a pair of gauntlets. Crystalline, and blue as a clear sky, Talon slipped them over his leather gloves, tightening the buckled straps around his forearms. Their dagger-like claws shimmered against the dancing lights, blue sparks trickling from their cool surface. Talon's eyes tingled as he sent a wave of magical energy flowing through his body, the familiar warmth and power amplified by the gauntlets. Staring at the wall ahead, he ran for the edge of town.

In the sea of people, Talon had lost his prey. Higher ground was required, so he bounded past the few remaining buildings that still stood. A jubilant snarling echoed behind him, his new approach trading subtlety for speed, several elves peeling off from the group to chase him down.

Ahead, another elf appeared around a corner, intercepting Talon with curved shortswords and a forked tongue laced with venom. As Talon approached, the elf stepped forward, swinging both swords in a unified sweep.

Using his momentum, Talon slid under the pair of diagonal cuts, sweeping the elf's legs with his arms. Hearing the crack of bone as the sharp edges of his gauntlets slammed into the elf's shins, Talon kept his eyes forward as his newest assailant crashed to the ground behind him. Shooting back to his feet, Talon continued down the scorched roads, ignoring the frustrated hissing that followed his retreat.

As the mob chasing Talon grew, so did the distance between them, Talon's heart-pumping sprint gaining ground faster than the mob climbing over each other. Tearing each other down, those in the back hacking away at those in front, the dark elves slowed themselves down. Talon hit the wall bordering Black Hollow, never slowing as he ascended, the protruding claws of his gauntlets digging in where his fingers couldn't naturally fit.

Every second that ticked by pulled at Talon's frustrations, baring his teeth against the agonizingly slow climb. But he stayed focused, eventually cresting over the ramparts of Black Hollow's walls.

The wind whipped at his face, now free of the confines of city walls and tight alleyways, tearing Talon's hood from his scalp. Long strands of silver glided in the wind, cerulean eyes staring down at the dark forest stretching out below.

A short clearing was all that Talon could see, the shadowy

forest hiding all those within under an endless canopy of reddish leaves. A thousand different pairs of feet stamped the clearing flat, the tracks indistinguishable from one another. Sparse groups of elves straggled from the confines of the trees, but most had already made their way inside the bulwark, and whatever else prowled the night stayed hidden from Talon's gaze.

His prey had escaped.

Clenching his fists into tight balls, Talon yelled in frustration, cursing their name under the clear night sky, scouring his throat. By the time the elves scaled their way to the top, these echoes upon the whistling winds were all that remained of the lone hunter.

That night, Black Hollow was left to fend for itself, abandoned to fester in darkness.

CHAPTER 1

The rotting warehouse within Shadowfen's old walls resounded with the pounding echo of slapping flesh and cracking bones. With each hit Torden took, the more addled his head became, the dwarf's eyes going cross as he took another heavy blow to the cheek. The smell of alcohol and vomit filled his nose, stuck in the heavy beard braided to his face, the natural auburn blotched with shades of bile. His tunic and breeches were in a similar state, the once-white linen browned from age and dirt.

"Where's the money, you damned dirt mouth?" Torden's assailant pulled his fist back for another blow, stopping only as a heavy hand gripped his shoulder.

"That's enough for now, Ivor. Anymore and you'll kill the drunk." The man known as Ivor pulled away from Torden, replaced by the bullish face of their leader, Rasfin. "Hello again, Torden." The minotaur crouched low, his snout blowing hot air into the dwarf's muddled face. "How are you feeling, old pal?"

Cocking an eyebrow, Torden snorted, spitting a gob of blood and spattering Rasfin's snout. "Doin' jus fine, ole Rassy."

Rasfin stood, huffing and glaring. "So it's like that, I see." With a meaty fist, he struck Torden, knocking him to the ground.

The ropes keeping Torden secured to the wooden chair strained as the dwarf clattered to the ground, a hairline fracture cracking along the back post. Coughing up blood and phlegm, Torden looked up at Rasfin with a toothy grin. "What's wrong?

Was just keepin' yer nose all moist fer ya, is all."

Grunting, Rasfin turned on his hoof. "Ivor, watch the oaf for a while. When he sobers up again, we'll interrogate him properly. If he can't pay us back the rest of the silver, then I'm sure we can find some kind of use for his body."

Ivor nodded, his fists still stained red with Torden's blood. "Will do, boss."

Torden grimaced, pulling against the ropes, hearing the subtle creaking of wood splitting as the crack in the chair widened.

Gregory grunted as he lifted the metal crate, the weapons within rattling and scraping the container's inner walls. The cacophony bounced around the small storage room, echoing against the various crates, scroll and knick-knacks stacked atop one another. The raucous noise was dampened only by the scrolls lining the shelves, each sheaf of parchment neatly rolled and bound with knots of string. After slamming the crate down on the bottom shelf, Gregory stretched and yawned, pushing his thumbs into the base of his back.

So enveloped in his own exhaustion that he failed to hear the door whisper open, panning his eyes across the neatly ordered shelves that he spent his days organizing. Nodding to himself, satisfied with the morning's work, Gregory turned–

A knife held to his neck as a hand slammed him against the shelf, scrolls tumbling from their pyramidal stacks as crates shook and bounced against their neighbours. "Scream, and I kill you." The voice burned with malice, almost hissing, each word as sharp as the tips of the man's crystalline gauntlets.

Gregory froze, a bead of sweat tumbling down his temple. "What–"

The ambusher put the barest pressure against Gregory's neck, drawing a thin line of blood that ran down the length of his weapon. "You will speak only when I tell you to. Answer my question clearly, and you get to live. Lie to me, or tell me that you don't know what I want to know, and you die."

There was no question, not even a threat in the stranger's words. Only a warning. Gregory swallowed, nodding as he desperately clung to whatever composure he could muster.

The ambusher cocked his head, silver locks falling out of place. "Good. Now, where's *Rat Ears*?"

Gregory bit back a retort, gulping down his breath to calm his nerves. "They... you leave this room and take a left. Their room is five, or maybe six, doors down, I don't remember exactly."

The stranger held his ground, grinding the blade against Gregory's neck. "Is there anything else I should know? A secret knock? Password? Any traps?"

"What? No. No! Of course not. We're just–" Gregory's mouth filled with blood as the stranger slit his throat, a trail of crimson following the blade's arc. Toppling to his knees, body shivering, vision going blurry, Gregory covered his neck with his hands. Blood seeped between his fingers, running down his arms and staining his tunic red.

"Thanks for the information," Talon whispered as the man tumbled face first into his own blood. "And sorry. But I can't have you alerting anyone that I'm here." Bending down, he wiped his dagger clean on the thug's pants, the corpse's gurgling filling the small room.

Pushing his ear against the door, Talon listened for any change coming from the hall outside. The old building creaked and whined, the decrepit wood that made up the walls waterlogged and rotting from within, ceiling held aloft solely by the stone brickwork that continued to hold strong. The floor had been replaced as needed, the scurrying rats underneath all the reason to keep the boards strong and fresh. Old parchment mixed with the scent of oil and iron, the blood coagulating into the floor overpowering the storage room's more subtle smells.

Hearing nothing of note, Talon slipped out into the hall. The scent of blood followed him, dissipating as he latched the door behind him. The hall was clear, the doors lining its length staying undisturbed. If anyone were nearby, they didn't care to check out the small disturbance.

Strolling down the corridor, passing doors both old and new, Talon placed his hand atop the fifth. The plain, iron door stood stock still, the room within quiet save for a muffled scritching. Pushing the door open, he was assaulted by the stench of unwashed fur, urine, and the unmistakable tang of mold. Wax candles circled the room, filling it with light and smoke, the subtle effects a pleasant undertone to the more blatant filth pervading Talon's senses.

A sea of paper layered so thick that it covered the ground crinkled beneath skittering paws. Full sheets mixed in with scraps, each piece covered in varied script, sometimes tightly ordered, others mindless scribbles. In the center of this mess hunched a lone figure, tossing aside one sheet only to scoop up another. A rough snout, more scar tissue than flesh, sniffed the parchment, dragging mucus across its inked surface. Dirty nails held the sheaf with a delicacy belying the creature's rough appearance. With an annoyed chitter, it threw the paper over its shoulder, replacing it with the next round of random scrabbling.

Talon slammed the door behind him, the figure's large ears twitching. "You must be Rat Ears," Talon said.

"Mmmm, yesssss... Heard you. Kill what's-his-name down the hall. Bull will be angryyyyy." The ratman looked over his shoulder, beady eyes glazing over Talon. Its thin tail unfurled from its waist, whipping the floorboards. "You look for me. What you want? Am busy, yes yes."

Crossing his arms, Talon got to the point. "I'm looking for someone. Heard you have a particular talent for knowing things like that."

Chittering, Rat Ears went back to sniffing its pile of parchment. "Hmmmmm. Know many someone. Must be more... specifiiiiic."

"A mage, in black robes." Talon took a step forward, hands flexing. "Last seen carrying a large case on his back."

Laying his own burden down for a moment, Rat Ears sniffed the air, smoke filling his nostrils. Breathing through his nose, the smoke reappeared, tinted a deep purple. "Yesssss. Me knows, I do. Hear many things. Many ears. Rats listen. Rats speak. Came through fen of shadows he did."

Talon took another step, baring his teeth in anticipation. "Where did he go?"

Spinning around to face Talon, Rat Ears crawled close on all fours, claws digging into the pitted wood. Sniffing Talon, Rat Ears licked his snout, "Information never freeeeee. Offer met for knowledge gained."

Talon took a step back, hand trailing towards his dagger. "What do you want?"

Sniffing more, Rat Ears circled around, tongue flicking out. "Much I smell on youuuu. Mmmmm... gold, silver, steel... strange something. New smell." Rubbing his nose against Talon's gauntlets, the ratman hissed. "Magic. Oooooold."

"Don't lay your filthy paws on those!" Talon jerked his hand back, snarling, more feral than the ratling before him. "You want payment, fine. I've gold aplenty, so just take it."

Retreating a step, Rat Ears held his arms up in a placating gesture. "Want no gold. Want no magic too! Clean. Too cleannnnnn."

"What do you want then? And speak quickly, I'm losing what remains of my patience." Talon tensed, fingers brushing against his dagger's pommel.

"Liiiiife." Reaching up, Rat Ears brushed his claws against the strands of hair falling from Talon's hood. "Blood tainted. Power within the bloooood."

13

Brushing off the dirty paw, Talon tugged his hood tighter in around his face. "I hope you realize that's my hair, and not my blood."

"Blood tainted!" Rat Ears shrieked, scurrying around the floor before picking up a random piece of parchment and shoving it into his mouth. The paper crunched and crinkled in their mouth, tongue becoming black as the ink stained its tongue, pupils dilating. The ratman thrashed around, tail whipping across its own body before they spit the paper out, beating its hands against the floor. "Blood tainted! Fitting price!"

Grabbing his dagger, Talon was halfway to unsheathing it when Rat Ears stopped.

Becoming still as a statue and quiet as a whisper, Rat Ears stared at Talon. "Strands three for knowledge seeked. Terms are these, less none. Tainted is your blood, thus life another is needed."

Talon found his back pressed against the door, unaware that he had been retreating from the pest. Swallowing down the lump in his throat, he fought to regain his composure. "Why my hair? What use does that have to you?"

Rat Ears made no attempt to answer, staring, eyes still for the first time.

Growling, Talon ripped off his hood, waves of silver cascading over his shoulders. "Fine." Counting out three strands, Talon plucked them between thumb and finger, grunting against the quick snap of pain. "Now take them, and give me what I came for," Talon demanded, holding the hair before him.

Padding forward, Rat Ears held his hands out, eyes wide as the hairs dropped into his palms. "Yessss. Life. Blood tainted." Turning around, cradling the strands like they were his children, Rat Ears took cautious steps towards the other side of the room. An ornate box sat on a rickety table, the small container the only piece of furniture not covered in bite and claw marks. Its varnished surface played against the dull candlelight, rippling as Rat Ears swung its golden hinges open. Inside were a small collection of teeth both human and not, rotting ears and tongues, and knots of hair. Blonde, auburn, black, and now the shimmering strands of silver that Rat Ears dropped into the box. With a chittering laugh, he closed the box.

A tingling sensation ran across Talon's scalp, like boney fingers raking through his hair. Gritting his teeth through the strange sensation, Talon spoke to distract himself from the pounding dread creeping into his head. "Great, so you got what you wanted. Now it's time to give me what I want."

Looking over his shoulder, a haze disappeared from the ratman's eyes. "Yesssss, yes. Deal made, deals to be maaaade." Turning around, Rat Ears crouched down, snout snuffling through the ocean of scattered paper, tongue lashing out to lick the occasional sheaf.

Talon covered his nose, a sickly sweet scent of rot beginning to overpower the room, the candles spread around the room nearly spent.

Rat Ears licked another piece of parchment, scabbed-over tongue dragging against the rough surface. His limbs froze in place, head cocking to the side as he tentatively tasted it a few more times. Nodding to himself, he picked it up with care, scuttling over to Talon. "Information seeked, information founnnnd."

Talon took the parchment, batting off the fleas from its surface before scanning its contents. The letters were scribbled with too much ink, creating splotches in places that made the inconsistent and warped alphabet far more difficult to decipher. "I can't read this at all!" Talon growled, tossing the paper at Rat Ears. "Decipher your blasted handwriting! Or I swear by every god that can hear me that your disgusting life ends right here and now."

Scrambling, Rat Ears caught the thrown paper, scanning its contents with its eyes. "It sayssssss," he hissed, eyes wide and darting, "that the seeked passed through here – the fennnn of shadows – not three monthssss ago. Rats he crushed through the passingggggg. Hate him they do. North headed, he did."

"North? Is that the best you can give me? Do you have any idea what's north? The whole bloody rest of Udrela, you pest!" Talon drew his dagger, taking a step forward. "Are you even sure that it's him?"

Rat Ears hissed, jumping back, eyes never leaving the contents of his parchment. "Yessss. Black wear, casket on baaaack. Headed forrrr... the Marble cityyyy."

Cupping his chin, Talon sheathed his weapon. "Marble city? Do you mean Marbleton? You must, yes. It's large, plenty of places to hide, and with plenty of people... plenty of fuel." Nodding, Talon turned from the ratman. "Pray to whoever you wish that we never meet again, and say nothing of my being here." Talon thought briefly of slaying the putrid creature, but disposed of the notion as soon as it crossed his mind. He may have need of the vermin's skills in the future, after all.

It was only as he stepped from the room, and the door shut behind him, that Talon felt the burning eyes of a hundred rats leave him. He wiped his face with the back of his sleeve, sweat staining the gray wool. Clicking his tongue, he made his way back down the hall.

A rattling of wood preceded a sharp yelp from behind one of the dozen doors, the frame shaking as something slammed against the closed entryway. Talon drew his dagger as a few lighter impacts battered the door, crouching into a combat stance as it burst open, a roaring dwarf knocking a human down to the ground with his burly fists.

The two rolled around the hall, lungs working overtime as they beat and bruised one another. Using his stouter build, the dwarf overpowered the human and stayed on top, vomit-stained beard blocking the other man's vision. With a series of hooks to the human's skull, resounding *cracks* echoing down the hall, the dwarf knocked out his adversary cold. Standing proud, fists raised into the air, he shouted. "Yarghhh! You face da might o' Torden Ironfist! Don'cha ever forget dat." With one hand on his hip, the dwarf pointed dramatically down at the unconscious human.

Talon stared in bewilderment. His composure broken, he couldn't help but respond. "What in the name of Los are you doing?"

Torden snapped his head towards Talon, a moment of clarity crossing through his hazy eyes. His mouth opened to speak, but was interrupted by the synchronized clattering of doors swinging open, knobs slamming against the walls and leaving dents in the poor wood.

"Intruders!"

"The dwarf's escaping!"

Talon and Torden looked at the thugs filing out into the hall, then back at each other, a moment of understanding passing between them. Without a word, they ran, fleeing their would-be captors.

CHAPTER 2

"Where'd they go?" One thug growled, breath heavy from the recent chase.

"They couldn't have gone far. Search every room, we'll find them!" Another answered, breath far less laboured than the other. The first ran off, the other tapping his foot against the floor as he grumbled. "Dung-spittin' dwarf, makin' me run around like this, wastin' all our time. When I find him, I swear I'll–"

The thug's voice tapered off as they began their search elsewhere, Talon's ear pushed against the door failing to pick up anything but incoherent noises. Slowing down his breathing, Talon turned towards Torden and the array of equipment lining the small armory.

The dwarf was strapping on his rediscovered breastplate, grunting with each tug of leather and buckling of steel. "Whorin' bastards caught me while I was drinkin'. Nerve o' dem!" Lifting up his beard, Torden slid his gorget on, the neck armour dull and lackluster, spotted with rum and grease.

Flexing and unflexing his fingers, Talon watched in cold silence, glancing around the small storage room that Torden's gear had been stuffed away into. Compared to the other one, it was bare save for a few open boxes filled with a dozen-or-so weapons, most covered in rust or chipped along the edges. The only weapon of significance was a two-handed battleax leaning against the wall, the blade broad and squarish, intricate engravings all along the shaft and blade. Its owner was obvious, even before Torden strapped the rest of his armour on and grabbed the ax.

With his arms recovered, Torden grinned, slinging the ax over his back, the weapon's size cartoonish against the squatty man. "Righty den! Guess we best be on our way, eh?" He tapped his thumb against his chest, grinning up at Talon, every word slurred. "Name's Torden Ironfist, proud warrior o' da Ironfist clan."

"I gathered that," Talon said, "especially when you yelled it out for the whole district to hear." Pressing his ear back against the door, Talon nodded to himself as silence greeted him. "We need to go now, before they circle back around and find us."

"Before dat, lad. I would have a name o' one I'd be fightin' with." Torden rolled his shoulders, the armour plating scraping against itself.

"Talon."

"Course it is," Torden muttered.

The door swung open with a metallic screech, Talon cringing against the noise. The old building made enough noise to counter the lack of competent security. The boards squeaked as the two slid from the storage room, the door's ill-fitted latch scraping against its splintered frame, the jostling of Torden's armour echoing down the barren hall.

No one arrived to apprehend them, however, so the two continued moving. Talon led the way while Torden took rearguard, his armour making him a far more effective meat shield. Talon heard the skittering of rats beneath the floorboards, keeping pace with the two, slowing down as they came to a bend. Peering around the corner, Talon spotted a pair of humans pacing the corridor, throwing doors open and storming the rooms. He held up his hand, motioning for Torden to stop.

The two thugs were heading in the opposite direction, but moving far too slow. The longer they waited, the higher their chances of being discovered. Drawing his dagger, Talon turned towards Torden. "Stay here," he whispered. Taking a deep breath, he waited for the thugs to begin moving away before dashing out.

Talon cleared the space with barely a sound, the padded soles of his boots muffling his approach. The creaking of the old floorboards were the only warning the thugs got, screaming alarms as Talon jumped. The two turned at once, the closer one gasping as Talon's dagger slid into his neck. With his arms around his kill, Talon kicked the second human in the face with both feet, snapping their head back and pushing them away as Talon and the dead thug fell to the ground.

Old and in poor condition, the wooden boards cracked and collapsed from the weight of two full-grown men. Pain arced up Talon's back as his tailbone crashed through the floor, rats beneath fleeing from the sudden impact. Gritting his teeth, Talon drew one of his throwing knives from his belt, tossing it at the still-reeling hoodlum.

Given the poor angle and the suddenness of the throw, the small projectile missed its mark, scoring the man's cheek, more annoying than lethal.

"Gah! You bastard," the thug cried, wiping the crimson trail from their cheek with the back of their hand. Drawing his own dagger, iron and dull, he charged at Talon, holding the weapon with both hands as they screamed in rage.

Talon grappled with another throwing knife from his belt, the small hilt catching on his wool tunic. Cursing under his breath, Talon braced himself, pulling his feet in, ready to kick out.

The attacker loomed over him for but a moment before Torden arrived. Jumping over Talon, ax held high over his head, Torden swung. Bone crunched and split beneath the squarish blade's weight, toppling the thug as Torden's feet hit the ground. Pulling down on the decorated shaft, Torden jerked the thug to his knees, shouldering the bleeding corpse off his blade. "Hah! Did ya see me, lad? Like Aggoth 'imself." Looking down at Talon, Torden stuck his hand out.

Scowling at the proffered hand, Talon untangled himself from his own kill before grabbing the dwarf's arm. "Well, you're efficient, at least."

With a chorus of grunts and groans, Torden pulled Talon out of the hole. Once Talon was back on his feet, Torden slung his ax back into its holster, wiping his hands clean against his trousers. "A little fun ain't such a bad ting here and 'ere before an escape, aye lad?"

Talon regarded Torden with cold eyes, blood still dripping from the dwarf's ax. "I suppose not. Let's just get out of here before we're forced to have anymore *fun*." Pushing past the dwarf, Talon picked up his pace to where Torden had to jog to keep up.

Sunlight greeted them as Talon pushed aside the square board leaning against the building, uncovering the gaping hole he'd sawed earlier. Stepping into the street, he stretched out his limbs, the overhanging structures of Shadowfen creating a maze of alleyways blanketed in shadow.

Torden followed soon after, climbing over more than stepping through the hole, its bottom curve too high for his more diminutive stature. "Hah! Now 'ere's da nice dirt I like. Solid an' soft."

"Could smell less like dung and corpses," Talon grumbled, dusting himself off before turning away from Torden. "Well, good luck with whatever mess you're stuck in." Pacing down the alley, Talon sighed as the clanking of armour followed him. "Why?"

Torden grinned, his rattling jaunt leaving prints in the wet mud. "Only way out o' 'ere, lad. Little company won't hurt'cha anyhows."

Conceding his first point, Talon left the second unremarked upon. Together, the two wound their way around cramped passages, cutting through derelict buildings when they could. Every wall was scoured from age, wood and stone bare save for a few fleeting paint chips still clinging on. Empty interiors squeaked and groaned, cleared of everything valuable, cheap furniture tossed aside or smashed into pieces. Sometimes the pair would come across a stray squatter, always passed out from exhaustion or so inebriated they went unnoticed.

Eyes found them when they finally broke out into the main street, a straight path from the southern and northern gates. People milled about, stalking about for their next prey or handout, the former far more common than the latter. Breathing a sigh of relief, Talon turned once again from Torden.

"There they are!" Someone shouted, stirring the ghostly silence into movement.

Talon didn't bother looking over his shoulder, sprinting on instinct, Torden huffing and puffing behind him as the dwarf tried to keep up with his stubby legs. There was no ducking and weaving, no subterfuge or disappearing into the shadows. Nothing but a straight run, the adrenaline of the chase, and the beating rhythm of blood pumping through Talon's head.

Shouts erupted from all around, Talon pushing past the throngs of people who got in his path, Torden barreling through. Commands to stop followed by threats of death followed as they fled the thugs chasing after them. The northern gate waited for them, its doors long fallen from their hinges, leaving it an open passage.

Huffing and puffing, Talon and Torden passed under the gate, skidding to a stop as they left the shantytown's boundaries. "Gods be damned," Talon cursed.

Just beyond the gate, leaning against an ax a head longer than Talon was tall, waited a Minotaur. Bulging muscles covered in tufted fur flexed, calloused hands hefting up the massive ax with a lazy swing. "Now, now, Torden. You didn't really think you could just leave without payin' off your debts, now did you?" His voice rumbled from the depths of his throat, rough yet elegant.

"Rasfin," Torden hissed.

Talon looked down at the dwarf, "You know him?"

"Aye," Torden nodded, avoiding eye contact with Talon. "I might, eh... owe 'im some coin."

"'Some' is low balling it a bit, don'cha think?" Rasfin huffed, tapping the shaft of his ax against his shoulder, dozens of old scars stretching beneath brown tufts.

Talon eased his posture, the pounding of boots against dirt approaching from behind, their pursuers finally catching up. "A bit foolish to give coin out to a drunk like him."

Rasfin nodded, giving a knowing smile. "Yes, a foolish move indeed. That is, if we didn't collect collateral. The dwarf's ax is pretty valuable, and would easily make up for what he owes us. Even the interest wouldn't be an issue."

"Over me dead body!" Torden bared his ax, miniature compared to Rasfin's.

"And that's the problem," Rasfin snorted, glancing at his men over Talon's shoulder. "Honestly, you've got some good stuff on you too, human. Drop everything you got, and we'll let ya leave in one piece."

"Piss off," Talon said.

"So be it." Rasfin nodded towards his men.

The calm exploded into violence.

Rasfin and Torden charged, roaring their own war cries, one in proclamations of honour, the other incoherent bellows. Ax clashed with ax, Rasfin's superior size and reach giving him the immediate advantage.

Talon spun in the other direction, loosing two throwing knives as he drew his dagger. He processed the battle as his body moved, moving on instinct. Two humans, one orc, the latter taking charge. One of the humans fell to the ground as a knife impacted against his chest. The second knife struck the orc's shoulder, slowing the green-and-gray skinned brute for but a moment. The other human overtook the orc in the charge, his cleaver meeting Talon's dagger, iron screeching against steel.

The orc caught up a moment later, Talon kicking away the human to parry the new attack. His blade bit into the orc's cudgel, the wooden mace knocking the dagger from Talon's grasp. Twisting his body with the arc of the orc's swing, Talon responded with a flurry of blows, the sharpened edges of his gauntlets biting into their toughened hide, leaving the orc reeling.

Talon's attention split once more as the human thug flanked him.

Kicking backwards, Talon's boot met the thug's shin, throwing him off balance. Grabbing the throwing knife stuck in the orc's shoulder, Talon spun, slicing the thug's neck, tearing a gash in the orc's skin at the same time. The human dropped his cleaver, Talon catching it just in time to once again parry the orc's cudgel. With the full momentum of his spin, Talon's heavier weapon split the orc's weighty stick, pulling it free from his hand. From horizontal to overhead, Talon spun his wrist, launching the cleaver straight down into the orc's unprotected head.

Bone crunched beneath the blow, the orc falling to his knees as blood spilt from the crater in his skull. Talon let the cleaver go, imbedded too deep in the orc's head to pull free. Turning away from his kills, Talon grimaced.

Rasfin was still alive, and winning. Torden parried and blocked what he could, attacking when he saw an opportunity, but the minotaur's superior strength and reach made winning an impossibility for the dwarf. Talon considered for a moment retrieving his dagger and legging it, leaving the dwarf to his fate.

This notion, and the opportunity, passed. Rasfin launched his fist into Torden's face, sending him skidding through the dirt. Torden coughed up blood, struggling to roll onto his side, possibly suffering a concussion.

"Well, seems at least one of you knows how to fight," Rasfin said. His snout split into a smile, pulling at more scars along his face, his eyes too feral to make the expression pleasant. "No matter. I've got more men, and I've been itching for a good fight." He rolled his shoulders, stepping towards Talon.

"What are the chances this can end peacefully and neither of us has to die?" Talon crouched down, baring the clawed tips of his gauntlets.

Rasfin's laugh was a hearty one, disturbing nearby wildlife. Birds fled from their perches atop the city's walls, rabbits in the grass hopping away. "Very, very small."

"That's unfortunate," Talon said, muscles tensing.

"So it is." Rasfin charged, swinging his two-headed ax in a wide, horizontal sweep. His size belied his speed, powerful muscles carrying the massive weapon through its clean swing. He leveled the blade at Talon's throat, who made no attempt to dodge.

CHAPTER 3

Chunks of the minotaur's colossal ax flew in all directions, acrid smoke filling Rasfin's lungs, eyes watering. The shockwave knocked him back, stumbling hooves clomping over and crushing the few grass patches surviving along Shadowfen's edge. Several steel shards embedded themselves in his fur, too shallow to kill but deep enough to bleed.

Talon vibrated beneath the aqua currents that danced around his body. Crackling blue energy poured from his gauntlets and eyes in a river of electrical smoke, popping and sparking.

The rogue's ethereal eyes pierced through Rasfin, and the minotaur reared back, his thick tufts of fur standing on end.

"All of this over some coin." Talon's voice echoed alongside the crackling energy. Phasing in and out of Rasfin's sight, gliding just within his powerful reach, the human flickered, disappearing.

Rasfin gasped, staring at the razor-sharp gauntlet protruding from his chest, his heart stuttering against crystalline fingers as they squeezed the precious vitae from his muscular chest, matted hair splitting open in a brutal display of death.

"In all honesty, I didn't want to burn myself out on some marauding beast, but I suppose one must do what's necessary." Talon tore his hand back, ripping through Rasfin's heart.

Blood exploded from both ends of the hole in Rasfin's chest, the minotaur falling to his knees, gurgling and choking before falling face-first into the mud.

An acrid scent filled his nose, the embers of his magical exertion still clinging to the crystal gauntlets, boiling the ichor dripping from his hand. Trying and failing to shake his gauntlet dry, Talon grunted, resigning himself to wiping it clean against his trousers.

Striding over to the dwarf, Talon bent down, smacking Torden on the arm. "Hey, get up! If you're dead, then *I'm* taking your ax."

"Ya ain't takin' not from me yet, lad." Slowly, Torden rolled over, shaking off some of the dirt that now clung to his beard and smeared his helm.

"So, you're still kicking. Goodie."

"What happun, lad? I get 'im?" The dwarf sat up, dazed, climbing to unsteady feet.

Looking between the addled dwarf and the mangled remains of the minotaur, hearty snout down in a pool of its own blood, Talon shrugged. "Yeah, you got him alright."

Clumsily pawing at his ax, the dwarf successfully grasped the handle upon his third swipe. After slinging the hefty weapon across his back, Torden puffed out his chest, fists pressing against stout hips. "Hah! Now ya see me true worth. Dat o' the Ironfist clan!"

Still stumbling, the dwarf produced a leather flask from his belt, fumbling as he uncapped it, the smell of cheap alcohol rising into the air. Throwing his head back, Torden plugged the flask between his dry lips, draining it in one long draft.

Talon watched the small display with amusement. "It's not going to be a problem when you run out, is it?"

Pulling the flask from his lips, a contented sigh escaping into the air, Torden wiped his mouth with the side of his glove before waving the question off.

"That's not an answer, you know."

Slinging his flask back at his belt, Torden grinned up at Talon. "Lad, da only problem I'll 'ave is gettin' some more down me gullet."

Nodding, Talon scanned the bodies bleeding around them, most still alive but slowly dying. "Well, this is certainly a mess we've created."

"Aye, lad. Things can get a bit messy 'round 'ere. Just part o' da culture." Torden walked over to Rasfin, nudging the minotaur with his boot. "Dis is sure ta cause a ruckus somewhere."

"Yeah, well, that's not my problem," Talon said, walking away from Shadowfen and its poor walls. "Good luck dealing with whatever you got going on."

Torden pattered after him, a wide grin spread across his alcohol-stained face. "Where we goin', lad?"

Talon stopped, put on the deepest scowl he could muster, and turned towards the dwarf. "Excuse me?"

"Lad, someone like ya has got 'trouble' written all over ya. And since I ain't gonna be very welcomed 'round 'ere fer some time, I might as well get inta some trouble meself fer a bit." Torden continued grinning, pounding his chest. "'Sides, I'm sure ya could use a sturdy dwarf by yer side, eh?"

Crossing his arms, Talon huffed. "I don't have time to be babysitting a drunk. My business is important, and I can't have you slowing me down."

The dwarf burst out laughing, still pounding his armoured chest. "Not very good at tellin' someone off, are ya? Important business, ya say? Well, now I'm doubly interested. And don't worry 'bout any trouble from me. I'll be not but a 'vantage fer ya."

Running his fingers over heavy eyelids, Talon sighed, turning from the noisy drunk. "I get the feeling there's no talking you out of this, is there?"

Torden continued grinning, his eyes sparkling.

"Do whatever you want, but don't expect any kind of compensation. It's a personal matter." Done with the conversation, Talon walked off, taking a moment to enjoy the silence that came after.

"Personal 'ow?" Torden asked, his booming voice disturbing the moment's serenity. "Ya on a quest, s'that it? I know quite a bit 'bout dat, lemme tell ya. We dwarves, aye, we prove ourselves by goin' on such adventures. Why, Magnar Silver-Eye, one o' da great kings of Stenhjerte, went and fought a whole army o' da undead leadin' only thirteen warriors!" Torden threw his arms up for emphasis, ignoring the blank stare from Talon. "'Silver-Eye's Thirteen' dey were. Wit axes and hammers dey slashed and smashed da way through thousands – maybe tens o' thousands – of da bloody corpses. Now see, at da center was dis necra... necker... neck..."

"Necromancer," Talon filled in, still massaging his tired eyes.

"Aye, das it! Now see, da necramancer had dis big staff wit' a big silver orb on top. Dey used it ta control all da corpsemen, and Magnar knew dat to destroy it would end da battle. So, when Magnar fought 'em, one-on-one, he smashed it with a single swing of his ax. Shattered it into a hundred pieces. Now, not bein' one to shy from da spoils o' victory, Magnar took one of da rounder shards, and shoved it right inta his eye! Now, both o' his eyes were dere, and workin, but how could one not want one of silver? And from dat day on, he was known as ole Silver-Eye."

"Fascinating," Talon said, his monotone not even attempting to hide his apathy.

"Truly a great dwarf," Torden agreed nonetheless. "Eh... remind me, why was I tellin' dat story? Bah, don't matter. Lemme tell ya 'bout Rimcka Stonefist next. Not related to me Ironfist clan, mind ya, but a great Warmaiden none da less. Now, she had dis big bird, which is strange fer a dwarf already-"

Talon sighed, walking slightly faster. It was going to be a long day.

CHAPTER 4

Brimlux thrummed with life, the morning sun bathing the cobblestone roads and the collage of buildings creating a kaleidoscopic panorama for migrating birds to enjoy. Second in size only to Udrela's capital, Aeternia, Brimlux housed many coexisting groups. From the stalwart Order of Paladins, to the curious College of Magi, the city bustled with merchant caravans and travelers of all levels hoping to gain from the various services on offer.

Overlooking a particularly busy street, embroidered flags flapping in the light breeze, the Adventurers' Guild's hall stood as a monument to their organization's unfettered success. Filled with warriors in shining armour, rogues hidden under leather cowls, and mages draped in colourful robes decorated in runes both new and ancient, Brimlux's guildhall, like always, was bustling with adventurers.

Among the many warriors, a giant sat undisturbed. Two-meters tall, with a sword just as long, the blade smithed from black steel. A bright-red hood draped his head, the loose cloak held in place by a singular button. His dull, brown eyes peeked out over a chiseled nose, his powerful jaw leading up into strands of black hanging out at his sides. Rolt was well-known amongst the Guild as one of the strongest warriors in Brimlux.

Uncomfortable atop the small stool, the large man was in a constant state of shifting and readjusting, trying pointlessly to stretch out his tree-trunk legs. A sturdy mug of wood and iron wobbled in his beefy hand, ale sloshing dangerously close to the rim with each movement.

"You realize you're stressing the poor thing, right?"

Looking up, the large man smiled at the sight of his friend.

Scarlett: a name matching both her appearance and personality. From her bustier, leggings, and arm warmers, to the sash dangling from her hips, every item bled a different shade of red. Her voluminous hair caught the light in such a pure, sheening crimson that the strands resembled a small waterfall of blood. A soft, white blouse created a stark contrast to the sea of red, held tight under her laced, leather bustier. She was a beautiful wound amidst the browns and grays of more practical adventurers.

Scarlett tilted her head, directing the hulking man towards the guildhall's front door.

Pushing off the stool, several nearby patrons jumped at the sound of his cracking knees. Rolt's joints were finally able to stretch out. Downing his drink, the giant slammed the empty mug against the surface of the small table, rocking the weak furniture. The possible damage was a minor thought as he grabbed his massive sword, slinging it smoothly across his burly back.

Scarlett led Rolt out of the guildhall, sauntering out into the busy streets that crisscrossed through their massive hometown. "We're heading north," she declared.

Turning, waiting for her to continue, Rolt hoped for no more than that she had found them good work.

"I've caught his scent. Reports from an old contact in Shadowfen say they spotted someone who resembled Talon pass through about a week ago, heading north. Apparently he got himself into some trouble with a dwarf."

His arms crossing, Rolt slowly shook his head, an inaudible sigh escaping his lips.

Holding her hands up in a placating gesture, hushing Rolt's

wordless skepticism, Scarlett pushed on. "I know, I know. But this won't be like the last... six times. If we just head north, we'll eventually cross paths with him. It's a simple, fool-proof plan, probably. Now come on, I already packed our bags with rations and spare clothes... well, spare clothes for me. There wasn't really anything in your size, so I just bought a big, new cloak for you. Winter's hitting us soon, and you could certainly use one."

Rubbing his temples, Rolt trailed behind Scarlett, the redhead beckoning him to follow her, leading him to the stables, where well-crafted walls of oak guarded the three-dozen horses inside from the elements.

Scarlett's horse, Ruby, neighed as her master stepped under the slanted roof, scraping her hoof against the dirt.

Hopping the distance to her mare, Scarlett landed with her hands playfully thrown into the air, coming gently down to pat the horse's muzzle. "Hey there, girl. How's it going?" Ruby whinnied, shaking her crimson-dyed mane back and forth. "Glad to hear it. Ready to move out?" Another whinny was all she got, but it was all the go-ahead she needed to toss on Ruby's saddle.

Huffing at the noisy pair, Obsidian trotted towards the entrance. Rolt's black stallion was too large to comfortably fit within the stable's confines, once his rider was atop the saddle. Swinging the gate open to let the beast out, Rolt pat Obsidian's muzzle, eliciting another huff, though this one far more amicable than the prior.

"Catch, big guy!" Scarlett tossed Obsidian's saddle, the heavy leather plopping down at Rolt's feet. "Whoops... guess I need to work on my underhand."

Shrugging, Rolt picked up the saddle, dusting it off before nodding to Obsidian, whom decided when he would be saddled. Standing over Rolt, and even most other steeds, Obsidian was massive, needing the extra muscle for Rolt to sit comfortably astride.

With the horses ready to move, the strange-looking pair led them away from the stables, mounting them as the open streets neared. With only the slightest pressure, Ruby began trotting forward, Scarlett looking at Rolt from over her shoulder. "Come on, big guy. We've got a lot of ground to cover, and we're already way behind."

Three days into their hurried journey, their peace turned sour. Dark, angry clouds swirled overhead, blotting out the sun and threatening a violent downpour. Teasing wind lifted their cloaks with icy fingers, piercing both body and mind.

Scarlett lifted one hand towards the sky, catching fat drops of rain in the palm of her leather glove. "Well, this sucks. Probably should've packed for this, huh?" Musing quietly to herself, resting a hand gently atop her thigh, Scarlett glanced over her shoulder towards her companion. "As much as I love riding wet, we should probably find some shelter! There should be an inn further down the road, if I remember correctly."

Four hours later, as the sun was beginning to set beneath an orange skyline, they found said inn.

Old and rickety, with bloating, rotting walls, Scarlett found the only word she could to describe the establishment was *shabby*. She squinted up at the weather-beaten sign, twisting in the wind, the only identifying image some indecipherable scribble over what looked to be a crudely-drawn depiction of a goblin grasping a knife. Or a unicorn. Scarlett wasn't sure.

"Not the most flattering place, but we've stayed in worse," She mused, leading Ruby into the stables, squeezing the mare beside the dozen-or-so other horses already packed into the small structure.

Rolt led Obsidian into the warm stable, leaving him to his own devices, gifting Scarlett a baleful glare. The black stallion snorted at the other horses, forcing them to move away, allowing the beast more room in the cramped space.

The adventurers gave their horses a brisk brush-down before filling their troughs with the cheap grain provided by the innkeeper.

"I envy knights with their squires who do all of the menial tasks, leaving the big boys to just drink and kill."

Rolt glanced at Scarlett before letting Obsidian waltz into the stable. He walked away, towards the shelter of the inn.

"Hey, wait up!"

As expected, the inn was teeming with the usual suspects - traveling merchants, bards, mercenaries, and mysterious characters cutting shady deals in dark corners.

Scarlett nudged Rolt with her elbow. "Let's find ourselves a room."

Rolt nodded, trailing the redhead towards the counter, where a portly man stood wiping a mug with a dirty rag. Catching Rolt's eye, he scowled, jerking his head in the direction of two empty stools, seated at the end of the bar.

Well, he's a welcoming one, Scarlett thought. Reaching the bar, she plopped down on the stool, putting her elbows down on the counter, cradling her head in her palms. "Good evening."

The round man grunted, slamming the mug down in front of her. "You only here to hide from the rain, or do you actually want to order something?"

Biting back a sarcastic retort, Scarlett leaned forward. "I *was* hoping for a room, though I'll gladly take some wine, if you've got any."

"We've got ale and brandy."

Scarlett gave a playful smile. "No water?"

With a snort, the barkeep pointed towards the door. "Plenty outside."

Just barely holding her smile up, Scarlett pushed on. "And the room?"

The innkeeper shrugged, waggling a thumb towards the gathering of warriors near the hearth. "All taken by the boys in blue over there. You want a room, you talk to them."

Scarlett's grin fell, twisting into a dour scowl. She had spent her younger years evading the law, missing the finer points of a young lady's formative years. Nevertheless, she could charm the scales off a dragon if she had to. Taking a deep breath, Scarlett pushed herself from the bar, strutting over to the 'boys in blue.'

Gold-trimmed surcoats of blue and polished chainmail reflected the hearth's light, golden doves circling atop the warriors' chests. Almost half of them had scarves or patches of pure red as part of their uniform, though for what reason, Scarlett couldn't identify.

The captain was easy enough to spot amidst the more undisciplined soldiers. Beneath his shorn, salt-and-pepper hair, black eyes drilled into Scarlett as she approached. His hawkish features reinforced the impression that she was no more than a mere mouse, caught in the sights of a deadly bird of prey.

She hesitated for a moment, just managing to smooth out her nerves as she came up to the table.

Most of the soldiers did little more than glance up before returning to their meals.

"Can I help you, miss?" The captain's voice was deep, though not unpleasant, flowing like rushing water against sharpened stone.

Mustering her most gracious smile, Scarlett bent forward, hands clasping playfully behind her. "Hello there, fine Sirs. Me and my friend over there were trying to acquire a room for the night, only to be informed that you'd rented them all already."

The captain nodded slowly, chewing his stale, buttered biscuit, waiting.

"And... I was just wondering, if you could possibly spare some space for us?"

One of the soldiers, sitting at the edge of the group, snorted. "Yeah, I could probably find some space for you, red. If you don't mind sharin' a bed together, that is." A few of the other soldiers cackled, all of those wearing blots of crimson, but their leader sat stern.

"Private." The captain's weight shifted. The old soldier's movement was slight, the table's mood tense.

"Whaddya-" The private yelped as the captain slammed the pommel of his dagger against his hand, fork dropping from his gasping lips. The other soldiers gaped, frozen before their captain's violent reaction.

Picking up his own fork, the captain straightened his shoulders, pointing the utensil at his bruised subordinate. "You dishonor not only yourself with your actions, but me and the rest of your squad as well. Remember that." He turned back to Scarlett, his eyes betraying nothing. "Unfortunately, as much as I would like to secure lodgings for you two, I think it'd be best if you kept your distance from this rabble."

Scarlett's smile slipped, but she kept the sullen pout off her face until she and Rolt reached the bar. Her friend slid a silver coin to the bartender, pointing at an empty mug.

As Rolt chugged his ale, the bartender turned his attention back to Scarlett. "Your friend don't talk much, does he?" The innkeeper pocketed the silver coin, watching with amusement as the large warrior drained his cup.

"Not a word." Scarlett drawled, her mood now a sour one. "So, about our accommodations for the night..."

"As I said, lady, rooms are all taken up."

"Yeah, I heard you the first time."

"Well, unless you want to lay with the horses, you're out of luck."

Scarlett sighed, shifting uncomfortably in her seat. "How much?"

Glancing over at the redhead, seeming to genuinely consider the price, the innkeeper rubbed thumb and index finger together. "Five silver pieces."

Feigning disgust, Scarlett propped herself up, knowing full-well he would high-ball it. "I'll give you two, and even that's being generous given how shabby your stables are."

The innkeeper glanced over at Rolt, who was quietly staring him down. Shrugging, ignoring the sweat that trickled down his back, the portly keeper relented. "Fair enough. Two silver."

With a satisfied nod, Scarlett handed over the money, ordering food for herself and Rolt. Given all that was being served were biscuits with honey, and meat stew, their options were limited, but they took what they could get. They filled their stomachs and retired for the night.

She awoke halfway through the night, nose wrinkling against the smell of horse dung and urine. Scarlett's wool blanket proved poor protection against the nauseating odours encasing the moulding stables. Looking over at Rolt, sleeping peacefully against Obsidian, Scarlett squirmed against Ruby, finding the poor quality of the stables' ceiling to be even worse than the overbearing smell.

Even tucked away into the back, near the piles of hay, rain dripped between old boards, soaking into Scarlett's blanket. Shuddering against the cutting wind, her teeth chattering, she nuzzled further into Ruby's coat. Tossing and turning, a miserable half-hour passed before the weight of her eyes overcame discomfort, and she back fell into a light slumber.

By morning the rain stopped, and at first light, Rolt rolled away from Obsidian and woke Scarlett, lightly shaking her shoulder.

She stirred almost immediately, welcomed by the familiar look of Rolt's thin smile. "Mornin', I guess," She mumbled, clumsily throwing her damp blanket from her aching body, and clambering to her feet. Stretching out, she noticed that the soldiers' horses were gone, allowing the adventurers space to walk about. "Well, at least the troop of arseholes is well on their way ahead of us. Hopefully we won't see them again."

Rolt shrugged the comment away, heading inside for his breakfast, Scarlett trailing just behind.

Absentmindedly stirring her meat stew, Scarlett found her attention focused solely on a motley-dressed bard, strumming through her well-practiced list of tales. Their next ballad started slow, progressing into a jaunty, energetic tune. She strummed her lute with light fingers, a soprano voice sing talking the lyrics.

> *O, listen well, who all sail west*
> *For the storm to come shall be one not bested*
> *With a crew two-hundred strong and a blade that bites deep*
> *Through the mists and the dead, Bloodbeard brings all to dread*

Scarlett's lips pulled up slightly, her thin smile parting as she ate a spoonful of stew.

> *With a sword of steel and a hand that steals*
> *Unabated by age or guilt, he took from all that had been gilt*
> *Silver or gold or even life, it mattered not to one free of strife*
> *His coffers never full, always starving for more*

Scarlett's foot tapped against the floorboards, following the song's rhythm.

Rolt glanced over, eating more quietly.

> *His eyes wandered free, from drink to trinket*
> *Until one day he spotted one worth more than tonnage*
> *A fair lady, hair like roses, brighter than Solis, our dearest sun*

And a face full of soul, too hard to bear without

Scarlett played with her hair, circling a finger through the thick strands, red as a rose.

But alas, she was hid behind walls
Too full of life and a willful fire
Once their eyes did exchange, and a connection was made
And from that day on, his course was then set

So it was decided, by ole Bloodbeard himself
That he would have what he wanted most
Under the night he did sail, only his lone self to carry the winds
His prize cast over castle walls, no climb too high for a treasure so fine

But alas, he was caught, trapped betwixt steel and ocean
Bested but not beaten, Redbeard planned his escape posthaste
Showing his tongue to be one of silver, he did meet his treasure
The woman of gold freed him heartily, and together they fled

For ten more years, did Bloodbeard sail before his end
His greatest treasure captured and never sold
His second greatest following to his grave, sunk into the deep blue
A legacy of murder and theft ending in flames upon the sea

The music died down, falling from its crescendo into a serene quiescent. Without a bow or a single clap from her audience, the bard set her lute aside, letting the room sit in its silence.

Scarlett stood from her seat, thumbing a handful of coppers, clinking together as she dropped the coins into the bard's bag. The two women shared a nod, and Scarlett strut back to Rolt, the giant of a man sipping up the last of his stew. "It's time we got back out there, don't you think? Talon's not going to wait around for us to catch him."

Rolt nodded, pushing himself up from the squealing stool.

With bellies full, and their clothes properly dried by the fireplace, the adventurers headed out. Taking their horses back onto the mud-slick road, the sun's rays reflecting off wet leaves, water dripping into puddles risen overnight, they moved on.

Their first day on the road having ended well enough, they rode without reservations, riders urging horses on.

CHAPTER 5

Selora, blood rushing to her head, foot aching from the rope snare, groaned. Barely out of her clan's territory, and she had already walked straight into a trap. The trees, old enough to remember her as a seedling, laughed at her misfortune. It was well deserved, she supposed. Temples pounding, she stared at her captors through hazy eyes, vision doubling.

One goblin fumbled around with the elf's bow. One picked at the arrows scattered around the dirt road. Two were fighting over her bag, its contents spilling out as they tugged, punched and kicked each other. Another cackled, poking at the rope keeping her dangling under the creaking branch.

"Don't touch!" A sixth goblin, this one taller than the others – a hobgoblin, Selora noted – shrieked at the poker. "Will cut down when it's time to eat." The hobgoblin snorted, tapping its studded club against the side of its horse, the animal whinnying against the light beating. "Shut it! Stupid animal. Will eat you too if you don't quiet down." The horse whinnied again but settled down after.

A conniving bunch, the elf thought, but stupid too. "Hey," Selora said.

"You shut it too!" The hobgoblin barked, baring its teeth and waggling its club. "Food don't speak. Food be eaten. Taste best that way."

"I'm not food," she stated matter-of-factly.

The goblins laughed, the raucous noise increasing the

pounding in Selora's head.

"Of course food!" Their leader declared. "Humies food. Dwarvies food. Elvies food too!"

"But look at me. Do I look like anything but skin and bones? No meat to be found here, and my flesh tastes especially bad too." Selora gestured towards herself, patting her flat stomach while trying to keep their eyes from her legs, well-defined muscles straining against her dangling weight.

"Bones good," the goblin with her bow slung on its back declared, bouncing and clapping. "Good for teef and tongue."

"Teef and tongue! Teef and tongue! Teef and tongue!" The other goblins started bouncing and clapping, their scratchy voices mixing and echoing through the forest's dense trees.

"Quiet!" The hobgoblin beat its club into its horse, voice shrill and sharp against the animal's whimpers. "See, elfie? Good for teef and tongue. Even if no meat, bones good. Even bad flesh good when cooked. We find meat later, if we want."

"Like them?" Selora pointed past the hobgoblin, unsure if her own eyes were deceiving her or not.

The goblins turned as one, staring at the human and dwarf standing apart from their noisy gathering. "Who you?" The hobgoblin demanded.

Without hesitation, the dwarf beat his fist against his chest, shouting proudly. "I am Torden Ironfist, proud warrior of da Ironfist clan!"

The human simply sighed, pressing his palms against dark-ringed eyes. "I do not need this right now," Selora heard him mutter.

"Hey," she called. "A little help here?"

"Oi! Wha'cha doin' up there, lass?" The dwarf shaded his eyes with his hand, squinting at the paling elf.

"Not exactly up here by choice," Selora called back, waving one arm at the rope and the other at the goblins.

"Silence!" the hobgoblin commanded. "Humie! Dwarf! What

you doin' here? Dis *my* territory." Smacking its chest, the hobgoblin huffed.

The human rolled his eyes, sighing. "And who are *you*?"

"Chük! The mighty Chük. This forest mine. This horse mine. The elf mine. And now *you* are mine too!" Chük, drooling and bug-eyed, waved his club over his head.

"Well, *Chük*, we're passing through your forest," the human said drily. "You know, so we can get to the other end? Now step aside."

"Perhaps we should get da lass down while we're at it?" The dwarf motioned vaguely at Selora, hand making circles in the air.

Raising his head, the human's eyes met with Selora's. Both bright and blue, his crackling with magic, hers shimmering like a clear sky. "What say you, girl?"

Her nose wrinkled at the condescension, but she couldn't really afford to skip over the help. "Would be much appreciated. Name's Selora, by the way."

"Haha!" The dwarf beat his fist against his chest again. "Well, nice ta meet'cha, lass. I'm Torden Ironfist! And dis 'ere is, eh, Talon."

"Strong names," she said, grinning.

"SILENCE!" Chük thrashed about his horse, sending the animal into a wild fit. "Elf is mine! No take! Only I take! ATTACK!" He shrieked, every word punctuated by a guttural rumbling, and the goblins charged, screaming as one.

Talon wiped his dagger with a strip of linen, tar-like blood slicking off in clumps. Tossing the cloth aside, letting it drift over Chük's grinning cadaver, the adventurer sheathed his blade. Crossing his arms, he watched as Torden patted Selora's back, the elf curled up on the ground, controlling her breathing. Letting the blood ease out from her head, he guessed.

"Ya doin' right yet, lass?" Torden asked, leaning over to get a better look at Selora's face.

"I..." She lifted her head incrementally, eyes shut tight. "Yeah, yeah, I'll be fine. Thanks for the help."

"Wasn't given much of a choice," Talon said, nodding to Chük, the hobgoblin's corpse already buzzing with flies. "What are you doing out here anyway? It's rare to find an elf separated from the rest of their clan, especially so deep into the forest."

"I was, uh..." Selora bit her lip, brow furrowing. "Scouting."

Talon raised an eyebrow, "Alone?"

"Alone," she agreed. "We're, eh, short-handed at the moment."

Talon went for another retort but shut his mouth as the elf jumped to her feet.

"Listen," she started. "Don't worry about me. What are *you* two doing out here?"

Torden beat his fist against his chest, gaining their attention. "We's just passin', lass. Promise. Ain't got no interest in yer forest or clan or whatever else ya might got tucked away out 'ere."

"Besides," Talon jumped in, motioning down at the dirt path. "We're sticking to the road, where your kind usually don't bother visitors. Which begs the question of why you're... scouting. So close to the road. Far beyond where your clan's perimeter should be."

Selora tilted her head, sweat dripping from her temples. "Well," she talked slow, dragging out each word. "I wasn't sent out to scout our area, per se, but the... outer lands. Human lands, I suppose."

Talon and Torden shared a look, the rogue scowling. "That doesn't bode well, regardless of circumstances."

"Aye," Torden nodded. "Lass, are yer people-"

"They're fine!" Selora blurted out. "We're fine. No problems. The elders, they just... they just want to know what the situation outside is, that's all. Completely normal reasons, I assure you." With eyes now drilling into her, the elf cleared her throat, looking away sheepishly. "Again, thanks for the help. I'm a little... out of my depth at the moment."

Talon grunted, muttering: "A little?"

"Aye, no worries, lass." Torden patted the elf's back, forcing her to take a step to keep her balance. "Just watch out fer more traps an' you'll be fine. An' look at dis beaut!" Toddling over to the horse, Torden spread his arms up and out. "Not a fan o' ridin' meself, but I bet dis lad... er, lass? Bah, who knows? Anyway, I bet dis one could fetch a pretty gold or two, eh?"

Talon stepped closer, scanning the horse. It was compact; short but heavily muscled, though its ribs were showing more than they should have been. Its tangled coat was spotted white and brown, dirt mixed into its coat. A jennet, maybe? It was certainly a calm enough temperament for that, considering its recent treatment. He shrugged the thought away. "Maybe, but this one clearly hasn't been fed well in recent days, and..." He crouched down, scowling. "And *she* is clearly not a work horse. Maybe light cavalry, or a messenger. Whoever their original rider was, they're probably long dead." He glanced over at the hobgoblin, arm twisted into an unnatural position. "Probably a messenger."

"Hah! A ridin' 'orse. Betcha wanna be on da road real soon again, aye lass?" Torden grinned wide, slapping the horse's rear.

She brayed, the supposed jennet rearing its front legs before bolting off, down the road back towards Shadowfen.

"Ah..." Torden's hand hovered at shoulder level, reminiscent of a regretful wave.

"Well, now *that* is unfortunate," Talon remarked drily, cupping his chin. "Don't suppose you want to chase it down? Get your gold or two somewhere down the road?"

Shoulders dropping, Torden let his hand fall to his side. "Nay. Lass is long gone."

Talon nodded, watching as the fleeing horse disappeared over the horizon. Without another word, he turned, starting back down the road.

"Hey, wait!" Selora shouted after the human, pulling his

47

attention back to her. "Um-" Her face became flushed, fingers fidgeting into knots as she bit her lip. "So, I don't really know much about the outside world, and since I'm... supposed to be learning about it, maybe I could... come with you?" She quickly flung her hands up, waving away Talon's deepening glare. "I won't cause any problems, I swear! And I- I'm quite good with a bow, I can track people and animals, and even have some skill whittling if... you... need that."

Talon considered her words, eyes drifting over to Torden, the dwarf still waving off to the horizon. Looking back at Selora, he grimaced, then sighed. "Do whatever you want. That one over there sure does." He waved off at Torden.

Selora perked up, her long ears twitching, a beaming smile overtaking her anxious fidgeting. "Ah, thank you! I promise, I won't cause *any* problems."

"You already said that." Talon turned his back to her, brow furrowing at her choice of words, and walked away.

Captain Evrich, leading his newest recruits back home from their first training excursion, twisted the dead hobgoblin's head around, examining the gash in its throat. It was hard to tell through the rotting skin and the maggots overflowing from the wound, but it looked to him like a blow from a dagger. "Why?" He wondered aloud. Looking up, he squinted down the road, taking in the smaller goblins, most of whom were in pieces. Heavy ax blows, from what he could tell. "Why are you different?"

The hobgoblin did not respond, its glassy eyes shifting and bulging from the bugs crawling behind them.

Standing up, he wiped his glove against his pants, thinking back to the redhead they'd met back at the inn. She'd had a pair of daggers capable of this, but she'd still been asleep in the stables when his party had left. Another adventurer then? An assassin? Or mercenaries? He shook the thoughts from his head, turning to his recruits, the rough men soiled from the hard riding, the jennet they had picked up on the road looking somehow worse than all of them. "Keep a look out for any other creatures; the forest is full of them. It's still a ways from home, you hear?"

The recruits all grumbled as a group, bobbing their heads.

Disgraceful, Evrich thought, jumping back onto his horse. If he was lucky, one or two of them might get themselves together before reaching Marbleton. He didn't need any more troublemakers like the Archmage's mercenaries running around his streets.

CHAPTER 6

If asked, Selora would proclaim that she isn't easily impressed, but as the city's walls came into view, her eyes began sparkling. "Wow..."

Marbleton. A sprawling city, filled with towering buildings of sanded marble and gilded statues. It stood as a gem amongst the rough terrain, and a common tourist spot for the wealthy.

Passing through the large, wooden gate, the town square opened up to them. A large fountain of stone with expertly sculpted doves intertwining the waterspout stood center in the circular area, opening into the town's large proper.

Shops and family residences filled the roads, packed tight on all sides, creating a maze of alleys and backroads. The main promenade, however, kept a straightforward path through the markets, webbing out through Marbleton's northern and western gates.

Guards walked around in pairs, marching in steel plate, holding halberds pointed rigid towards the sky. Their surcoats were a bright blue with gold trimming, a pair of golden doves circling a white circle on each of their chests. Wearing conical helms, their faces were in plain sight, humanizing the guardsmen while showing the wide range of ages and expressions present amongst them.

Standing above all of this, however, was the Duke of Marbleton's estate. Tucked away in the back of the upper-districts, where scholars and nobles chipped away at their days, the duke's mini-chateau stood tall amongst even the College and other assortment of manors and noble quarters. Even taller than the duke's estate was a large, spiraling tower. The Citadel: the headquarters of Marbleton's Prime of Law, and main office of governance and bureaucracy for the shining city.

"I never knew human cities could be this pretty," Selora said, the adventurers striding through the market streets, the elf's gaze longing for the wonders out on display.

Talon shrugged, "You've seen one, you've seen them all. It's just what happens when money filters through. Now keep your ears pricked for talk of mages."

"Aye, so yer lookin' fer a magic-man." Torden pursed his lips, nodding.

"Are they common amongst humans?" Selora asked, leaning forward and dropping her voice.

Talon cocked an eyebrow, "They're... uncommon, but not rare. Regardless, any information is better than none."

Farther down the road a gaggle of citizens gathered around a raised stage. A man dressed in drab, brown robes waved his arms toward the crowd in dramatic patterns.

Torden pointed, gathering the party's combined interest. "Whad'ya s'pose dat noise is?"

"Looks like a local problem." Dismissing the man and his amassing crowd, Talon tried to walk past, stopping as he saw his two companions no longer following him. "Are you *that* curious? For everything it's worth, it's probably some prophet shouting about a coming evil, or some such nonsense. You tend to get those types in bigger cities."

A smirk crept over Selora's face, "Well, only one way to find out. Come on, let's go check it out." She grabbed Talon's wrist, dragging him to the edge of the crowd before he could object.

The man in brown robes was loud, his raspy voice carrying

through the air as panicked shrieking. "-they think to stomp on us, these brutish newcomers! With their bloody pikes and red banners, they consider themselves above us commoners. But I say nay, this is our town, not theirs!" Each word was accompanied by some swing of his arm, each motion emphasizing his speech.

A majority of the crowd mumbled agreements, others simply nodding. A sparse few shook their heads, exasperated.

Selora leaned in towards Talon, whispering. "This doesn't sound like any kind of prophet; more like a call to arms."

"Yeah, it's not what I was expecting." Talon's eyes flickered as a hint of red fluttered in his peripheral, accompanied by the clanking of plated armour. "Though, maybe I'm the prophet, 'cause I just spotted some trouble incoming."

A group of soldiers, clad in steel and crimson, pushed through the crowd, stopping at the base of the stage where the disheveled man in brown stood. From the mass of dull red and glistening metal stepped a grizzled man. His beard was overgrown and messy, his hair turned white from age, face covered in faded scars. "Alright, alright, break it up! You lot have disturbed traffic long enough for today. Either return to your homes or get back to your business."

Stepping to the edge of the stage, the man in brown wasted no time, "*This* is exactly what I'm trying to tell all of you! These *guards* stomp around without a care about us, the people. Looking down their noses at us, they plan to take everything you own. Your money, your home, your children!"

The grizzled warrior signaled to his men, two of which detached from the group of eight to restrain and carry the man away. "That's enough! I said to disperse. Don't make me say it a third time."

Grumbling, the crowd broke apart, trickling away one by one, until only the adventurers remained, the mad orator shouting obscenities as he was dragged away.

With a derisive snort, the grizzled guard turned towards the adventurers. "By your clothing, I'm guessing that you're outsiders. And by your weapons, I'd say mercenaries, or adventurers."

"Well, you know your crowds, at least." Selora huffed, crossing arms over chest.

Clicking his tongue, the grizzled guard puffed up his chest. "Given your attitude, I'll assume you're new in town. If so, let me give you a warning: don't cause any trouble. Go about whatever business you have and leave." With a huff, he made to turn away.

"Hey!" Selora called out. "What was with that old man? He seemed pretty adamant about you guys being, well, problematic."

The guard waved her off, "Don't listen to the geezer. He's just set in his ways, and doesn't like the fact that our company's been hired as extra guards."

Talon stepped forward, eyes sharpening, "I didn't think there was such a high crime rate to need extra guards."

With a sigh and a shrug, the guard reiterated. "My company takes care of major disputes and deals with the assignments and organization of the old guard. So, it's not that there's more crime or anything, the guards just needed better organization; that's what the Prime of Law said, anyway. Now, if you're done wasting my time, enjoy your stay in Marbleton. Try not to cause any trouble while you're here."

Sticking out her tongue, Selora rested knuckled fists upon her hips. "Are all humans this grouchy and... unfriendly?"

"Get used to it," Talon said, glaring after the group of shuffling armour, watching close as they turned a corner, disappearing from his sight. "Though I will admit, mercenaries like them are usually a lot worse than the town's natives. And I highly doubt they'd be useful in 'organization.' No, we'd best be careful while we're here, no telling what trouble they could cause us."

"If ya lot are done talkin', let's go find us a place ta eat." With stomach growling, Torden began his march through the streets, his taller companions following him, letting the dwarf take the lead... until they realized that Torden had no idea where he was going.

Talon took the lead again, bringing them back to the main street.

To Evrich, Captain of Marbleton's old guard – a title he wore with a petty sort of pride – the sight of the city's towering walls was always a welcome one. The yawning gates, imposing sentries of iron-banded oak, greeted his company as they cantered into town. Through the courtyard, past the immaculate fountain of sculpted stone, down the main road, taking a left into the center of that half of the city, stood Marbleton's barracks.

Two stories high, the stone building stood steadfast as a shield between the inner and outer districts, sheening windows reflecting sunlight in scattering rays.

To the garrison's side sat a sizeable stable where his men unloaded, the new recruits taking markedly more time to unsaddle and brush down their horses. A stableboy was on hand to deal with such things, but the captain thought it prudent that each guardsman be well acquainted with the horses available to them; it also helped in wearing down the new recruits, leaving them less energy to harass the townsfolk. And thus, it was as Evrich finished rubbing down his own steed that a young woman, dressed in the regular garb of a guardsman, strut into the stables.

Lilyana, one of the last entered into the old guard, stood rigid, her short, auburn curls framing soft features scrunched in discomfort. She was tall for a woman, lean muscle hidden beneath layers of armour and cloth, her leather-bound hand resting atop the handle of her sheathed sword, a slight tremble from tightly-wound digits. "Captain?"

"Private." Not prone to questioning her own ability or authority, Lilyana's awkward, yet defensive stance told Evrich enough for him to guess at what she was to tell him. For there were only two people who could leave his subordinates in such a stone-like state.

"The Prime of Law, Sara Hawse, is here, Sir. She awaits you in your office. Said to fetch you immediately when you arrived."

"Thank you, Private. And how long have I kept our dear mistress waiting?" Voice dripping with venom, Evrich made no attempt to hide his disdain for Marbleton's ultimate judge of law from his men, enjoying the sense of control he got as he felt tensions in the stable rise.

Hesitating for only a moment, Lilyana shrugged. "Less than an hour, if I were to guess. I did not see her arrive, was simply told by Lieutenant Sigurd to retrieve you as quickly as I could."

Nodding, Evrich finally allowed the stableboy to take the reins of his horse for feeding. "I suppose I will be on my way then."

Lilyana's shoulders dropped slightly as she relaxed, her message delivered.

Evrich smiled, "Curious thing, though, that she would know the approximate time that I would arrive, even though we weren't slated to return for another three whole days. That spellslinger of hers must be watching us all through a crystal ball or some such device, don't you think?"

For a moment, everyone in the stables halted, taking in the joke as though it were an indubitable fact. And it was with that suspicion that Evrich left his people, strutting out and around the building, towards the barracks' main entrance.

The chattering of the city bustling about inched into range as Evrich distanced himself from the comfort of the stables, leaving the cacophony of open streets behind the thick oaken boards and closely-laden bricks of the barracks. A slight draft carried the noise inside, but it was distant, and muffled, and even this slight buzzing dissipated with a few mere steps into the bowels of the guard house.

Down a short hall, the building opened up, a moderate-sized lounge acting as a hub for five branching paths, leading down more hallways lined with doors, each entryway leading into a shared bunkroom for Evrich's men.

The central path was bare of any extraneous posterns, the torch and banner-strewn hall leading to the captain's office. A pair of heavy doors stood at the end, guarded by a man in blue on each end: Evrich's men. Nodding to each of them, he pushed open the doors, well-oiled hinges swinging in on a whisper of scraping metal.

Its decorations were minimal, a few shelves lining the walls, filled with reports and the occasional trinket. A painted portrait of Marbleton's Duke, Arthur Giles, hung upon the west wall between shelves. A large window in the back let in light from the sun, though it only opened to a series of interconnected alleyways, the architect having clearly not been in talks with the city planner when the building foundations had been laid.

Evrich's mahogany desk sat a few meters in front of the window, the backboard depicting, in heavy detail, the goddess of life, Lei'Vania. Resting upon her side, looking inward, one arm reaching slightly towards the sky, the deity's depiction was covered by the flowing silk of Sara Hawse's dress.

"Good afternoon, Captain." Her voice slid out smooth, sweet as syrup, slender body slithering towards him, pushing away from the fine desk. Gliding across the breadth of the room in seconds, willowy fingers pushing aside hair of woodland brown, the Prime of Law stood proud before the captain.

In deference to her rank, second only to the duke himself, Evrich bowed his head. "Mistress Hawse. To what do I owe this unexpected visit?"

Chuckling, the sound a spine-chilling prickle of honey-sweetened deception, Sara Hawse traced her fingers gently across Evrich's surcoat, following the path of the doves woven on his chest. "I got word that you would be returning soon, and wanted to so *desperately* see you." Full lips quivered against the last words.

Evrich scowled. "I do wonder how you heard of my arrival, though I can probably guess. And as I have said before, Mistress, the implications of your actions are not lost upon me. *And* you understand that, given our positions, keeping our feelings out of the picture would be for the best, in keeping things amicable between us."

Her smile curled, becoming cruel, nails scraping against the blue-and-gold of his surcoat as her hand pulled away. "Oh, my dear Evrich, if only you would loosen up, you would enjoy life so much more. But very well, I suspected you would give your usual answer. So, down to business, as usual." Pacing the perimeter of the room, the Prime of Law stopped before the duke's portrait. "You have filed several more complaints to the Citadel, and I wish to address them."

Resisting the urge to roll his eyes, Evrich crossed the room, sitting behind his desk. Even within the steel plating of his armour, the cotton-stuffed cushions felt like clouds caressing his back, helping to loosen his muscles. With a sigh, he broke the silence. "Which complaints specifically are you referring to?"

Without turning, she spoke, her temperament once again even. "You have raised concerns about disappearing townsfolk, lacking resources to hire more guards under your authority, and you have also completely ignored my request to stop sending in reports on *my* regiment of sellswords."

Letting the silence settle, Evrich picked up his letter opener, examining the delicate blade gifted to him by one of his privates. Gently placing it back down, he made sure to announce his displeasure with a scowl. "From the sounds of it, you aren't going to answer any of my inquiries or requests, and are simply going to once again request my silence."

"You're partly correct. I must, once again, ask that you

stop questioning my decisions on Marbleton's security, though I understand that not only is it your main concern, but your job to worry about the city's safety. You would not be so loved by the people were it not so. Thus, I doubt you will heed my words on that front." Turning, graceful as a dancer, Sara Hawse stared Evrich down with an emotion he had never seen from her before: conviction. "I wish to inform you that your concerns about the noted 'disappearances' are no more than the duke's decision to move the homeless into the inner district, where he has had a shelter prepared for them, and for the more troublesome criminals of our fine city to be moved into the dungeons beneath the Citadel."

Evrich froze, bewilderment crossing his features. The Citadel, central hub of Marbleton's government, had a dungeon? "What do you mean? Since when did the Citadel have a dungeon? And why would you move 'the more troublesome criminals' so close to yourself, and the duke himself?"

The Prime of Law's lips lifted up into a genuine, kind smile, and Evrich, a hardened warrior, felt a chill run through his body. "The Archmage requested the dungeons be built so that he could keep a closer eye on them. Truly a noble man he is."

Having seen his ragged robes, the tattered cloth a mix of fresh black and faded grays, Evrich doubted that from the bottom of his heart.

Twirling, Sara Hawse turned her back to Marbleton's captain, "I have answered your questions, and given you what I can. Please try to reduce how many forms you submit to the Citadel. Though I understand it is protocol to do so, and that you know how much they annoy me, I have already responded to them, and my answers will not be changing. However, if you ever wish to request something more personal, you may send your letter directly to me." Winking over her shoulder, she stepped towards the front of his office, knocking on the door with a quick rasp of her knuckles. Moments later, the guards just outside the office opened the doors for her, and the Prime of Law let herself out.

The doors closed once again, and Evrich was left with his thoughts, in a room that suddenly felt like not his own.

"What about this one?" Selora pointed towards a comfortable-looking inn, *The Flying Bear* scrawled on the sign under a depiction of a bear in freefall. "It's got an interesting name."

"Well, the only way to get business in a big town like this is to stand out." Talon pushed the door open, introducing them to a familiar scent of sweat, alcohol, and honey-soaked meat.

The establishment was finely furnished, filled with enough tables and chairs to seat roughly sixty people, giving just enough space between the furniture for someone to squeeze through. The adventurers walked up to the bar, where eight stools sat perfectly spaced apart, a burly man and a luscious woman hunched together behind the counter, conversing in hushed voices.

As they each took a stool, Torden needing a moment to clamber up to the top of the raised seat, the two staff members took notice, breaking off their conversation. Waving off the woman, the burly man stepped up to the counter. "Welcome! Welcome! What can I get for you three?"

"Rum, if ya got any," Torden started.

Producing a wooden mug from under the counter, he poured a substantial amount of booze into it before sliding it smoothly across the bar's lacquered top, flashing a quick smile. "Anything I can get for you two?"

Selora shook her head, "I'm good, thanks."

"Some coffee, if you have any," Talon said.

"Yeah, I think we got some left. Give me one moment to go check." The large man wandered off to the back room, through a door just behind the bar, appearing a minute later with a mug filled near the brim with the rich, brown liquid. "Here you go."

Talon nodded his thanks, sipping his drink.

The bartender eyed Talon for a moment longer than what might be considered polite, measuring up the deadly air that stirred around the roguish figure. Glancing around the establishment, he leaned forward, whispering. "You lot wouldn't happen to be adventurers, would you?"

Talon nodded, his words slithering out in a similar level to the bartender's. "We are."

Biting his lower lip, the bartender nodded. "I see. Good. I got a job that needs doing, if you're interested. But not here. If you'll hear me out, I'll let you three take one of the rooms upstairs for a night... free of charge."

The three turned towards one another, eyes meeting in what became a silent understanding. Talon turned back to the large man, slow and deliberate in his movements. "Deal." Not like they had to accept, after all.

Producing a key from one of his pockets, the bartender slid them across the counter with exaggerated care, Talon sliding them beneath his fingers before anyone could see. "Go up the stairs, and head for the last room on the left. I'll meet you up there to discuss details. After supper, of course."

"Of course." Pocketing the key, Talon returned to nursing his coffee.

After finishing his drink, Talon spent the rest of the day's light asking around town for information about the black-robed mage. His findings were sparse.

Everyone he asked either fidgeted and avoided the question, or were simply dumbfounded by his line of questioning. Something he'd taken notice of was that the closer he got to the upper-districts, the more fidgety the people got. A sign that not only had the mage passed through the area, but that he'd made his actions more noticeable as he headed deeper into Marbleton.

After hours of asking around, gaining no useful information, the sun set and the streets emptied. Talon's expression was, as usual, somber. His frustration, rising with every dumbfounded stare and stammering non-answer, was threatening to boil out; his fists were clenched tight, his lips pressed into a thin line. Trying to calm himself, he forced his body to relax, releasing his fists and letting his jaw loosen. By the time he'd made his way back to the *Flying Bear*, Selora and Torden had already returned from their day of interviewing. They'd found no more than he had, as he had expected.

Enjoying a hearty dinner downstairs, they made their way upstairs with full stomachs. Having finished their meals quickly compared to most of the other patrons, they had to wait for a good hour before the bartender slipped into their room, checking around the hall before shutting the door behind himself.

Licking his lips, and pacing the room, the bartender hesitated.

Scratching his chin, observing the man in silence for a moment, Talon broke the ice. "I'm getting that you might need a moment, but we'd like to go to bed sometime tonight. So, if you could hurry this up, that'd be very much appreciated."

The bartender scowled, not taking kindly to the dangerous man's approach, but he hurried nonetheless. "Okay, so look. There's, uh... there's been a... problem, lately. A town problem, specifically. Do you know anything about the... brutes that recently started supervising the city guard?"

Selora clicked her tongue. "We had a run in with them, yes. Seems they've stepped on more than a few toes during their time here."

With a harrumph, the bartender regained some semblance of his confidence. "If that were the limits of it, we'd be blessed. But unfortunately they've stirred up a hornet's nest, and some people haven't taken too kindly to it."

"Can't blame 'em. Hate bugs meself." Everyone turned

towards Torden, staring at the dwarf in silence as he drained his rum-filled waterskin before returning to their conversation.

Shaking his head, Talon pushed ahead. "I'm guessing the point you're trying to get to, is that you want us to deal with the new guards."

"Violently, I hope," Selora chimed in.

"Well, uh, hopefully not." The bartender swallowed hard. "I just, uh... okay, look. Ever since those brutes took over, people have started disappearing. It started with the homeless, and then the thugs and mercenaries; y'know, the types people tend not to miss much. But then there weren't enough of the unmissed to take, and people started disappearing from the streets at night. People wandering back home after a good run of drinks, kids running last-minute errands for their parents, and even the occasional guard – the *old guard*, of course – started up and vanishing."

"Quick question," Talon didn't wait for any kind of go-ahead. "How is it that *you* noticed people went missing at the beginning, when others didn't?"

The bartender scowled. "I said that no one *missed* them. Kind of hard not to notice when the beggars stop begging. Besides, as the proud owner of a... somewhat-successful establishment, it's my business to notice these things."

The lack of stuttering, and the sudden burst of confidence put Talon off, but he made a point not to mention the burly man's sudden change in tone.

Following a subdued yawn, Selora cut in. "So, what's the job? You said that there would hopefully be no violence involved, so I'm guessing right now you just want us to track down where these missing people have been whisked away to, right?"

"Discreetly, if possible." The bartender began to fidget about. From his pocket, he produced a small bag of jingling coins. "Six silver pieces, as an upfront cost. I'll give you twice this amount once the job is done, if that's acceptable for your services."

Talon opened his mouth to object, but Selora beat him to the punch. "That'll do for now."

The rogue glared over his shoulder towards the knife-eared girl, the elf ignoring his caustic gesture.

"Of course, if any strenuous complications come up, we'll be expecting adequate recompense," Talon said.

Selora's face scrunched up, and she cleared her throat to grab Talon's attention.

The two adventurers eyed one another for a moment, their stares only broken due to the bartender's stuttering.

"Uh, w-well yes, of... of course. That, um, that makes sense." Handing Selora the bag of silver, the bartender slowly began to back away towards the door. "I'll let you lot rest now, and you can begin your search tomorrow."

"Will do." Selora nodded, waving the burly man off as he slipped away into the hall.

Talon slowly turned towards Selora, his nostrils flaring. "Look, I get that you're just following along, and that you're new to this whole thing, but there's this little thing called *haggling*. Besides, there's a far more important mission that needs taking care of."

Pocketing the coins, Selora turned from Talon. "I don't have the luxury of being choosey, for as you can imagine, I have very few of these coins that are so precious to humans. I'll take care of it, don't worry. Won't get in the way of your mission, but I'm also not here to get that done for you."

Pinching the bridge of his nose, Talon sat down on one of the beds. "Fine, yeah, whatever." Too tired to lecture her on the finer details of business, regardless of how much a novice mistake like that annoyed him, Talon stripped off his cloak and weapons. Kicking off his boots and slipping under the bed's covers, he rested his hand atop his dagger, hidden beneath his pillow.

Walking over to the table in the center of the room, Selora

clicked off the glass-encased lantern that illuminated the room. She glanced over at Torden, peacefully snoring in his chair. Deciding not to wake him, she moved to her own bed, unstringing her bow and leaning the weapon against the wall. She fell quickly into the world of dreams, sleeping peacefully enough through the night.

She awoke the next morning to a sharp pain in her side.

CHAPTER 7

To the average person, Marbleton was a beautiful city, filled with opulence and opportunity. But to a pirate's daughter, the sparkling city was like a living vault. In the upper-district, pockets clinked with gold, while expensive jewelry and priceless gems glittered beneath a cloudless sky. The finest horses pulled elegant carriages, its passengers too old or too self-important to dirty their feet walking.

Down in the lower-district, however, it was the same as any other town. Guards mulled about, supervising the shops and working people, occasionally glancing at someone they deemed suspicious through their open helmets. Children ran about while their parents took care of the morning shopping. A pair of muscular carpenters carried heavy beams of wood further down the street, and someone was passing out hand-made flyers to advertise a new shop.

Looking around the busy streets, Scarlett realized that she had no idea where to begin their search. Glancing over her shoulder, she could see that Rolt was having the same thought, his eyes moving erratically from one person to the next. "Come on, big guy. We should find a place for these two to rest, and start asking around."

Rolt nodded, steadying himself as he adjusted his vision towards the buildings lining the street, urging Obsidian onward.

They found a large inn, *The Golden Crow*, that was easily able to house their horses. It was run by a rather portly woman, with a rough attitude and confident stride. She was set in her prices, and Scarlett was unable to haggle her way down, so the pair were each out three silvers for Ruby and Obsidian to rest. While the stable boy attended to their steeds, Scarlett and Rolt began asking around for Talon.

Well, Scarlett asked around, at least. Rolt stood menacingly behind her, shrugging occasionally to keep his sword from sagging.

She started her search street-level. "Have you seen a man, average height, with long silver hair, and crystal gauntlets, seemingly irritated by his own existence?" And by the end of the day, she'd spat this question out a good hundred times, without any new information to go on.

As the sun began to set, Scarlett found herself relaxing on a wooden crate, situated on the side of the street where fewer and fewer people passed through every hour. "I know we were unlikely to find him right away," she started, turning slightly towards Rolt, who'd remained standing, "but to not get a single lead is a little annoying, you know?"

Rolt shrugged.

A crash and clattering of fruit down the street gained their attention.

"Hey! Watch it!" A crimson-robed guard, visibly shaking with rage, had drawn his sword at a middle-aged man dressed in sweaty work clothes.

The working man was stolid, palms held open before him, unbothered by the other man's bare blade. "Now just calm down, it was an accident. Besides, you were the one who bumped into me."

"Don't tempt me, old man!" The guard's hand was shaking, the tip of his sword wavering, struggling to not skewer the man in front of him.

Taking a step forward, gripping his own sword, Rolt's advance was halted only by Scarlett's hand, deftly laid upon his arm. "Hold on there, big guy. Let's see how this plays out. I got a feeling it'll be worth the watch."

The man's wicker basket, now empty and on the ground, was still close enough for him to wrap his foot under its handle. As the guard stepped forward, a vein popping out across his forehead, the working man kicked his basket straight up.

Surprised at the sudden motion, the guard slashed, catching the basket and throwing it to the side, tearing through a good chunk of the woven reeds.

Taking advantage of the opening, the man launched himself forward with a swift elbow to the guard's exposed nose, throwing him off balance. In one deft motion, he disarmed the reeling guardsman, grabbing the sword before it could touch the ground.

Just as the guard regained his balance, the older man smashed the iron pommel into his temple, throwing the armoured man to the ground in a clattering mess. Regulating his breathing, he threw the sword to the ground, crouching down to collect his dirtied food.

Scarlett smiled at Rolt, "See. Everything worked out fine." Standing from the crate, the redhead strut from her perch, the man glancing up at her approach. His movements were clean and precise as he picked up the spilt food, dropping it into his damaged basket. Crouching down herself, Scarlett gently picked up an apple, putting it back into the man's basket with a smile. "You handled yourself well. You a soldier?"

He raised an eyebrow, staring unerringly into her eyes for a moment before speaking. "I was, until about three years ago. Been working as a guard since... well, until *these* bastards came in and began kicking out members of the old guard." He waved his hand, indicating the unconscious guard, his surcoat the shade of blood.

"That the reason he started the fight?"

The man clicked his tongue in disgust, collecting the last of his fruit. "That blubbering idiot would've started the business with an old woman if he'd felt the urge. No, most of these buffoons don't have anything against the old guard. They're just lacking a few nails up in their heads. Can't tell a warrior from a cripple, that lot."

Scarlett smiled as he eyed her, his gaze moving from her armour to her daggers, then quickly flickering over to Rolt, who kept an unsubtle watch over them.

"You're an adventurer – from out of town, at that," he said.

A coy smile played at the redhead's lips. "How do you figure?"

"Your garb is carefully chosen; you're going for a specific image, even your friend's garbled mess of a wardrobe is designed to intimidate. Your weapons are decorated, but not overly so. Your friend, on the other hand, is carrying around possibly the largest sword I've ever seen, yet wears a suspicious lack of armour. These things tend to point to either adventurers, or fools. And, I bet you both have some kind of tag on your person to dictate your rank in the Guild."

"Well, you're a perceptive one." With Scarlett chuckling, the two stood, the redhead pointing down at the unconscious guard. "So, what're you going to do about him?"

"Bah! I'll avoid this street for a week or two and he'll forget all about it. This isn't the first run-in I've had with this type of lout." Waving the question away, the former soldier took a single step before stopping, turning back towards Scarlett. "Name's Rickard, by the way."

"Scarlett. The big guy's Rolt... well, that's what most people call him, anyway. No idea what name his parents gave him."

Hearing his name, Rolt stepped forward, nodding towards Rickard in greeting, who nodded back.

"Well met, adventurers Scarlett and Rolt." The former soldier bowed his head slightly. "Hopefully this town treats you better than it has me in recent times."

Before he could walk off, Scarlett stepped forward. "Hold on!

Before you go, can I ask you something? We're actually looking for someone – a friend of ours – and we're pretty sure he's somewhere in town."

Rickard considered her words for a moment, nodding his understanding. "Yeah, maybe I've seen them around. What do they look like?"

"He has long, silver hair, usually hidden under a cloak, with a middling build, and constantly has this look on his face that looks like he's about to kill someone. He has blue gauntlets that look like crystals, and from what I last heard, might be traveling with a dwarf. Have you seen him?" Him leaving with the dwarf was the only new information she'd come across during their short trip through Shadowfen, a more reliable source of information than Rickard, whose eyes glowered with confusion.

"My apologies, but I've seen no one by that description. You'd be better off swinging by the Guild and seeing if he's stopped by there." The old soldier sighed, scratching his white-speckled beard as he fell into his thoughts.

Scarlett relaxed her breathing, steadying shaky hands. Brimlux's relationship with its other guildhalls was a strained one; the chances that Talon would have stopped there were almost in the negative. "Well, thanks for your time. Come on, Rolt, let's get back to the inn. We'll ask around there before we call it a day."

"Ah, wait!" Rickard called. "I just had an idea."

The adventurers turned around, Scarlett not too pleased at being stopped but, preferring to not cause any further of a scene, listened with artificial patience.

"Look, I still have a few contacts in the city guard, and I'm well trusted within Marbleton. So, maybe I could pull some favours, and have a few more pairs of eyes looking for your friend."

Scarlett's eyes widened slightly but were quickly thrown into a cold caution as Rickard continued.

"I do, however, have a job that requires a more... discreet

application than what I could provide at my age."

CHAPTER 8

Selora tumbled from the rented bed, gripping her side with both hands, attempting to ward off the stabbing pain that now wracked her ribs. Gritting her teeth, she looked up to see Talon looming over her, tapping the toe of his right boot against the ground, shuffling his footwear back into place.

"Get up."

"The shit is your problem?" She groaned. Eyelids still heavy, she struggled to her feet. Looking through the single window bleeding light into the room, Selora guessed it to be about six or seven in the morning. "Why are we getting up so early?" Her words came out cracked and uneven.

Talon rolled his eyes. "*You're* the one who has a job to do. While you're taking care of that, I'm going to continue looking for my mark."

Still rubbing her side, she looked around the room. "What about Torden?"

"Couldn't wake him. He sleeps like a rock. I even tried kicking him, that just made him snore louder." Thumb over shoulder, he pointed towards Torden.

Sprawled on the floor, his chair toppled over next to him, Torden snored; and it *was* obnoxious.

"If you want to try and wake him, knock yourself out." Just before heading out, Talon spoke over his shoulder. "If I were you, I'd start by investigating around the guard barracks, maybe go through the captain's desk or something. If any place is going to have recorded information about missing people and where they might disappear off to, it'll be there. But be careful. If you get caught, you're pretty much dead, so wear a hood and leave your bow, it'll just get in the way."

Talon shut the door behind him, his absence leaving the room somehow warmer.

Mentally exhausted from his meeting with the Prime of Law, Captain Evrich was able to carry only a light conversation with his two closest subordinates as they patrolled the streets. A conversation his younger escort, grinning from ear to ear, was happy to start.

"So, how was your meeting? Exciting, I hope." Private Goddard was an oddity to Evrich; charming and full of energy, yet fully content with the uneventful work of standing guard for hours on end. Aside from the occasional scouting run, Goddard never left Marbleton. He even refused the offer to come with them during their latest excursion down south, missions high-ranking guards would often take to gather good will with other cities.

Nonetheless, Evrich liked the young private, often humoring him to keep relations positive. "If you find the prospect of sitting in a stuffy room, discussing budgets and guard routes exciting, then yes, very."

Goddard chuckled, his voice full of mirth and youthful energy. "Oh, yes, that sounds exhilarating. Almost makes me want to become an accountant, with all those numbers and... routes." The youth trailed off as he realized he'd chosen the wrong analogy, looking over to the second of Evrich's escorts for assistance. "Do accountants decide routes of any kind?"

Lieutenant Sigurd sighed, the gruff, older man having little patience for idle chit-chat. "Not to my knowledge, Private, no."

"Pity. Who, then, decides both budgets *and* routes?"

"City planners, and guard captains, apparently." The lightest of smiles came across Captain Evrich's lips as Private Goddard snickered.

Annoyed as she was, Selora wasn't stupid, and knew genuine advice when she heard it. So, as she hopped into the stone building lined with beds, wooden chests and weapon racks, the elf tugged on her cloak's hood, casting her face in deep shadow. Crouching as she went, glancing around corners with care, Selora also began to understand why Talon had said to do this so early. Most of the guards were either out for morning drills, or stationed at their posts around Marbleton. Few, if any, remained in the barracks.

Passing by dozens of nondescript lockers and trunks, Selora headed for the captain's office. Given the symmetrical design, it wasn't hard to guess its position.

Her soft, leather boots padded against the rough stone floor, making nary a sound as she crept along, hand trailing gently against the walls of stone and mortar. The dead halls echoed the clunking armour of a straggling guard, rushing off to wherever he was supposed to be. By the time he'd passed by Selora, she lay flat beneath a cot, hidden from the guard's sight.

The distant clicking of a shutting door alerted Selora to the passerby's leaving. Sliding out from below the bed on the tips of her fingers, she continued down the halls, unhindered by any further interruptions. Through the large, central room that acted as the guards' lounge, she found the captain's office, the large set of doors standing out from the rest of the barracks' singular entrances. No guards stood sentry, allowing the elf to simply slip in.

The scent of crusty parchment and ink wafted into Selora's nose as she was greeted by the sight of chaos. Stacks of bundled papers littered the office, covering the surface of the mahogany desk facing the doorway. An empty inkwell sat next to the stacks of parchment, holding a stained red feather. A stamp, depicting two circling doves, laid next to several sticks of gold wax, one of which had been used down to a stump.

Creeping around to the front of the desk, Selora began rummaging through the piles of documents. Scanning for anything that might seem out of the ordinary, she found little of note amidst the countless reports, invoices, and letters of complaint.

In her haste, Selora's elbow knocked over a stack of papers, scattering them across the floor. Hissing, Selora crouched down, eyes landing on an intricately-designed envelope, its crimson seal broken. With a gentle touch, she picked it up, pealing the flap back to read the letter folded within.

Scarlett skirted her way around the barracks, threading through the alley leading directly to the captain's office; exactly where Rickard had said it would be. Slipping her dagger through the crack of the two window panes, she popped the latch, leaving only the barest mark upon the polished copper. Sweeping aside the aqua drapes blocking her path, Scarlett froze.

Rickard's job had been a simple one: search the guard captain's office for something, anything, that would incriminate the new regiment. Something substantial enough to take further action upon. Standard burglary, done it a hundred times before. Not anticipating action, she'd sent Rolt back to the inn; she would be completely alone.

Yet, there was a girl. Crouched over a pile of spilled papers, an opened envelope in one hand, and neatly decorated paper in the other. Staring, wide-eyed and mouth agape. "Uh…"

Scarlett smiled. "Hey there. Don't mind me, and continue your rummaging. I'm just here for some blackmail." Swinging her legs into the room, she let the curtain fall slack behind her.

"Oh, uh… yeah, sure." The girl muttered, pulling her hood tighter around her face.

Scarlett began searching through the drawers of the large,

ornate desk. Catching the girl in her peripheral, Scarlett bit her lower lip. "You know, scrambling like that only makes more noise."

She *was* scrambling, trying desperately to stack the papers, having resealed the envelope she'd been looking at, and pocketing it. It was almost pitiful how out of place she was. "Oh... sorry."

Shaking her head, Scarlett found her own bundle of similarly sealed envelopes, bound together by a crossing of thin strings within the bottom drawer.

As the nervous girl put the restacked pile of papers on the desk, Scarlett went to undo the binding on the stack of envelopes, stopping as the office doors clicked. Scarlett moved quick, spinning on her heels, using her cloak to conceal her back as she dived out through the window.

So, as the door swung open, and a trio of guards entered, they saw only the novice thief and a shadow leaping from the window. "Halt!" A booming voice commanded.

The nameless girl leapt outside moments after Scarlett, landing hard on her shoulder as she tumbled to the ground.

Not risking turning around, Scarlett sprinted down gave a silent apology to the girl she was abandoning. Every criminal for themselves, she thought.

Selora scrambled to her feet, shoulder burning from her bungled landing, ears pounding from adrenaline. Gathering her breath, she kicked into a full sprint, the redhead long out of sight.

"Stop!"

"You're under arrest!"

The guards continued shouting for a good minute, eventually going quiet as they realized that she wasn't going to stop. Into the city streets and through the marketplace, the only sound between the three was their haggard breathing. Selora weaved between the shopping masses, civilians jumping back to avoid her. Some were then quickly knocked over as the guards barreled through them, angry shouts hurled as they got to their feet.

"Sorry!" Selora shouted back once before deciding it best the guards not hear her voice.

As a battle of attrition, the elf, dressed lightly in her leathers, outpaced the bulky humans in their plated steel. She slipped through a small alleyway, far too cramped for the armoured men to fit through, even her lithe form put under pressure by the tight fit.

"Go around!" A guard commanded as the other one tried to squeeze into the alleyway after Selora. He pulled back quickly as he failed to fit, disappearing from Selora's sight. She reached the other side and was treated to a dense crowd of shoppers.

Breathing a sigh of relief, Selora tugged her hood from her head. Untying her cloak to blend in with the crowd, she pretended to go about her business amidst the stalls.

Having made their way back to base without incident, Evrich's mood had lightened, Goddard's charm and energy having done wonders in lifting the captain's spirits.

Lieutenant Sigurd, however, was on edge the entire way through town. "Something just hasn't felt right, that's all," he said.

It was a sentiment Evrich knew well, as recent events over the past month had led to strange, and rapid changes within the city. All having started at the appointment of the new Archmage.

There was no time to elaborate on the thought as he pushed open the doors to his office. A small girl, her features hidden in the deep shadows of her hood, was slouched over a stack of his papers, another cloaked figure vaulting from the window, disappearing. Instinct and training kicked in, Evrich and Sigurd's swords drawn in unison as the captain shouted. "Halt!"

His command only pushed the girl into action, turning to dive through the window. As the fastest among the three guards, Private Goddard was the first one out, vaulting over the windowsill with ease, his armour looking almost weightless in his movements. "Stop!"

Sigurd rushed after the two, vaulting the window. "You're under arrest!"

Leaving his subordinates to the chase, Evrich began digging through his desk, horror overtaking him as he saw what had been taken. After a moment, his horror turned to anger, and with a beastly roar he smashed his fists against his desk, his outburst chipping the fine mahogany. "Damn it! Damn it all!"

Goddard and Sigurd returned within the hour, having lost both the girl and the letters.

Rolt sat stock still as Scarlett pushed open the door, holding up the stack of envelopes she'd pilfered.

"So, bad news first: I didn't find any concrete dirt on the new guard. Good news, is that I found something to keep us occupied for a little while." She plopped the stack down of envelopes on their room's table and sat down. "Let's get to it, big guy."

Silently, Rolt reached for the stack of envelopes, opening the first of many letters.

CHAPTER 9

"Please, j-just leave me alone!" Tears ran down the guard's whimpering face, mixing with the blood dripping from his split lip. Sprawled in the dirt, back to the crumbling wall, the guard nursed his mangled knees. Fresh blood mottled the deep crimson of his surcoat, the twirling doves bleached in the spilt life.

Talon crouched down, the sharpness of his stare sending a shiver down the sentry's spine. Using his thumb to wipe away the blood that had splattered on his cheek, he ran it against the guard's twisted leg. "I'm going to ask again." Standing back up, Talon grabbed the guard's right arm, tugging on it, placing a foot on his shoulder to keep it rigid. "Where's Viktor?"

"I don't know! Why would I?"

Clicking his tongue, the adventurer began twisting the guard's arm, forcing it straight, his other hand applying pressure to the tautened elbow. "The deeper I go into the city, the more distant people become when I ask about a mage. In spite of this, I've still managed to gather that you lot have a new Archmage; it's quite clear to me who that probably is. Given that, and how new you guys are, I can only assume you're related. Now where's Viktor?"

The guard smacked his left hand against the ground, fighting through the pain with gritted teeth. "I don't know." He screamed, the sharp exertion covering the snapping of his tendons as Talon smashed his elbow, leaving the arm useless.

Sliding his hand over the guard's, Talon took hold of the man's first finger between his own. "Where's Viktor?"

Weeping, the guard refused to answer, shaking his head as tears and snot ran over his lips.

Sighing, Talon bent the guard's finger back, listening for the harsh *crack*. He waited for the guard to quiet down before asking again. "Where?"

Hard, raspy breaths escaped from their lips, the guard's eyes wide as he tried to regain himself. "I... he... I don't... I don't know."

Talon frowned. "He?"

"No! I-I don't know what y-you're talking about!" The guard's eyes dilated, mental barriers faltering against the physical pain.

Huffing, Talon took hold of the guard's thumb. The tendons snapped, and the guard hiccupped, his teeth clamped together trying to cover up the burning agony. Without waiting for him to regain his composure, Talon snapped the middle digit, and then the ring, finishing off with the pinky. Each broken finger led to another pained yelp, and when the man collapsed on his side, Talon finally stopped. "Where. Is. Viktor?"

"Please... I don't... I *can't*..." He stopped, feeling the warmth of Talon's leather gloves, the cold edge of his gauntlets brushing his skin, hands pressed against the sides of his head.

"You're pitiful, you know that? Falling to the mind-control of a failed magic-slinger. Though, it's not really *his* magic, but I doubt you know much about that." Talon moved his left thumb next to the guard's eye, the sharpened tip of his gauntlet held threateningly still next to the quivering, gelatinous orb.

"W-what are you-"

"All it takes is to overload the brain with pain so that it overrides the caster's control. Unfortunately for you, your body's resilient, and you have a high tolerance for pain. For a mercenary, you were trained quite well, sorry to say."

With his still-working hand, the guard tried desperately to claw at the adventurer's arm. The effort was wasted, as he'd already lost too much strength to even budge the silver-haired man. "Wait. No! PLEASE!"

Talon didn't hesitate, nor did he look away, feeling no sympathy or disgust as he pushed down.

With the guard shivering on the ground, his uneven screams lost amidst Marbleton's depths, Talon took this chance to wipe the blood from his gauntlets, most of which had collected at the knuckles, a few specks staining his face. "Damn. Going to be difficult to hide all this." He looked around the alleyway, appreciating the solitude it afforded him. In such a derelict spot, so far into the depths of the labyrinthine city, the chances of being found were low.

Especially with the regular townsfolk keeping a wide berth, after the disappearance of so many undesirables.

A fitting spot, Talon thought.

Within the minute, the screams had faded into hoarse whimpers, but it took another ten before the half-blinded guard was able to think straight enough to talk.

Crouching back down, Talon draped his arms over his legs. Cocking his head to the side to get a better view of the blood-stained face, the guard's unbent hand gripped over his new cavity. "Ready to talk?"

The guard took slow, shallow breaths as he looked up at Talon with a tired, hateful eye. "Y-yes," he croaked, shifting back up to a sitting position, grunting all the while.

"Where's Viktor?"

"He's... made himself... a good spot... in... the Citadel. Next... to the duke." Every word was a struggle for the mutilated man, his eye unfocused as he tried to keep contact with Talon's shimmering blues. "You'll never... make it... to him."

"We'll see." Talon hung his head in thought for a moment

before looking back up, both his eyes locked on the guard's intact orb. "Thanks for the information."

The guard nodded, his mind so out of it that he seemed to forget the pain he'd been inflicted only moments ago. "Tired. Need... to rest."

The adventurer sighed, pushing himself back to his full height. Looking him over, Talon knew that he would die without immediate medical attention. However, carrying him through the crowded streets to a herbalist or healer would risk his discovery and possible arrest. He unsheathed his dagger, staring solemnly at the dying man.

Talon kneeled, putting the edge of his knife to the guard's neck, his helmet already tossed to the side after their initial scuffle. A quick slice through the unconscious man's throat, and he died. "May you find peace in the Lands of the Dead," he muttered.

Wiping the blood off on the corpse's pants, the rogue sheathed his blade. Pushing himself to his feet, Talon walked away, back through the maze that was Marbleton, back towards the inn, where he thought of Selora and Torden fretting over his absence. He snorted at the fantasy.

Looking towards the afternoon sky, he spotted the Citadel, its peeking tip framed by the light of the setting sun.

The scent of smoked ham and buttered bread wafted into Talon's nose as he slipped back into the *Flying Bear*, giving a slight nod in the barkeeper's direction. Avoiding eye contact with the muddled patrons seated throughout the spattering of tables, Talon made his way up the creaking stairs towards his shared room.

Opening the door, the rogue caught Selora pacing back and forth around the room. Torden sat at the little, though still-too-large-for-him table, looking over a letter. "Anything interesting?" Talon asked, surprising the two.

Selora snatched the paper from Torden, dashing over to the

human and handing it to him. "This was the only thing I was able to get from the barracks, but I think it was worth the trouble." Her prideful grin was enchanting, Talon thought for just a ghost of a moment, grabbing the letter and skimming through its contents in the next. Every word was scratched out in a flowing, flowery script.

Captain Evrich,

In light of your recent concerns towards the new guard, I have made it my duty to try and quell these misguided views and help you come to an understanding with your new men.

Firstly, I understand that they lack the charm and rigidity that your former retinue of men possessed, but they are loyal to Duke Giles entirely. In this, I am certain.

Secondly, though many of them served for years, a good third of the former retinue had uncertain loyalties. In this aspect, you should understand why they needed to be let go.

And finally, the safety of Duke Giles, along with all members of the Citadel's upper court, take precedence over any other matter, civil or otherwise. Thus, having men who understand their purpose as swords is just as important as those who act as shields. This is why the Archmage has taken up residence within the Citadel's crowning office, so close to the duke's property: to protect him.

If you have any other concerns, please don't hesitate to send them my way.

Yours truly,
Prime of Law, Sara Hawse

Talon read and reread the letter, digesting every word, every detail. It was a simple letter, giving nothing he hadn't learned on his own. But it did *confirm* what he'd gathered, which was just as important. The edge of his lip tugged, baring his teeth in a wicked snarl. "Not what you were looking for, it seems, but this is still useful. Good work." His voice came out thicker than intended, more venomous, more bestial.

"Uh... yeah, well... you know." Selora brushed a few strands of hair from her face, glancing away from Talon's unsettling features for a moment before recomposing herself, sweat beading down her cheek.

"Did anyone see you?"

Selora scratched the back of her head. "Well, not my face, at least. But a pair of guards chased me pretty far through the marketplace."

Talon folded up the letter, walking over to the table where he saw the opened envelope, slipping it back in. "Well, that'll have to do, since we really can't have you just lazing around here 'til it's time to go." He glanced down at Torden. "Sentiment going double for you. Since you've decided to tag along, I've decided that I can make use of you."

"Aye, don' worry. I'll be ready when 'eads need mashin'." The dwarf flashed a toothy grin, and, for just a moment, Talon considered throwing him out the nearest window.

"Selora," Talon said.

The girl jumped. "Yeah?"

"Good work."

One might usually express joy from a companion's praise, but Selora's tight face described the opposite against his cold and apathetic tone. "Uh... yeah. No problem."

Talon nodded, plopping down on his rented bed.

"Is there, um, something you need us to do?"

"For now, just wait. I have questions for our employer. Information I need before planning our next move."

Nodding, dumb and without purpose, Selora sat down on

her bed. Sitting across from Talon, the colour having left her face, she waited.

It was well past dinner by the time the tavern calmed down enough for Talon to get a word in with the bartender. Seated at the bar with a cup of coffee, the silver-haired adventurer tapped his foot, cold eyes piercing through the burly man's back as he worked at cleaning the cups.

The barkeep cleared his throat. "So, you needed something?"

Talon sipped at his cup before answering, "Just some information. Nothing too arduous."

"Well, ask away." His eyes darted to the side, avoiding eye contact with Talon's lethal stare.

Leaning in, Talon kept his voice low, eyeing the few patrons still nursing their evening drinks. "I need information on the Citadel."

The bartender froze, his hand finally stopping in their repeated wiping of cloth on glass. He set the glass down, his expression made of stone. Glancing around, he leaned in as well. "You find something?"

"Something one of my partners found mentioned it, and it piqued my interest."

"What do you want to know?" His voice was shaky, eyes warbling as he failed to keep his cool, fear pervading his every action.

"Everything you know, starting from the beginning. Any little detail could be useful down the road."

The bartender whispered through gritted teeth. "The Citadel is like Marbleton's, eh, court of law, I suppose. They run the show, basically, deciding how public relations with other places are going to be handled, make any final decisions on any new laws, or taxes. Basic stuff like that. Those part of the Citadel answer directly to the duke, and even the Captain of the Guard has some connections to them. Mostly, they're a good thing."

Talon nodded along.

"Though lately, something's changed. Not sure what, but tensions have risen in the past few weeks between Evrich and the Prime of Law." The bartender shook his head, despairing at the thought. "Those two always seemed to get along well enough before, but any time you see them in public now, their words are cold, and short. I don't know, but it seems like something between 'em has gone south. Least, that's what I've heard down the vine. Can't say I've seen them too much myself."

Talon nodded. "And how does the duke's newest Archmage fit into this system?"

"Ah, so you know about that, do ya?" Talon's stare was harsh and unwavering, enough so that the bartender's eyes continued to flicker away. "Right, well, I don't know too much about him. The last one left town; disappeared actually, but it's an easier story to sell if people think he had somewhere else to be." He shrugged. "Either way, this new one's bad news. Has this feel about him, like he's always angry or distant when he has to make public appearances. It's almost a mandatory gesture when you work directly under Duke Giles. Aside from that, I don't know too much. He keeps himself well away from people, and even most of the guards who come around my place seem anxious over him."

"When did he show up?" Talon drummed his fingers against the counter, glancing over his shoulder as a pair of drunken humans stumbled passed him towards the exit, slurring botched lyrics for a local tune.

Once everyone was out of earshot again, the bartender answered. "Few weeks ago, actually. Around the same time people started disappearing."

Smiling, Talon patted the bartender on his shoulder. "Looks like our price just went up. I'll start figuring out how to get into the Citadel tomorrow, so make sure to have a big breakfast prepared.

Going to need a lot of energy to find those missing people."

Swept up in the adventurer's sudden burst of energy, the burly man nodded, dumbfounded.

Tilting his head in farewell, Talon headed back upstairs, unable to suppress the sneer spreading across his face. Things were lining up well, and he wouldn't allow the mage to get away again.

CHAPTER 10

Rickard flipped through the letters with a hurried vigour, his expression grim. After hearing about a thief caught stealing documents from the guard barracks the day before, he tracked down Scarlett and Rolt, his hunch confirmed as she handed him the stack of tampered envelopes.

The ex-soldier read with flared nostrils, each letter building up his rage, one offense at a time. There was no indication to the order of which they'd been written, but he was slowly piecing it together. Detailed letters from the Prime of Law, as well as the duke's Archmage, made it clear that the decay of the old guard was neither Evrich's idea, nor within his authority to fully stop.

Eventually, he set the stack of papers down, reluctant to consider the full meaning of them, for the horrors that could spell out. Pinching the bridge of his nose, he looked over at Scarlett and Rolt, whom sat together, waiting. "I'm going to be honest. I was hoping against hope that all the recent troubles had just been coincidence, and that Marbleton's government hadn't fallen to such a state, but you've confirmed it for me.

"So, while I spread word around to look for your friend, I have another request. It's one that I have no leverage on, and ask in the simple hope that you'll accept: please, confront Duke Giles on my behalf, and find out what's caused this radical change in his behavior."

"No." Scarlett replied immediately. "Look, this place's

problems aren't ours, and while I understand how terrible these things can get when left unchecked, I don't work for free." She didn't look away, bowing her head to the side a moment later. "Sorry."

Rickard sighed. "It's fine. You did what was paid for, and it was selfish of me to ask anything more of you." Not one to sulk, he shrugged. "Very well. I'll just have to-" Before he could finish, Rolt stepped forward, leaving Rickard in an awkward silence.

Quickly, Rolt pointed over his shoulder at Scarlett, then shifted his finger towards the letters she'd acquired, finally pointing towards himself.

"Uh..." Rickard stammered, glancing between the indicated items. He almost jumped as Scarlett groaned, a little louder, and more dramatic than was necessary.

"He's saying that 'since he hasn't done anything to earn the information you're going to provide, he'll do the job'." She shook her head, exasperated. "You know, you're way too nice for this line of work."

Rolt shrugged.

Shock apparent on his face, Rickard took a moment to wet his lips before speaking. "While I appreciate the offer, you're not the most reliable person when it comes to... negotiation."

Without hesitation, Rolt turned towards Scarlett and rubbed his index and thumb together. The redhead groaned again. "Fine, I get it! We'll head out tonight, forty minutes before the guards change their shifts."

Rickard's eyes bounced back-and-forth between the two adventurers.

Seeing his confusion, Scarlett explained: "The big guy's going to pay *me*, to help *you*. Like I said, he's too nice."

"I see." Rickard looked over Rolt, nodding. "Well, thank you."

Rolt tilted his head; a sign of understanding, Rickard thought.

—•—

RETRIBUTION

Based on Rickard's information, Duke Giles's private chambers lay on the top floor of his estate, near the center of town, deep in the upper-district.

Guards patrolled the city in pairs, marching back and forth along their assigned routes. Furthermore, they were set up in a way that certain streets were almost always occupied, having patrols enter as another left. Seen as one of the strictest cities in Udrela, Marbleton's rate of crime was kept incredibly low, with punishments executed without delay and without mercy, often at the perfunctory decision of the Prime of Law. The upper-district, however, applied even stricter rules, with unauthorized persons imprisoned or executed on sight.

Even as daylight faded, and the first moon began cresting over the city walls, this didn't change. What did change was the guards' ability to see, and Scarlett knew how to exploit this. Once night fell, one in each pair of guards lit a torch. The advantage of this was an increase in visibility; the disadvantages were that it made it incredibly easy to spot the one holding it, as well as blinding them to anything past the flame.

From the darkness of a cramped alley, Scarlett licked her lips, eyes squinting in concentration.

A large wall of marble, resembling the one that protected Marbleton from outside threats, circled the upper-district, separating it from the rest of the city. The only ways in and out of the upper-district were two sets of heavy, double doors: one entered from the south end of town, the other from the north. To make things more difficult, there were no buildings within a hundred meters of the wall, and all greenery was kept cut down, leaving that stretch of land flat, and without cover.

Given enough time, Scarlett had no doubt she could scale the wall, it being a good bit shorter than the outer one, but not without abandoning Rolt. For as much as she didn't mind going in alone, if something that required brute force came along, she'd rather have her giant of a companion next to her.

With that said, they'd need a distraction.

A small guardhouse, nestled against the edge of the flattened land. Next to it, some stables, a pair of horses snuffling, whinnying, and kicking against their wooden confines.

Perfect, Scarlett thought.

Before rounding around to the stables, Scarlett whispered to Rolt, "Rush the door the moment the guards leave. I want it open by the time I make my way back around."

Rolt cracked his neck before sharing a toothy smile, nodding.

Skirting around the perimeter, slinking through alleyways and behind waist-high fences of piled stone, Scarlett slipped over to the guardhouse, and into the stables.

Two mares muddled inside, snorting at her approach, secured to their posts by knotted ropes. Stacked against the back wall was a small pile of hay, settled beside a broom, brushes, and buckets. Tiptoeing over to the horses, Scarlett pushed at the posts, testing their grip on the dirt; one gave way while the other stayed stock still.

The horses snorted and neighed, eyeing the redhead with curious eyes.

Crouching next to the loose post, Scarlett took hold and braced her feet. Heaving, the post slowly came out before suddenly popping free. Hissing at the indents left in her fingers, she went to work at the ropes holding the other horses. With them freed up, she began working at the pile of hey with her flint and tinder.

"Okay, let's see if I still remember how to do this." Striking the flint, sparks took hold of the dry straw, smoke rising as flames began to crackle. Behind the adventurer, the horses continued whinnying.

She waited for a few moments and, unsatisfied with the flame's growth, threw the broom and brushes into the fire. The flames expanded, consuming the straw in moments, spreading fast to the wooden structure around it. Soon, it would be a raging inferno.

Scarlett turned to see the horses pushing themselves against the exit, crying out as they made their way out into the open and fled. Scarlett followed, slipping past the noisy animals before slinking back into the shadows.

In the distance, she heard the rising voices of guardsmen, shouting out to one another as they rushed, scrambling to put out the fire. Scarlett ran, abandoning stealth in favour of speed. Hopping over fences and dashing through alleys, she hesitated only for a moment as she reached where she'd left Rolt, sprinting out into the open towards the gate that would take them into the upper-district. The guardhouse burned like a pyre now, guards trying to both put out the fire while chasing down their horses.

Smirking to herself, Scarlett slipped through the narrow opening of the rusted gate, hinges grinding behind her as Rolt pushed his entire weight against the door, separating them from the chaos just outside. "Good work, big guy." Scarlett smiled, turning around and patting her friend on the shoulder, Rolt grunting. "Right. Now, let's head towards the good ol' duke's place."

Rolt tapped her on the shoulder, pointing between the two of them and then at the gate they'd just passed through, shrugging.

"Oh, right. How *do* we get back out? Hm... Well, we'll worry about that when the time comes to worry about it."

Rolt sighed, and the adventurers made their way towards the duke's manor.

They skulked through empty streets filled with high-end shops, eventually leading into the residential area, where expensive estates were separated by iron-wrought fences. The Citadel, hidden away in the northern end of the district, became larger as they neared the center, eventually coming upon the duke's home.

Crafted from the shimmering marble that the town was

known for, the building stood two stories tall, four superficial spires at each corner of the property. Half-a-dozen guards in red surcoats patrolled the premises, warding off any potential thieves that might have the idea of sneaking in.

More than mere thieves, Scarlett and Rolt were professionals, and refused to be put off by such low-level protection. Leading them around the perimeter, Scarlett made sure the two were well out of the sentries' line of sight, hurrying to the eastern side of the manor, crouch-running up to the spike-tipped fence of black iron.

"Lift me over."

At the redhead's instructions, Rolt crouched down, cupping his hands together, Scarlett placing her foot safely within his grasp. Whispering, she counted down from three. As she finished, Rolt lifted her into the air, Scarlett subsequently kicking off his hands and shoulders, launching herself over the fencing.

Slipping her fingers between the spikes, Scarlett swung over the fencing, landing safely on the other side, now crouched within the boundaries of the duke's property. She glanced over her shoulder, watching with amusement as Rolt wrapped his hands around the spikes and hauled himself over the fence, the sharp edges digging into his calloused palms yet never cutting them. With both adventurers safely over the barrier, Scarlett waved for her companion to follow her as she headed for a line of bushes.

Ducking behind the shrubbery, Rolt having to lay almost completely flat, the two waited until a lone patrol turned his back to them. Scarlett tapped Rolt's shoulder twice, the warrior rising from the shadows like a spectre. With surprising speed, Rolt smashed his fists into either side of the guard's head, the shock of crumpling steel cracking bone, spilled blood running in rivulets from the crushed helmet. They hid the body behind the bushes, moving to the manor's side.

Using one of her daggers, Scarlett popped open the latch on a small window, slipping through with ease. She motioned towards

Rolt, twirling a finger in a circular pattern. "Circle around and look for a back door. If one exists, I'll see about opening it from inside."

The giant of a man disappeared around the corner.

Scarlett took in her surroundings, her eyes adjusting to the darkness. She could barely hold back her disgust. Put simply, the place was a mess.

Stacks of crusty books, covered in piles of discarded laundry, and rotting half-eaten food, littered the room. The red velvet couch and guest chairs served as makeshift counters, housing the foul smells and unwashed items that now invaded Scarlett's senses. She covered her face with her palm, hoping to stave off the odour and taste of foul air.

The scent of iron catching her attention, she approached one of the many stacks of books littering the room, sheathing her dagger before picking up a leather-bound journal, its deep brown long faded. A streak of dried crimson stained the edges of its binding, the scentless blemish cracking beneath the redhead's touch. Whether it was blood, or wine, Scarlett wasn't sure.

Flipping through the crusty journal, she found horrifying sketches of a twisted monster devouring people whole. The written entries inside were less intelligible, starting off as harried research before quickly devolving into mad ramblings.

"Probably blood," Scarlett whispered, throwing the journal onto a different stack of books. Her curiosity unsated, she continued to poke through the old, weathered pages. They varied greatly in age, authors, and even value, some easily worth hundreds of gold pieces given their fine print and wonderfully-decorated covers, and others seemingly nothing more than the scribblings of madmen bound in bundles of musty parchment.

The single connection between them all was the reference of the horrific beast. Its name, mentioned exclusively in those journals penned by someone known as Archmage William, was scratched out in heavy ink. Someone had tried very hard to keep the creature nameless. Though the portrayal of the beast's physical form differed from work to work, several things stayed the same: its sudden appearance in each area, to the tough but fleshy exterior, its carnivorous eating habits, the beast's frightening ability to "recruit" certain humans, and its singular eye. Whatever this creature was, Marbleton's duke had a strange fascination with it.

As she began to sink into her thoughts, a light tapping brought Scarlett back into the real world, her ears twitching as she picked up on the familiar rhythm. *Knock knock knock... knock... knock knock.* Smiling, she followed the rhythmic tapping, finding a door with a simple latch keeping it locked. Turning the small dial, she swung open the door to see Rolt standing just outside, his muscular body blocking most of the moonlight from entering the manor.

Before Scarlett could say anything, Rolt pointed down to where he was standing, mimicking a guard standing at attention, then smacking his fist into his open palm before pointing over to a tree, where Scarlett could just barely make out the unmoving form of another guard.

Scarlett gave Rolt a thumbs-up with a smile plastered on her face as she backed away. "Let's head upstairs."

Rolt nodded, beginning the awkward process of squeezing through the cramped door frame.

Once he was through, Scarlett took her position at the lead, tiptoeing up the long stairway tucked away at the front of the house.

Through the open living space, the two passed by every manner of painting, sculpture and tapestry they could identify, and several neither recognized. Clearly, along with his obsession for a flesh-eating monster, the duke was really into art. *Expensive* art, specifically. Scarlett's lips pulled into a scowl as she scanned the wanton waste of wealth surrounding her.

Reaching the second floor, Scarlett raised her hand, halting

Rolt as she peeked around the corner. Staring down the hall, she watched for any sudden movement, catching nothing but the dull rays of moonlight through a square window at the end of the corridor. Clear, the two intruders passed the bend.

Down the hall were three doors, two on the right and one on the left. "Wait here until I give you the signal to move," Scarlett whispered, moving forward, a single dagger drawn as she slowly inched open the first door.

Peeking in, she could see the barest outline of a wooden tub, large and circular, shoved to the back of the room. An iron chamber pot sat closer to the door, filled to the brim with waste. Swallowing back her retching, she closed the door to the bathroom, heading for the room farther down the hall, where a nearby window illuminated the inside as she pushed on the door.

The duke's personal library greeted them. Each shelf was tightly packed, books pressed in flat rows, organized by shape and color. Atop the duke's desk sat uneven stacks of old journals, chaotic compared to the clean organization of the shelves. So many books crowded the room's lacquered floors that walking would be a difficult task, explaining why so many books were spread around downstairs.

Scarlett considered for a moment looking through some of the closer laid titles, but backed away and shut the door instead, feeling Rolt's gaze on her from down the hall.

Stepping up to the third door, she motioned Rolt over, pushing at the handle. The knob turned smooth in her hand. She reeled as stale, fetid air assaulted her senses, eyes watering as she pushed through. Moldy, half-eaten meals sat around the room, flies buzzing around the old food.

On the edge of his massive bed, unblinking, the Duke of Marbleton sat. Rocking to an inaudible rhythm, hands clasped so tight his knuckles turned white, Arthur Giles muttered to himself. Atop the bed lay a woman, throat sliced open, splattered blood staining the pillow and sheets around her mummified corpse.

The duke stood at half the height of a normal man, yet carried twice as much fat. His twirling moustache and thick goatee were speckled by crumbs, standing out against the graying brown hair. The duke's clothes, wrinkled and stained, sagged against his sweating body, the simple buttoned shirt and straw-strung breeches contrasting against his elaborate hair. Blue and white stripes stretched across the portly man's width, yellow and brown spots staining his lower half, adding to the collage of smells. The duke's eyes, so gray and so drab, strained against his sockets, threatening to pop out at any moment, pupils mere dots against the bloodshot canvas of his eyes.

Scarlett and Rolt stepped into the bedroom, closing the door behind them, a large window lighting up the room. Silk curtains lined the large bed, drawn back to reveal the oversized mattress covered in several layers of expensive sheets, pulled by the clawed digits of the murdered woman. Getting closer, they saw the duke's hands were stained red, skin cracked and peeling beneath the blood.

Scarlett scowled as she stepped forward. "Hey." Her voice was soft, lips trembling.

Duke Giles didn't respond, continuing to mutter.

"Hey!" She raised her voice, almost barking from the building unease, but still the duke refused to respond.

Crouching down, the redhead focused in on the duke's crazed mutterings, his wet slurring a disgusting smack of incoherence. "Come to me. Come to me. Come to me." Over and over the duke repeated the mantra, his voice cracking and changing pitch with each repetition, sometimes so mangled that the words barely resembled human speech.

A chill ran down her spine, Scarlett shooting back up to her feet. It wasn't the words themselves that started spinning alarms in her head, but something *behind* the words, like a gnawing presence pushing out, thickening the air.

Her skin tingling, teeth aching, Scarlett reached out, her hand hovering over the Duke's shoulder, hesitating. She gasped as Rolt took hold of her arm and pulled it away, shaking his head. She rarely ignored Rolt's warnings, his instincts sharper than most, but they needed whatever information the duke had, and needed to shake him out of his trance. "Don't worry, big guy. I got this."

Holding her gaze for a few moments longer, Rolt finally released her arm, taking several steps back, hand reaching instinctively for his sword.

Pulling in a deep breath to steel herself, Scarlett reached out. "Listen up, pork-brains, we need-"

Scarlett's hand gripped the duke's shoulder, and he screamed, pupils dilating against the agonized shrieking tearing through the air. He clawed at the sides of his head, dead skin peeling up beneath dirty fingernails, the man thrashing, tartar spraying from his yellowed teeth.

Scarlett reared back, catching the near inaudible sound of steel against leather as Rolt unsheathed his sword. "Hold on a minute, we still need answers!"

Voices rose from outside, shouts and commands mixing into a jumbled mess. The floor rumbled under their feet, clunking footsteps and ringing chainmail charging up the stairs from below.

Scarlett growled. Twisting, she ran towards the rays of moonlight seeping in. "Through the window!" Drawing her dagger, she pried at the square portal, the frame unmoving against the lithe blade.

Rolt charged, grabbing Scarlett in his arms as his shoulder crashed through the glass, the shattering impact chiming like a bell in the silence.

Sword held firmly in his hand, Scarlett wrapped around his opposite arm, Rolt landed on his feet, powerful legs taking the brunt of the impact. The yelling of guardsmen surrounded them, screams of horror booming from the duke's room. Rolt bolted for the property's edge, bounding across the open courtyard with sword in hand.

Rolt raced around the corner, building up speed as he closed in on the iron fence. With one mighty leap, he crossed the spear-topped barrier, spinning his body midair to clear it, landing hard on his side. Scarlett rolled from his arm, Rolt's body cushioning the blow for her. Crawling to their feet, the pair heard the distinct sound of a dozen bows being drawn in unison.

"Halt!" A high-pitched voice cracked as it commanded, the speaker standing between a retinue of guards, twelve with bows, six others wielding a mix of halberds and swords. "You have entered the upper-district without proper authorization, trespassed on private property, and worst of all, have been caught red-handed attempting to assassinate Duke Arthur Giles. Any further resistance will be met with immediate, and lethal force."

Cursing under her breath, Scarlett's dagger slipped from her fingers, aching from the iron grip she'd kept during Rolt's mad dash.

CHAPTER 11

The Citadel pierced the low-hanging clouds, standing proudly over Marbleton, its surrounding walls separating it from the lower-district. It would be a near impossible task for the average person to sneak through, without a major distraction. Worse yet, a fire had broken out near the southern gate, meaning that the guards would be on the lookout for vandals.

Talon pulled himself up the dividing wall, gritting his teeth against the rope knotted around his shoulders. Selora climbed alongside him, just two meters to his side, slamming his extra set of climbing picks into the smooth marble, a similar length of rope rubbing at her torso.

Torden, on the other hand, hung far below his companions, hanging limp within the rope-fashioned harness tied firm around his body; a jury-rigged solution to the dwarf's inability to scale a wall. The dwarf displayed clear indignation at being lugged around in such a manner, but bit back the shame against the greater disgrace of missing a fight.

This course of action had been decided just after Talon had returned to their room. Using his two sets of climbing picks, they scaled the dividing wall between the upper- and lower-districts, infiltrating the Citadel directly. When they made it to the upper-district, they'd need to sneak through the residential area, up and around the hill where the Citadel sat, scaling up the tower before any patrols took notice. Once inside, Selora and Torden would search the lower levels, learning whatever they could about Marbleton's missing people, while Talon split off and searched for the duke's Archmage.

A simple enough plan, Talon thought.

Now, halfway to the ramparts, Talon regretted bringing Torden along this far. Even if the dwarf was useful in a brawl, he doubted it was truly worth the effort of hauling him up the twenty-meter-high wall. Focusing his anger towards Torden distracted him from the cramps forming along his arms.

Swinging one of his picks into the smooth marble, his thoughts turned towards his old companions, toward Scarlett, who could have scaled the wall with the same ease that he did, her nimble body and dexterous hands propelling herself upward in the same manner that birds took flight. She was a capable thief, having picked up every lesson he had to teach her in their younger years.

Then he thought of Rolt, the colossus with a body tougher than stone. That colossus caused them no end of trouble with his unusual sense of morality pushing him to jump into trouble they had no business meddling in.

There were others, of course, but those were the two Talon had spent fifteen years of his life bonding with, risking life and limb for each other over petty things like money and prestige in the Guild. Fifteen years that he had discarded when he laid his career as an adventurer to the side to chase his own personal vendetta, over three years prior. To kill Viktor, his old friend and fellow trainee, for the gravest betrayal.

His knuckles brushed against the bottom of the parapet, and his thoughts returned to the present.

Talon swung his pick over the top of the rampart, hauling himself over the wall, a mere second after Selora. "Hey," he called over to the elf. "Give me a hand." He gripped the rope keeping Torden suspended, tugging it for emphasis.

Exhausted, Selora nodded, gripping her own end of the rope.

Even without his armour, Torden's heavily muscled body made hauling him difficult, Talon reminding himself how much worse their struggle would be had he not convinced the dwarf to abandon the steel plates against their insistence that "a dwarf's armour is their pride embodied." Together, they heaved the dwarf over the wall, the trio huffing as they plopped to the stone walkway, never so grateful to undo some rope knots.

Selora, gasping for air, looked over at Talon, her wary eyes wavering in the evening sky. "I never want... to do anything like *that*... ever again."

All he could do was nod, his lungs and heart struggling to settle.

Allowing them all a moment to catch their breath, Talon struggled to his feet, crouching over the inner edge of the bulwark. He peered into the darkness beneath, his eyes picking out details within the blackness. Devoid of light and shadow, Talon's eyes picked out shapes in bluish outlines, like a flat drawing. "Alright, you two. Like we planned."

Selora groaned while Torden waddled forward, the three stretching the rope to its full length.

Talon pulled out a similar length of rope from his pack and knotted the two together. Redoing the knots around Torden, Talon nudged the dwarf towards the wall's cliffside. Motioning for Selora to stand behind him, Talon gripped the rope.

She did so, standing behind Talon with wide-planted feet, grasping the rope and gritting her teeth. "Ready," she muttered.

Talon nodded, then turned to Torden. "Alright, go... slowly."

With a quick thumbs-up, the dwarf started to clamber down the wall. "Now don'cha go an' drop me, ya hear?" He didn't wait for an answer, and let go of the wall's edge, dropping like a stone.

Boots ground against the marble beneath, tearing the wind from Talon's lungs as he braced, Selora pulling the rope back far enough to balance him.

"He's the size of a toddler; why is he so heavy?" Selora groaned as the rope's coils rubbed her palms raw, leaving lines of red down the inside of her fingers.

Talon hissed through clenched teeth. "Imagine if he still had his armour on."

Selora chuckled, then grunted, nearly falling as she fed out too much rope. The weight pulled the elf forward, bumping against Talon, who leaned back at a forty-five degree angle, keeping them both from tumbling over the edge.

Torden's feet touched the ground after another minute, unfastening the rope and tugging it.

Talon began pulling the rope up, coiling it around his arm.

Selora stretched, popping her back with a groan. "I'm next, I hope."

"Yeah, yeah," Talon said. Collecting the rest of the rope, he wrapped it around Selora's waist, giving her a moment to waltz over to the wall's edge.

"Ready," she called softly, inching backwards down the wall.

Talon fed the rope quickly, supporting her weight with laughable ease.

Selora touched the ground next to Torden, undoing the rope and tugging it, just as he had done mere minutes ago. She stepped back as Talon dropped the rope, letting it coil around the ground before hiding it in a nearby bush.

Above, Talon steadied himself, the fatigue in his arms dissipating as he gazed up at the sky. Twin moons peaked from behind shimmering clouds, washing away his worries. With only a moment to soak in the peace, he leaned over, swinging down the edge of the wall, descending towards the ground with his picks.

Talon picked his path cautiously, each strike of his picks another dull ringing in his muscles. His thoughts ran dry from the strain of holding himself up, the smooth marble allowing no rest from his descent.

Only once his toes brushed against the tips of grass did Talon relax, pulling his picks free of the cracked stone. Fingers cramping up, and stomach tightening, Talon grit his teeth against the pain. No time for a break, he thought. Turning towards his companions, he found them staring at him, waiting for instruction.

"So," Selora started, shifting her weight back-and-forth between her feet. "What's next?"

Regarding her in silence, Talon turned his attention towards the Citadel, seeing now how tall the tower truly stood, looming over the city, peaking above the massive walls like a beacon of order. Like every other building of note, its exterior was made of fine marble. Three lines of protruding stone spiraled around the structure, forming a connected spear at the tip, threatening to pierce the heavens.

Each twisting column depicted a prior age: the *Age of Gods*, the *Age of Strife*, and the *Age of Heroes*. Gilded in elaborate detail, the gold-plated stories displayed the birth of the gods, their war, and the resulting rise of the Eternal King at the end. Windows dotted the length of the tower, sparkling between the aging depictions.

Talon pointed towards the tower. "You two are going to sneak into the lower levels. Look for a basement of some kind – it's usually where these kinds of places keep their prisons – while I make my way up to the top floor. I'll work my way down, and once I've done what I need to, I'll make my way to your position. If the mage escapes from me, we can catch them in a pincer attack; I expect you two can manage without me until then."

"Ignoring the implications of that last comment, I'm on board," Selora declared.

Torden tapped the length of his battle ax, grinning. "Aye, don'cha worry 'bout us, Lad. We'll be fine. Just make sure not ta waste too much time on yer own tussle."

"Alright, then follow me. And do *try* to be quiet."

Torden snorted, Selora turning away, hiding her smile.

They prowled through the upper-district's empty streets, the silence eerie amidst the dark homes and unmanned stalls. They slipped from building to building, but no one appeared along the roads towards the Citadel, guard patrols missing alongside the hustle and bustle that would normally bring such a district to life.

The silence bothered Talon, but he had no time to consider its implications.

As they approached the Citadel's base, the first pair of guards showed themselves, each wielding a halberd in hand and arming sword at the waist. The crimson surcoats wrapped around the tower, another pair arriving just as the prior disappeared from sight. Several lone guards stood sentry around the grounds, each listless or lost in thought.

Hiding behind a line of bushes, the trio took their time examining their surroundings. Talon scowled, scanning the top of the waist-high shrubbery, no guard checking behind the obvious cover. Sloppy, Talon thought. Good.

"I'll go first," Talon whispered, visualizing the best route to take. Even with his speed, moving across the twenty meters from the bushes to the tower wouldn't be an easy task. "Go ten minutes after me, understand?"

"Yeah." Selora nodded.

"Don'cha go takin' too long, lad. We'll be in-an'-out 'fore ya know it." Torden's words were boisterous as usual, but at least he toned his volume down.

Leaving the two behind, Talon worked his way towards the Citadel, each step taken with purpose, never rushing, preserving his only advantage within the shadows. His goal, the next line of bushes, pushed within steps of the tower's base. With each rotation in the patrols, he stopped, letting the darkness consume him, their relaxed strides filling his own steps with confidence. Even through the brush, their crimson surcoats bled into his eyes, their torches illuminating them, searing targets amidst the void of night.

Soon, they made their final circuit around the tower of law, Talon's body crackling with energy as he charged, a mere eight meters between the line of bushes and the guards. One lazily turned his head, their scream stifled as Talon's dagger slashed through his neck. The guard's death alerted the other patrol, already several steps ahead of his partner, swinging his halberd in a horizontal arc.

Ducking under the polearm, Talon lunged, letting magic course through his body, illuminating him with crackling energy. Thrusting his dagger under the guard's chin, Talon heaved the man up, blood bubbling from their mouth. Their body slackened, falling at Talon's feet where their blood pooled.

Cerulean energy dissipated from around Talon's body as he loosened control of his innate magic. He wasted no time hiding the bodies, dragging each one to the line of bushes, tossing them within the brush. With the field emptied of corpses, he waited next to the corpses for the other two patrols to pass before continuing.

Cracking and stretching out his fingers, Talon cleared his head before pulling out his picks, beginning his ascent to the Citadel's top floor. A silk curtain covered the second story window, and the third's led into a storage room, filled with crates and long sacks piled together; it smelled vaguely like meat. Disgusting.

He cleared each gilded indent with collected calm, jumping and hooking his picks at the top of each, before leveraging himself up the Citadel's length. Clearing window after window, he reached the top, the final window poised at the tower's peak.

Talon stopped.

Looking down, he spotted Selora and Torden skulking towards the tower. Nodding to himself, Talon slid his dagger between the dual-window panes, unlatching the lock and pulling them open. The red curtains fluttered out of view.

The office, like most offices, housed a large desk, lined with shelves full of books and oddities. Gold-threaded rugs and banners decorated the floor and walls, splashing the bare walls with hints of colour. The desk was devoid of any busywork, illuminated by a few errant candles.

As he took in all the little details of the room in – the antique vase filled with dying tulips, the bronze bust of a now-deformed man, a crystal ball nestled in a velvet cushion – he heard the hinges on the doors creak. Ducking below the window, Talon held his breath.

"-question your methods, I must say the results have been promising." A woman's cold, sultry voice bled into Talon's ears, a subtle bite hidden beneath her relaxed tone. "But we're walking on thin ice here, and Evrich's not going to put up with much more."

A familiar voice chuckled, and Talon's hair stood on edge.

"No need to worry. It's almost done with our appetizers, and once it's had its fill, what the captain thinks won't matter."

The door slammed, sending a gust of wind that battered the curtains aside as the wooden chair scraped against tile.

"Speaking of, how goes things with the captain? You had another meeting with him recently, after all." Viktor chuckled, his voice filled with venom.

The woman sighed. "Oh, he's being his usual stubborn self. Can't see the bigger picture. Honestly, I'm terrified of telling him anything, seeing as how much he's already resisted over the smaller things."

"Yes, that stubbornness is truly a problem, isn't it? He's too tough to control, too popular to accuse of treason, and too well-protected to simply dispose of with a few thugs." Viktor, the betrayer, cracked his knuckles, the sound echoing around the stone room. "But he's been passive enough so far, and soon he'll be under my thumb."

"You mean your pet's, right?"

The mage harrumphed, his chair scraping against the polished tiles. "If anyone's a *pet* in our relationship, it's me. That much I understand; always have."

Sadness bordered his words, and Talon's knuckles whitened.

The woman chuckled, her heels clicking with each tentative step. "You still haven't answered my question."

"You know the answer," He shot back, the soft padding of his boots disappearing as he settled into his desk. Viktor was seated. Close as he was going to get, and vulnerable.

Talon breathed slowly, drawing a trio of throwing knives from his belt, legs building up strength. He couldn't let this chance escape; couldn't let him escape. Not again. Kicking off from the smooth marble, Talon launched himself through the tower's opening, leaving his picks hanging within the wall. A fluttering of black grabbed his focus, and he let his knives fly, all leaving his hand before his feet touched the floor. Drawing his dagger, Talon hurled one more knife from his belt.

His first knife flew wide, passing to the right of his target, giving him just enough time to raise his hand to block the next two projectiles. A humming wall of energy appeared in front of him, stopping the knives dead in their flight.

"Assassin!" The Archmage shot to his feet, chair toppling to the floor, blazing hatred from his red eyes piercing through Talon like a needle. He turned towards the woman, "Get the guards! The informant was-"

Talon propelled himself over the desk, body shooting straight for the woman. 'In open combat, dispose of the easiest targets first, thinning their numbers,' one of the first lessons his master had taught him. She gasped, having no time to do anything else, Talon's elbow smashing square into her face. He flicked another knife at the mage, bouncing off the magical barrier, before slamming the pommel of his dagger into the woman's temple, knocking her to the ground in a heap.

As the woman fell at his feet, Talon looked over Viktor. He hadn't changed much since the last time their paths had crossed.

His face was gaunt, his long, messy hair still black as charcoal, eyes bloodshot and rimmed with ebony, turned manic under *its* influence. His robes were ragged and gray, weathered from their original black, a thick leather belt of a similar colour cinched around his waist, an abundance of potions and pouches attached to it.

Huffing, hate and anger threading through his veins, Talon bared his teeth. "So, Archmage is it? I see you're moving up in the world, *Viktor.*"

Viktor's lips cracked as he sneered, the seething within his eyes dissipating. "Ah, so we meet again, Talon. I knew it would be you who's been scrounging around these past two days."

Cocking an eyebrow, Talon spread his arms out, the gesture a mocking one. "But of course. Who else has the ability to make you sweat the bed at night?"

Viktor began circling the room, Talon following his lead, the two like opposite ends of a spinning staff. "You certainly have a high opinion of yourself. No one can say you lack confidence, though you do seem to be lacking in common sense."

Talon's left eye twitched.

"What'll this be, the fourth attempt you've made on my life now? Isn't this getting a little old?" Viktor smiled.

Talon's rage bubbled to the surface once again, a seething wave of caustic emotions threatening to overcome him.

Viktor cackled. "Though I guess you are one to hold grudges. Twenty years now, and you still can't get over how I *gutted* our dear master."

Talon snapped, rushing the length of the room before his mind could warn against it.

With a quick weaving of his fingers, Viktor loosed a bolt of magic.

His reflexes working faster than his head, Talon ducked under it, jumping to the side, a second bolt zipping past him. The spellslinger didn't have enough time for a third missile as the rogue entered within cutting distance, flicking his dagger's blade at Viktor's palm, sending a spray of blood into the air. Slashing at his chest, slicing through the ragged robes, a distinct rattling of metal links echoed as Talon's dagger struck chainmail.

Grimacing, Talon stepped forward, attempting a clean stab at the mage's neck before dancing back, a sudden buildup of pressure under his foot pushing him away. A pillar of magma shot from the ground, melting its point of entry, splashing across the ceiling before falling like molten rain.

Talon tumbled to the edge of the room, his cloak sizzling. Rising to his full height, he wiped the bloodied dagger against his pantleg. "You've gotten faster at casting that one."

Viktor's smile spread wide, and it disgusted Talon. "Well, I can't let you overtake me too much. That would just be disgraceful."

Crouching down into a more centered stance, Talon steadied his breathing. "Yeah, like you have any pride." With a quick flick of his wrist, he sent the last of his throwing knives towards Viktor, stealing just behind them.

CHAPTER 12

Selora spotted Talon for the briefest moment as he dove into the tower with knives flying. Not exactly sure if ten minutes had passed, Selora skulked towards the Citadel, Torden's plodding feet following her graceful strides.

The bodies Talon had dumped unceremoniously in the brush had started rotting at an unnatural pace, patches of their skin already turning green, blood, black as tar, running from their nostrils. Torden seemed unbothered by the malodorous corpses, but Selora's sensitive sense of smell made the scent near unbearable, the elf scanning ahead for more patrols with less care than she might have otherwise done so. They'd have to wait for the break in the guards' pattern that Talon had made before moving.

Staring up the length of the tower, Selora guessed that she could make the climb up with the same ease Talon had, with or without some fancy set of picks. Glancing down at her side, a far bigger problem presented itself: Torden. His stocky build, while strong, was unsuited to making such a climb, and the window on the first floor was just a series of punctured lines, just wide enough to let some light slip inside. They broke from the brush, leaving the building cloud of rot for the relative comfort of the Citadel's exposed side.

They would have to go through the front.

Torden following her lead, Selora slid along the building's side, peeking around until she saw the first guard standing sentry at the front entrance, hand over his mouth as he let loose a long yawn.

"Hey, don't fall asleep on me now! It's boring enough out here without me having to listen to your damn snoring." The second guard's voice wrapped around the Citadel's wall, his gruff demeanour peaking the other guard's attention.

"What're ya so worried 'bout? Not like anythin' ever happens 'round 'ere." Waving his companion's concerns aside, the first guard spoke through another yawn. "We could take a good long nap, and nothin' would be any different when we wake."

Hearing the other guard click his tongue, Selora slid further back into the shadows, shoving Torden back even deeper.

"Have you been around town lately? Everyone's on edge, and they're starting to notice the missing townsfolk."

"What, the drunks and homeless folk shoved in the cellar? It's not like anyone would actually miss 'em; you must be imaginin' things." He chuckled, leaning back against the Citadel's walls. "Though, ya do gotta wonder what the Archmage needs 'em for."

"He said it's to help 'clear the streets', but I'm not sure I completely buy that. Now shut up and stay sharp. The walls have ears, and all that nonsense."

Selora and Torden glanced at one another, nodding in unison. Moving slow as to reduce the sound they would inevitably make, the two shifted their weapons into position.

With surprising speed, Torden rushed around the bend, smacking the brunt of his ax squarely into the closest guard's stomach, crunching through his armour and knocking the wind out of him.

Selora jumped out, three arrows drawn as the second guard came into her line of sight. He opened his mouth to yell but was cut off as her first arrow pierced through his throat, filling his mouth with a gurgle of blood. The elf's second arrow went through his eye, her third left nocked on the bowstring. She heard the crunch of Torden's ax as it caved in the other guard's head, tensing up at the sound of splintering bones. "So gross," Selora muttered to herself, collecting her arrows from the pinpricked guard.

"Aye, ya get used to it." Torden whispered back, sliding his ax over his shoulder.

"I'd rather not." Selora motioned towards the front door. "Come on."

Together, the two dragged the guards inside the Citadel, the door swinging silently on its bronze-plated hinges. They now stood in a large, circular room, lacking any notable features. The walls were the same marble as everything else, with a few sconces to hold up torches for light. A blue rug lined with gold thread centered the floor, and some barrels hidden under the stairs, where they hid the bodies, were the only other furnishings. They latched the door shut behind them.

Selora crinkled her nose as she looked around, focusing on the rug in the middle of the tiled ground. "A cellar goes down, so..." She crouched down and pulled back the mat from its resting place, revealing the same pattern of tiles as the rest of the ground. "Well... that's disappointing. Guess it *would* be a bit more hidden, huh?"

Torden snorted, "Who'd be fool 'nuff to hide sumtin', and make it *dat* easy ta find?" He moved next to Selora and began tapping his knuckles against the tiles. A rhythm of solid beats echoed around before a hollow clacking played out, Torden tapping several times in a circle to gather the area of the hole. "See?" He grinned up at the elf, quite proud of himself.

She shrugged, deciding to humor him a little. "Good work. Let's start pulling out the tiles and see what comes up."

"I t'ink what goes down would be da more 'portant question, wouldn't ya?" A playful smile spread across Torden's face.

Selora rolled her eyes, "Just pry the tiles off already."

Huffing, Torden used the blade of his ax to pry one of the tiles out, allowing the two to get to the main body of the work.

Several tiring minutes of work revealed a boarded square door, a rung of iron bolted at its edge. "Ha!" Without a moment's hesitation, Torden grabbed the rung and swung the cellar door open, releasing a thick puff of dust into the air.

Used to such things, Torden remained steadfast and relaxed. Selora, on the other hand, began coughing up a fit, her lungs unadjusted to the choking minerals that now invaded her lungs. Her hacking and wheezing echoed around, disturbing the silence enveloping the tower.

After a minute, she calmed down, and the two froze, listening for any sign that they had been discovered. Save for the slightest rumbling coming from the top floor, there was nothing. Yet still, they waited.

Her shoulders slumped, Selora put on a weary smile. "Give me a warning next time you do that."

Torden nodded, a genuine sense of guilt portrayed across his stiff face and pursed lips. "Aye, sorry 'bout dat. Wasn't t'inkin'."

Her lungs cleared, Selora bent forward, peering over the shaft as it descended into an impenetrable abyss. "Well, this is... dark."

"Yer eyes'll adjust once yer under." Torden motioned towards the tunnel. "Lasses first."

"Just don't fall on me, you hear?" Clambering into the tunnel, gripping onto the cold, iron ladder, Selora's head dropped just under ground-level when a loud explosion rang from the top floor, briefly shaking the tower. "Oh, what's that dust-head gotten himself into?"

The front door shook, its lock rattling as a pair of voices rose up from just outside the building. Torden looked down at Selora, "Go quick now, Lass!" and slammed the wooden door over her, the crash of wood and metal ringing in her ears, echoing within the confined passage.

From above, she heard the guards rush in, their words garbled as they shouted warnings and threats at Torden. More clearly, she heard the dwarf answer back. "Let's get dis over wit, you louts! Y'know it's rude to keep da Gate-Keeper waitin'."

Selora tried to press the cellar door back up, but it was too heavy for her to manage. "Hey!" The elf's voice rang hollow in her ears, words faltering against the earthy tunnel. "Damn him! What's that idiot doing?" The muted sound of ringing steel and Torden's battle cries found their way to her sensitive ears. Gritting her teeth, Selora began her descent down the ladder. If he lost, there would be no advantage in her staying where she was.

Making her way down the ladder's length, the tunnel's temperature rising with each bar that passed, Selora eventually settled into a comfortable warmth. She lost track of time, the minutes burning away, her muscles aching.

Her soles found solid ground, and she dropped from the ladder, finding herself in a dark, winding cavern. Given a few seconds to adjust, her irises opening to the edges of her aqua eyes, her natural night vision faintly outlined the edges of the cavern. Selora's depth perception disappeared completely, save for the almost nonsensical order of corrugated lines in front of her.

Selora pushed forward, her bow unslung, arrow nocked.

The winding passage allowed no forewarning to the presence of enemies, and no space to shoot her bow. A nightmare for any archer, every bend and shadow ample cover for foe or trap.

Stepping around one such corner, Selora's nose wrinkled, catching the subtlest hint of a disturbing, yet familiar, scent. Selora picked up her pace, her cautious crawl turning into a light jog, anxiety knotting her stomach.

Each step she took disturbed loose stone, throwing up puffs of dust, the soft pitter-patter of her leather boots turning into a horrid *squish* as dirt turned to mud, the ground sinking beneath her feet, throwing her off balance. Flailing her arms, the elf dropped her nocked arrow as she stumbled forward. "Shit," she hissed under her breath.

Forging ahead, Selora slipped a new one from her quiver. She moved slow, taking measured steps, nose crinkling with each inhalation of the stale air, on the edge of remembering the familiar scent. Selora stepped out of the claustrophobic tunnel into the light. Eerie emerald flames flickered from sconces lining the curved walls of the large, domed chamber.

Selora's eyes shook while her stomach churned, the floor beginning to pulsate with a lifelike fervour. Chest tightening, her thoughts became disjointed, struggling to draw in breath.

Flesh, that's what she'd smelled. Pulsating, veiny flesh covered the floor, crawling up the walls in lines of black and blue beneath the pallid skin.

Selora looked up, croaking as her throat clenched up.

A fleshy cocoon swayed, dangling from the domed ceiling, a morbid chandelier. Swinging back and forth, it stared at Selora with its singular, bloodshot eye. Larger than a man, and full of rage and desire.

Selora's vision blurred, arms shaking violently, swallowing back the vomit threatening to spew from her stomach.

The fleshy cocoon twitched, a bump forming on its side, stretching out, fingers splayed against the taut skin. Next to the constrained hand, a face came into being, undefined features screaming out. Then a foot kicked out, opposite the face. Then hands, innumerable, pushing against their prison. Then more faces, their muffled screams mixing together, forming a deranged melody of pain.

Dozens upon dozens of people cramped into the fleshy cocoon.

Were the missing people in there? The 'undesirables?' She choked up, thinking back to the upper-district's empty streets, its homes silent and without life.

Selora gulped, breaking into a cold sweat.

Drooping down, ropey tendons stretching and thinning,

the mass of flesh descended.

Selora's heart raced, panic taking over, tendrils beyond the creature's physical form reaching out. Her head pounding, thoughts jumbled and vague, she drew, the arrow flying before her conscious mind could release it. The sharpened tip plunged deep into the dangling sack of flesh, one of its captives now motionless within, the wooden shaft embedded deep within their neck. Blood, black as tar, slid down the arrow's length, dripping to the earth below. Another figure, just behind the one she'd killed, began flailing, their shrieking audible even through their confines.

The abomination's stringy meat stretched taut before snapping, the ball of flailing bodies hitting the ground in rippling folds of fat and splashing fluids. Mucus seeped from its pores, tracing its path as it righted itself. Its eye rolled around freely within the inflamed socket, taking in its surroundings, focusing in on Selora, staring the elf down.

She froze, spine tingling as though a thousand spiders crawled beneath her paling skin.

Dozens of legs began to push out from the mass of mucus-coated flesh, lifting it up as it leered, the agonized moans from within turning to grunts of exertion as it lurched across the cavern floor. Bones snapped under the weight of so many bodies, the creature's gait unsteady.

Backing away, her breathing erratic and her arms shaking, Selora nocked another arrow. Pressing her lips tight, Selora raised her bow, drawing it back with trembling fingers. Aiming as straight as she could manage, she lined up her shot alongside the lumbering abomination's eye. Taking several deep breaths, steadying her arms, she pulled and loosed.

The arrow struck true, shaft shattering as it impacted. Wood splintered, leaving dozens of scrapes against the surface of the eye.

The beast wailed, thrashing around, its victims screaming

beside it, a monotonous melody dancing through the chamber.

Selora covered her ears, shutting her eyes on reflex as thick fluids splashed up, her head suddenly cleared of the creature's psychic stranglehold.

Rolling, the creature charged into the cavernous walls, smashing the bodies within to pulp. Hands pushed out, as though attempting to stop the mass of twisted flesh from smashing into another wall. These twisted and fractured too, hundreds of feet skittering across the floor, dragging the abomination from one wall to another. With each impact, the screams hit a crescendo, quieting down moments later, the collage of voices less and less.

Cutting through the air, aimless in their approach, the dozens of separate arms began to crack and crumple together, compressing then stretching out into bone-crushed tendrils. These tendrils ripped apart, scabbing over and forming into talons, shaping two vicious pairs of hands that began clawing at the cavern's edges. The spherical mass began to take a more complex shape, a long, spiny trunk sprouting from the creature's center, pushing the eye out into the air, forcing the arrow out as it reformed.

Through the abomination's transformation, with all the cracking bones and stretching flesh, the screams from the townsfolk died out, silenced by a singular wailing. An elongated arm swiped at Selora with long, scabby claws, lopping off the ends of her hair as she weaved away.

Selora ran, the tunnels shaking from the creature's violent outbursts. A gust of wind tickled her neck as talons raked the air, ragged breaths becoming gasps. The tunnel shook, rubble breaking away, dislodged pieces pummeling Selora.

Wrapping her arms over her head, she fled. Back through the tunnels, and up the cold ladder, praying that wherever the abomination came up, she wasn't within chomping distance of it.

CHAPTER 13

"On your knees." The commanding guard brandished his sword.

Scarlett cursed under her breath, but did as she was instructed. Rolt followed, though was much slower, more methodical, taking his time to rattle the nerves of the men surrounding them.

The guard tugged nervously on the collar of his hauberk, shifting the chainmail around as he bit his lower lip. "I said on your knees!" His voice was high, almost cracking.

Scarlett spotted the faintest of smiles appear across her companion's face as he finally got down, placing his weapon on the ground.

"Hands behind your head." His confidence restored, the guard relaxed, waving his sword around with authority. And, as the two adventurers followed his instructions, he lowered his blade. "Now, I have some questions for you two. First, on the whereabouts of your other friend."

Scarlett squinted. "Excuse me?"

"Don't play dumb with me, wench. We've been well aware of your time in Marbleton; all three of you." He lifted his sword and pointed it at Rolt. "A menacing human in a hood," then over to Scarlett. "and a roguish elf girl. Now, where's the dwarf?"

She could almost laugh; they'd been mistaken for Talon and the dwarf, and from the sounds of it, he'd picked up an elf along the way. Apparently, whoever had been keeping an eye on them, had neglected to point out Talon's size, and Scarlett's hood kept her ears securely hidden. "Well, info was good this time, at least," she muttered.

Rolt chuckled in response.

"Silence your muttering and answer me!" The guard blustered, his face turning beet red as he began waving his blade over his head, to the embarrassment of his men.

"You're new to this, aren't you?" Looking around, Scarlett noticed the general lack of respect for the commander, who sounded fairly young under his helmet. "I mean no disrespect by that, it's just... you seem to be lacking in years to be ordering around people twice or even thrice your elder."

Shaking, his teeth bared, the guard stepped forward. "I am Lieutenant Trevor Cornell, commander of the third squadron of Marbleton's City Guard, and my age is of no concern to mere criminals, much less *assassins*."

"Third? How sad, not even good enough to lead the B-team." Scarlett feigned pity for the man, shaking her head, forcing back the smile itching to spread her lips. While the young commander, Cornell, continued to bluster, Scarlett continued. "So, what does that make those guys behind you? Old men and cripples, perhaps?"

At this, even the older guards could not hide their aggravation. Some grit their teeth and tightened their grips on their weapons, while others just sighed. One of them even stepped up behind the young leader, whispering into his ear. "Sir, we should continue with the questioning. Do not let their simple insults rattle you so; it is unbecoming of someone in your position."

Taking a deep breath, Lieutenant Cornell sheathed his sword, allowing his men to keep guard over the captives. "Yes, yes, you're right. My apologies. That was, admittedly, a tad disgraceful." He strode over to the pair, tugging at the cuff of his glove. "So, picking up where I left off: where's the dwarf?"

Scarlett shrugged. "Probably digging up some rocks or

something. You know how they are." She could faintly feel her companion rolling his eyes at her, but felt far more clearer the guard's knee smashing into her face, sending her sprawling to the ground.

Rolt jerked at the sudden attack, stopping at the straining of bows still aimed at him.

With the exaggerated swagger of a spoiled royal wearing their new pair of boots, Cornell crouched next to Scarlett, bundling her hair in his left hand, the blood-coloured strands bleeding between his leather-bound fingers. "I'll ask again. Where. Is. The. Dwarf?"

She began to shake against his cold grip, chuckling at first, soon turning into full-blown laughter.

The guards looked around, eyeing one another, their commander looking to them for help, only to be met with the softening eyes of the confused. Even behind his helmet, Cornell's expression was burning.

Straining against his grip, leaning towards the guard's face, she dropped her voice down to a whisper. "You hit like a *child*."

Cornell snapped, gauntlets flying, steel smashing into the redhead's face, snapping it back, one blow after another. Scarlett laughed along, the hysterics interrupted with each punch she was forced to roll with. Her taunting laughter soon subsided against the lieutenant's rage-fueled assault, the air becoming somber as she turned silent.

Behind the blanketing pain, Scarlett felt her lip split, a tooth crack, and the myriad of bruises beginning to swell across her face. Blood pooled up in her mouth, only dispelled as her head was whipped from side-to-side, shooting out from between her teeth. Time distorted, every second filled with pain, but the blows came to their eventual end.

Cornell stood, chest heaving. With a flippant wave of his hand, Cornell's guards moved to surround Rolt.

Connor Kimbley

Eyes watering, Scarlett nearly snarled as the young guard crouched beside her.

"So... will you answer... my questions... now?"

In a final move of defiance, Scarlett tried to spit a gob of her blood into Cornell's face, but the guard slapped her before she had the chance, shedding the build-up across her face, spilling to the ground. The rest slipped down her throat and she was racked by a horrendous, bloody cough. Head resting on its side, bundles of her silky air shifted, Scarlett's ears bare against the cold air.

Cornell shot to his full height, whipping around to the rest of his men, eyes so wide they almost popped from their sockets. "She's a human! These two aren't the–" He bit his tongue as the ground began to shake, growing from light tremors into violent rumbling, throwing the guards off-balance, arrows beginning to slip from the archers' hands.

Rolt was fast, picking his rattling sword from the ground as he rushed towards the guards, slashing horizontally with both hands. One guard didn't get the chance to panic as his head was cleaved from his shoulders; the man next to him, however, only took the blade shoulder-deep. His yelp of pain dragged everyone's attention.

With Cornell distracted, Scarlett dug her fingers into the dirt and kicked out, the heel of her boot smashing into the back of the young lieutenant's knee.

Cornell collapsed with a grunt, his joint cracking against the plates of his armour as they hit the ground. With a feral growl, he spun around, drawing his sword from its sheathe. He was quick, his blustering backed up by daily training, yet Scarlett was faster.

Still on the ground, she twisted, swinging her leg out, the toes of her boot catching Cornell's knuckles. She heard another crack just before he lost his grip, dropping the sword only half-drawn. Bracing, the redhead swung her leg out and back like an ax, hitting the guard's face dead-on. Blood spurted from his nose and

126

he reeled, crashing to the ground in a squirming heap.

Clambering to her feet, Scarlett scrambled around the ground, fingers gripping the worn handle of her dagger. Metal clanked behind her, and she turned.

Cornell held his sword high, charging.

Scarlett ducked, diving towards him.

Cornell forced himself to stop just as Scarlett crouched before him. She tossed her dagger upward, forcing the lieutenant back, drawing the second from her belt. She slashed, Cornell leaning forward just in time for the knife to tear through his throat.

Cornell dropped his sword, hands clamping tight around his neck, blood gushing between the gaps of quivering fingers. Even through his gurgling, anger was evident in every menacing step he took towards Scarlett. Hands falling to his sides, Cornell collapsed, blood bubbling from his mouth.

Bruised and bloodied, Scarlett turned to help Rolt.

The giant man stood over a half-dozen bodies, sword splashed in red, the remaining guards fleeing. Shaking his head in disappointment, Rolt turned away.

Then *it* appeared. Off to the north-east, towards the large tower in the city's center, the ground exploded. From the rising cloud of dirt and stone, a nightmare ascended, an abomination of glistening, wriggling flesh. With a menacing array of tentacles whipping through the air, it pulled itself to the top of the tower, its singular eye moving erratically, scanning its surroundings. Stone crumbled and fell as the creature's massive weight tore at the bricks holding up the intricate walls, gripping the cracks and tearing them open.

And throughout the city, its horrendous screams echoed, a tsunami of psychic energy washing over Marbleton.

Scarlett fell to her knees, the contents of her stomach emptying from her bruised lips. Eyes watering, she strained her neck to look at the beast, vision blurring each time she tried to focus on it. "By the gods..." She croaked.

Rolt put his hand on her shoulder, nudging Scarlett as he stood beside her.

"That's what Talon was after, wasn't it? Why he left us?"

Rolt shrugged, helping Scarlett back to her feet, wiping his blood-stained sword along the side of his pants. Giving her a moment to collect herself, Rolt strode towards the crumbling tower and the abomination that clung to it.

Her face still swelling and her vision still a blur, Scarlett stuck close behind.

CHAPTER 14

Talon huffed, his clothes singed, his blade scorched black. His body crackled with blue energy, minor wounds sealing within moments, but drained of energy. His knuckles turned white around his dagger's grip.

Viktor's sneer had long left his face, replaced by a less offensive scowl. His left arm hung at his side, rivulets of blood running down the length of his arm, down to the tips of his fingers. Viktor swayed, eyes darting, wavering.

Chaos surrounded the two. The desk no longer existed, blasted into splinters, its contents fluttering through the air. The shelves and their contents suffered a similar fate. Fire wafted along with the night air, let in by the multitude of holes now peppering the walls.

"You... are surprisingly resilient, for a mage," Talon admitted, stretching his neck with a satisfying *pop*. "But I can tell you're just about done. Cast any more spells and you'll black out."

Viktor bared his teeth. "Like you're in... any position to speak down to me. Your reserves aren't limitless either, and you're... just about spent."

"That's true." Talon stepped forward, holding up his weapon. "But *I've* got a knife." He felt the side of his lip curl up as Viktor snarled, the fire in the mage's eyes dimming. "No more running. We finish this. Right here, right now." Another step forward, and the Citadel began to shake.

Walls rattling, more bricks shook free, cratering against the already shattered tiles. Scattered books flew open, the *shik shik shik* of snapping pages deadened by the tower's cacophonic tremors.

Talon stared at Viktor, watching the mage's face contort through different emotions. Watched as Viktor braced himself, Talon mimicking him mere moments before a massive tentacle swept the ceiling away.

The wriggling mass slithered around the opening, tearing away more bricks, tossing them high through the air. Heaving itself up, the abomination's singular eye peered over the edge of the office, puckered skin writhing. Glistening and bloodshot, its gaze shifted quickly between Viktor and Talon.

Sepulchre was awake, and it was much bigger than the trunk it had been in months before.

Talon's throat clenched, cold sweat running down his back. "What have you done? Viktor, you bastard!"

Viktor spun around, jaw tight. The perfect chance to kill him, wasted. "*Me?* It was one of your fool companions who shot it! It was perfectly happy staying underground while I fed it scraps. Do *you* have any idea what you've just wrought upon us, you foolhardy brute? Death and destruction, that's what!" Throwing his arm wide in anger, Viktor's face went taut, Sepulchre groaning, responding to the mage's gesture.

Slick tentacles forced their way further into the chamber. Soon enough, the tower would bulge and crumble apart.

Talon dashed, single-mindedly, with dagger held at his side, for Viktor.

But fast as he was, Sepulchre was faster. The sudden movement spurred the abomination into action, and it whipped one of its tentacles into Talon's side, tossing him across the room and into one of the crumbling walls. Talon heaved, coughing up blood. His arm felt numb, twisted in the wrong direction, ribs aching.

Even through the haze, he heard Viktor begin to laugh, his sudden mirth underpinned by his shaking fear. "You're as simple as ever, I see. Even faced with such a terror, you think only of killing me! I should be honored that you think so highly of my presence, but I'm more astonished than anything else."

Clenching his teeth, fighting through his pain, Talon made out Viktor's shape sauntering towards him, the even strut betraying his former exhaustion. How much was Sepulchre in control now, he wondered, and how much of the creature's power was pushing Viktor forward? Through his hazy sight, the mage's form distorted, stretching and splitting, lurching ever onwards.

Talon wheezed, gagging on his blood as Viktor's boot dug into his side. Twisting, Talon caught Viktor's next kick against his twisted arm, continuing into a roll until he heard the clinking of his dagger against the tiles.

Gathering his remaining strength, Talon swung. It was clumsy, barely catching Viktor's leg, but it was enough. Blood dripped down the knife's subtly-curved blade, and the mage jumped back in surprise, slipping on one of the many books scattered across the room. Falling upon his backside, Viktor's tailbone smacked against the ground, and he recoiled in pain. "You whoreson!" Viktor shrieked, struggling to crawl back to his feet, slipping on his own blood as it dripped from the cut in his leg.

Even with the few moments of respite he'd bought himself, Talon's body was struggling to stitch his injuries, focusing only on the immediately lethal ones. Cursing himself for his continuous weakness, he heard Sepulchre begin to shriek once more, only moments before the door to the Archmage's quarters swung open.

"Talon!" A familiar voice called out, weaker than he remembered it.

Scarlett and Rolt crashed through the heavyset doors,

131

huffing as they stumbled into the Citadel's bottom floor, Scarlett looking up along the tower's spiraling staircase. Cracks ran along every wall, rubble and debris scattered across the floor and ascending steps. Noting the puddles of blood staining the entrance, the two raced up the stairs. They got halfway up the tower before its shaking became violent.

Back and forth the tower rocked, slamming the pair against the wall, Scarlett bouncing off, her foot slipping against a broken step. Shouting, she wheeled her arms around, throwing her weight back towards the wall, swinging the airborne leg back onto the crumbling steps.

Rolt's face reflected her own: drained of its colour, eyes wide with panic. The tower's shaking receded back to its usual rumblings, and the redhead braced herself against the wall once more. "I'm fine... just a little... you know."

Considering his companion for a moment, Rolt nodded, warily, before continuing his methodical ascent.

Scarlett mirrored Rolt's path, heart pounding in her ears with each step. Every door they passed greeted them with silence, save for one, a violent gurgling and sloshing singing the two passed.

Just as she felt like she was going to collapse, they reached the top, stopping to catch their breath just before the large wooden doors; it was splintering, and looked as though it had endured a small typhoon.

They braced against the door, leaning into the frame just as a bone-rattling shriek hit them. Muscles surging, they threw the sagging doors wide, hinges screaming.

Chaos played out like a poorly orchestrated theatre show. Sepulchre rocked against the walls, throwing bricks in every direction, tile exploding under the raining projectiles. Two men stood on the room's far edge, one baring a knife on his side, the other screaming, the words inaudible beneath the explosion of ceramic and screaming flesh.

Scarlett charged, baring her teeth. "Talon!"

Rolt ran past her, sword raised, muscles flexing as he swung at Sepulchre, its writhing mass whining, mouth quivering.

Without even realizing it, she'd drawn her own weapons, closing in on the black-robed man.

The man in the black-and-gray robes crossed his arms before him, Scarlett's downward thrust shearing through his ratty vestment, the blade screeching against the iron links of chainmail beneath.

Scarlett dropped down, bracing her knuckles against the floor as she swung her leg. Her boot smashed against the side of the man's knee, her fist flying into his chin as he stumbled, knocking him to the floor. Leaving him there to nurse his new set of bruises, she ran towards Talon, sheathing her weapons as she slid next to him.

Welts and lacerations covered the rogue's body, the color from his clothes scorched away. Talon wheezed and croaked, his lips moving but forming no words. His eyes wavered as they met with Scarlett's, his eyelids closing as his breathing slowed. Magical energy continued crackling across his body.

Balling her fists, Scarlett stole a glance over her shoulder, just in time to see Rolt slicing at one of the dozen fleshy tentacles whipping through the Citadel. His sword, sharp as it was and swung from arms that could put a minotaur to shame, bounced off the abomination's exterior, the skin seeming to harden the moment before his blade struck.

Flicking his blade with grace belied by his size, Rolt grit his teeth as a tendril knocked away his sword, sending it flying. A moment later, another tendril struck him in the ribs, sending him skidding several meters.

His sword struck a wall, falling to the ground under a pile of rubble. Finding it would be a problem.

Scarlett snapped back to her own surroundings, catching

sight of the man in black jerk upright, limbs snapping into position like a puppet on strings. Snarling lips revealed blood-stained teeth, every word he spoke accentuated with undiluted rage. "You... whore!" Fists balling and face tightening, the man squinted with such effort that his eyelids wrinkled, veins popping along his face. Smoke billowed from his fists, twisting grays and greens swirling through the air.

Throwing his hands forward, power exploded from the mage, a sickly green smog dancing discordantly to the rhythm of whipping winds. Waving his arms, the mage released a blast of raw energy, sparks of emerald flashing from his pale fingers.

Too drained to dodge the arcane blast, the magic missile slammed into Scarlett. Born from powers ancient and inhuman, the blast numbed her thoughts and sense of self. Behind the blast's eldritch power, a single thought formed: *Sepulchre*. And thus, the beast was known to her, its name etched into her memory through a psychic explosion.

Lifted off her feet by the impact, flying straight over Talon's crumpled form, Scarlett hit the ground hard, skidding to a stop half a dozen meters away. The hate and resentment that fueled the blast filled her mind, the emotions coursing through her so vivid that she thought for a moment they were her own.

Pushing her back against the wall, Scarlett forced herself to stand, legs wobbling. Blood ran down from her forehead, tasting copper as it slid down to her mouth. Her world span, blobs of green and black shifting in her vision. Ears ringing, her back arched as a voice bounced around her head, each word a needle stabbed through her brain.

You will pay dearly for your arrogance, *mortal*.

The voice dripped with venom, Scarlett grabbing her head as though it would keep the words contained.

To damage my pet,

She choked, a cold hand gripping her neck, lifting her from

the ground.

Is a grave insult.

Scarlett's vision wavered into focus, her emerald eyes met by those of inky black.

The mage's body twisted into a disfigured parody of himself, skin pale and ashy, veins spiderwebbing along the length of his arms. A sickly green pulsated beneath his veins, thick wisps of magical energy oozing out of his eyes. His left moved independently from the right, bloodshot and erratic. Snarling, he revealed a set of sharp, yellow teeth behind his blistering lips.

Scarlett drew her daggers, stabbing frantically at the arm that kept her caged. Her blades, sharp as they were, bounced right off the corpselike man's now-leathery skin.

Struggle all you want, it will avail you nothing.

Scarlett kicked and struggled, tears running down her face, the grip around her neck tightening. Arms dropping to her sides, her daggers slipped from failing grips, hitting the floor with a dull clink.

Then she was on the ground herself, gasping for breath.

Rolt, his shoulder hammering into the man in black's side, grappled with the twisted figure of a man. Using his superior size and inhuman strength, Rolt tried with desperate fervour to throw his foe back, his bare chest now just a large bruise from the beast's tentacle.

The mage lifted Rolt, their disfigured limbs slamming the adventurer against his knee before swinging him towards the ground.

Weak! Foolish! Always thinking of yourselves as above what you truly are.

Rolt braced his feet, smashing the back of his fist into the mage's chin, snapping his head back. Pushing his advance, Rolt grappled with his growing opponent.

Scarlett glanced at Sepulchre, guessing it was the source

135

of the mage's strange and inhuman strength. Looking warily at the creature, examining it, watching its tendrils whip around erratically as they smacked against the tower, she saw how aimless the strikes were. Each one shook the Citadel, but only because of their size, none making solid connections with the tower they clung to. Stranger still, no attack came too close to the struggling mortals before it.

Scarlett scrunched her face, gaze moving back-and-forth between Sepulchre and the man in black. Its puppet.

However it was controlling the black-robed man's body, it was an arduous enough task to leave its main body stupid and senseless. She picked up her daggers, fingers squeezing the leather grips.

Too small, she thought, staring at the overgrown eye rolling back in its socket.

She needed to hurt it. It was the only way.

A simple task, she thought dryly. Not easy, but still, simple.

She scanned the room, assessing her options. Talon's crumpled form still lay twitching atop the broken tiles, his breathing easier. On his way to recovery, but still in no condition to fight. Rolt, still in the midst of his own one-sided fight, would also be of no help. Gritting her teeth, Scarlett saw that she'd get no assistance against the slavering creature.

Daggers firmly within her grasp, Scarlett moved cautiously, sweat dripping down her face, some drops turning pink as they glided over the mostly-dried blood staining her face. Stomach churning and lips quivering, Scarlett focused in on the creature's glossy mass, tears welling up at the edges of her sight.

Squirming appendages wriggled beneath its skin, layers of mucus breaking apart as the occasional limb pushed out, wriggling arms and legs stretching the taught canvas of skin entombing them, before being swiftly crunched into another tentacle.

Many beasts ate people to survive. This one was no

different, she told herself. Lied to herself, ignoring the screaming faces pushing out against Sepulchre's skin, grasping hands calling out to her for release.

Eyes stinging, Scarlett glanced around the room, looking for any reason to avoid staring at the horrors she approached. Step by step she closed the distance, hyperventilating as she neared, her mind clogged, unable to properly devise a plan. Then a glint in her peripheral stopped her, and the most basic of thoughts rung inside her head: *Stab it.*

Rolt's sword lay only a few meters away.

CHAPTER 15

The city rumbled, civilians screaming as blades bit through bone, steel clanging together as the old guard fought to protect them. Buildings set alight with flame burnt to cinders as marketplace stalls were hastily looted, left toppled in the streets, corpses hanging over them like the beginnings of a demented pyre.

Shivering in his hastily-donned armour, Captain Evrich sliced through one of the dozens of enraged guards that had begun to swarm them, a psychic humming always present in the back of his head, egging him on to greater acts of violence. "Everyone, head for the barracks! Men, protect the citizens at all cost!" Growling, he fought off two more of the crazed guards, his training from years of war easily overcoming their erratic strikes. Evrich prayed that the townsfolk were smart enough to run behind the wall of guards that *weren't* chopping in their direction.

"You heard the captain. Get moving!" Lieutenant Sigurd's gruff commands pierced through the veil of noise, splitting up the enraged and scared, the latter soon running for the protective wall of emblazoned armour. "Captain, we need to retreat!"

Evrich knew that all too well, but still he wished to fight, even as sweat ran down his face, stinging his eyes and blurring his vision. Even as his mind faded, losing focus with each glance he took at the abomination, clinging so desperately to the Citadel. "Just hold them off until everyone's safely behind us!" Gripping his sword in both hands, fighting back his fury, he stood his ground and prepared for the oncoming onslaught of rushing citizens and berserk mercenary-guards.

Rickard parried one blow, dodging another, turning the motion into a clean decapitation. Heart pounding, covered in sweat, he charged another of the crazed red-guards. All around him, people rushed from their homes, awakened from their dreams by the sudden chaos.

Another mercenary-guard danced along to a cacophonous melody resonating throughout the whole city, every step and swing of their sword playing to the discordant tune. Harmonizing with the shaking of the ground and the rumblings of the abomination clinging to the sky, the guard took a clumsy step forward and swung, roaring with an inhuman voice.

Rickard stepped aside, knocking the weapon from his bulging arms with a quick slap of his meaty hand. Grabbing the sword before it hit the ground, Rickard cut down his attacker with one powerful swing.

With only a moment to pull himself together, Rickard stared down at the corpse, noting its glassy eyes and leathery skin, so dry that it cracked like glass. Their arms had become large and unwieldy, veins popping against barely contained muscles. Whatever change had taken hold of it had given it little time to agonize, transforming both its mind and body within seconds.

Rickard threw back his shoulders, tossing aside the worse of the two swords he now held. Glaring at the tendrils of flesh battering the Citadel, he marched off.

His retirement, short-lived as it was, officially ended.

Sigurd struggled through the barracks' heavy doors, leaning against Evrich's shoulders.

Goddard shut the doors as his superiors joined the rest of the downtrodden escapees. "Captain, I think we're in trouble."

Goddard's voice shook, his eyes watering against the smoke bleeding through the doors.

He'd reacted the worst to the abomination's sudden appearance, almost dropping to his knees at the sight of it. The manic shouting of his captain and lieutenant kept him grounded, however, and he managed to retreat with the civilians, turning his back to the creature to protect them.

"I'm very much aware of that, Private." Evrich helped Sigurd onto his bed, the lieutenant's twisted leg bleeding over his sheets. "You okay, Lieutenant?"

Stubborn as he was, Sigurd nodded. "The bastard caught me from behind, that's all... thanks for the assistance, Captain."

Evrich smiled warily. "Well, it's just one of my many jobs, saving your arse. Now rest up; you'll be of no use in this fight with that busted leg."

Gritting his teeth, Sigurd motioned towards the barrack's front doors. "Prop me up against the wall with a spear, and I'll do just fine."

Evrich patted his friend on the arm, "Funny. Now hush up and rest; we'll find someone to tend to your leg." He spun on his heel, face hardening as he stood, his posture rigid and authoritative. "Alright, listen up!"

Both civilian and guard turned his way, the captain's voice cutting through the hushed murmurs.

"We can assume the chaos outside, both the guards slaughtering people and the citizens setting the town aflame, is due to the creature clinging to the Citadel. Meaning we can also assume that, theoretically, killing the creature should snap them back to their senses. Thusly, following that logic, the plan becomes simple: we will march towards the Citadel, and eliminate the beast." Evrich said all of this without concrete evidence, but a giant flesh monster was usually bad news, and killing it would give them all a goal they could aim for, regardless of whether its death helped or not.

Fearful mutterings began to stir from the civilians. "Does... does that mean you'll be abandoning us here?" A middle-aged woman, her expression tense, clenched and unclenched the grip on her dress, repeating the motion like a ritual.

"Not to worry. I'll leave a contingency of men here to protect you all while we take care of the creature. That said, if you wish to come along and assist us, there are plenty of spare swords and spears stored around the complex." By the wary glances shared amongst the civilians, it was obvious to Evrich that none would offer their help against the abomination. "Actually, you should all arm yourselves regardless. Even here in the barracks, there's still a chance you may have to defend yourselves."

More muttered voices echoed around the room, and a man in a leather smock stepped forward, grabbing one of the many spears.

Blood pounded in Rickard's ears, teeth bared, muscles aching as he cut through his city's aggressors, adrenaline fueling his single-minded rampage.

More guards, staggering along with their backs turned, loosing eerie moans, fell to his blade. Even as he cut them down, one by one, they marched for the city's center, unaware of his presence. Hadn't they been more aggressive simply moments before, hunting down innocent civilians? The old warrior assured himself that this were the case, and their sudden retreat, if it could be considered as such, troubled him in its own way.

Regardless, he cut them down, his body never hesitating whilst his mind pondered. Were they regrouping to a designated spot, or was something calling to them? Considering his options, Rickard continued his slaughter, never stopping until the last of Marbleton's killers was dead.

—·—

Twenty-two guards marched, Evrich leading the charge with his usual, stern composure. Sigurd, with his busted knee splinted, had been left at the barracks, along with seven others who simply couldn't muster courage enough to come along.

Goddard, on the other hand, marched nervously beside his captain, the private gripping his unsheathed sword so tightly that his knuckles went white beneath his shivering gauntlets. The other twenty marched behind in four lines of five, their stolid faces betraying their abject horror. "You could've stayed behind, you know," Evrich whispered. "No one would have blamed you, had you done so."

Keeping his gaze forward, Goddard forced a thin smile. "A little late for that information, Captain. Besides, my sister would never let me live it down, were I to cower and hide while others die in my place, though she would be ever so sad if I perished doing something foolish." His posture rigid, gait uneven, Goddard remained on his feet through pure force of will. "And what about you? Were you not allowed to stay behind? You keep casting your gaze downwards, every time you catch a glimpse of the creature."

Evrich had thought his wayward glances less noticeable under his helm, feeling shame at his show of weakness. "Were that I could. But, as your and everyone else's captain, it would set a poor example were I not leading the charge."

"It sounds like a difficult task, being in charge."

"Never was there a time when it wasn't, unfortunately. Though maybe you'll one day appreciate the honour of carrying such a burden, long as you make sure to outlive me." While Goddard seemed stiffer for their conversation, Evrich found himself relaxing, their banter distracting him from the grim reality of their advance, allowing a certain clarity when viewing the streets ahead. "Goddard, don't the streets seem calmer than they were a few minutes ago?"

"I noticed that myself, Captain. Was kind of hoping that the wayward guardsmen had come to their senses and just skipped town, or perhaps went to go kill the creature themselves." Goddard shook his head, a grim expression crossing his features, the private finally breaking his northward gaze. "I have a feeling that's not the case."

"Then you've prepared yourself for the worst?"

"It's not difficult to do so, when you can see the damned thing, scraping the clouds with its putrid form. No, I've not prepared myself; don't think I ever could. But I know what we'll be facing, so at least I won't be surprised when I'm forced to stare it down."

"Some advice, Private: don't look directly at it."

With each swing of his sword, Rickard took down another of the shambling guards. A dozen patrolled the inner gates, doors standing wide open while all others stumbled through. Creating a half-circle around him, they attacked.

Rickard deflected a horizontal cut, flicking his sword in a circular motion to parry another. Running the blade of his sword down his opponent's, Rickard threw the mercenary off balance before stabbing through their neck. Kicking out, he smashed in a knee, spinning to cut off an arm.

Someone grazed Rickard's shoulder and he killed them in response. Another sliced just above his eye while a third caught the side of his neck. Stepping back, Rickard let loose a flurry of swings and stabs, cutting down the pair pressing down on him. Resetting his stance, he dodged and parried a collection of clumsy swipes from the rest of the assailants, cutting each one down in order.

The last fell at his feet, and Rickard was alone. Breathing hard, he grabbed his arm to stop its shaking.

Picking up a new sword, he threw his bloody, blunted weapon to the ground, taking only a moment to wipe the sweat from his brow before passing through the inner gates which separated the peasants from the lords.

He could be forgiven his trespassing, he thought, given the situation.

CHAPTER 16

Arms shaking, Scarlett heaved aside rubble, the sharp debris tearing up her gloves, the thick leather protecting her palms from ruin. Rolt's sword, its shimmering blade reflective of the night sky, peaked out from between the blue- and gold-veined stone pinning it down. Gritting her teeth, she grabbed hold of its thickly wrapped handle, heaving with her whole body. Muscles straining, the stone shifted, the black blade sliding from its trappings. Grinding, screeching, obsidian sawed through cracked marble, finally tearing free, Scarlett stumbling with it.

Tired and swollen, she barely kept her feet, letting the massive weapon's tip rest against the ground. Seeing double, Scarlett shut her eyes tight, trembling hands and wobbling legs never steadying, even as her head cleared, and her vision returned. Her grip wide, she hefted the massive sword from the ground, five kilos swinging an arc through the air, the flat of the blade smacking hard against her shoulder. Knees buckling, Scarlett barked in pain, every nerve on fire.

Behind her, beyond Rolt and the puppet-mage, their exchanging blows hammering against one another, Sepulchre continued its wild thrashing and screeching.

Turning on her heel, holding her breath lest she topple, Scarlett gathered her strength and charged. Each thumping step shot pain up her legs and spine, teeth clamped so tight they threatened to crack beneath the pressure.

Still, she ran.

With each thunderous lash of the abomination's tentacles, Scarlett stumbled, dirt and debris bruising where they failed to cut and stab, vibrations threatening to knock her feet from under her.

Still, she ran.

Fueled by adrenaline, her legs pumped away on reflex, likely to fail her if she stopped. A rock smacked her temple, only a few meters from the gigantic eye rolling towards the sky, blinding her. Warm blood trickled down her ear, the pain overridden by the ringing echoing in her skull.

And yet still, she ran.

Clearing the short distance of the office in seconds, though it felt like minutes to her, Scarlett swung Rolt's sword from her shoulder. Leaping just as the point fell straight, she braced for impact, the last of her strength dissipating.

The hilt of Rolt's sword stuck out from the creature's eye, the weathered leather leaving Scarlett's hands as she flew across the room, one of Sepulchre's tentacles knocking the wind from her.

Sepulchre screamed, an inhuman screeching further shaking the tower.

Somewhere from her side came a more humanesque screaming, a combination of searing pain and uncontrollable rage that echoed in her ears with a hollow din. Expecting to meet the hard ceramic of the Citadel, she was pleasantly surprised when she felt her body fall into the rough cradle of Rolt's arms, his feet sliding across the uneven ground as he landed from his lopsided jump.

Skidding to a halt, Rolt set Scarlett down, her legs sprawling under her. "Thanks, big guy," she managed to wheeze, still fighting to recover her breath.

The giant man simply nodded, as he always did.

Sepulchre retracted its tentacles, coiling them around itself in a protective embrace, leaving the tower quiet.

"You despicable cur!" The words erupted from two voices, one booming, one echoing just a moment after. **"I'll pay that back in spades, I promise you *that*."** The man in black's left eye bled as he marched towards them, crimson drops running down his face in rivulets, his pupil gray and cloudy.

Rolt stepped forward, dragging his worn body to shield Scarlett, taking a mere three steps before collapsing to his knees, grunting in pain as his joints smashed against the shattered ceramic. Strong though he was, Rolt was still mortal, and the multitude of welts and bruises covering his body spoke to the severity of his earlier beating.

Weaving his hands through the air, the man in black chanted, "Hic me, Solis, et inimicos exurere in cinerem! Neminem relinquas aduersus me manu mea." The air around grew cold as an extreme heat built up within his palm, searing the pale skin to a charred black, a mass of smouldering stone forming between his fingers. Like ashes piling together, particles built up into a long blade, volcanic energy spreading through the obsidian sword like veins. **"I think this weapon shall suffice for you, swordsman."** The revenant lifted the crackling sword high above his head. **"Be thankful that your lives end at my hands, mortals."**

Something whizzed past Rolt, slamming into the mage's collarbone with a loud *crunch*.

The man in black staggered back, green mist leaking from the throwing ax in his chest. "AGH! Whoreson!"

A booming voice slurred, "Looks like I got 'ere just in time."

Selora kicked up dirt, sweat running down her back, unblinking as she took in the abomination filling the sky.

She emerged from the rumbling tunnel into a field of bloody corpses strewn about the Citadel. The dwarf's fate didn't even cross her mind, fear and shame driving her straight from the tower, into the open air.

She ran for a lifetime, each step like pushing through tar, invisible hands trying to pull her down. She fled further and further from the abomination, its tendrils slithering towards the moons, the cracking of bones and squelching flesh booming across Marbleton. Her legs no longer able to carry her, Selora collapsed near a large house she barely saw, heaving out her insides in a violent torrent.

She watched as her dinner spread out in a puddle, breath uneven. Glancing over her shoulder, Selora quickly turned, crawling through the dirt on hands and knees to escape the singular eye baring down on her. She collapsed only a few meters from her vomit.

There she sat, staring blankly at the writhing mass wrapped around the spiraling tower of crumbling marble, unable to focus and rid herself of the haze that enveloped her vision. Brick by brick, the abomination's whipping tentacles tore the Citadel apart, mutilating the few living bodies that still remained within its calloused carapace rubbing against the beautiful stone. It droned on, mindless in its assault, lash after lash, minute after minute.

In the distance, Selora spotted people shambling towards the chaos, streaming through the southern gate with erratic movements, into the central plaza. From civilian to members of the new guard, their red surcoats standing against the dark of night, individuals mobbed together, pushing ever forward. Behind them marched a small battalion of the old guard, organized, their training betraying the feelings of abject terror the elf imagined they were all feeling.

Feeling empty herself, and unable to muster any more strength, she resigned herself to staying where she sat, watching as events moved along without her intervention. They can handle it, surely, she thought bitterly. I'd just make things worse if I got involved again anyway. Tears wetted her dirty cheeks, salt stinging her tongue through gritted teeth.

Torden scanned the room. Giant monster, angry pale man, two humans he didn't know, and Talon crumpled on the far side of the room. Brandishing his battleax, the dwarf stepped forward, nodding towards the unconscious Talon. "Looks like ya gotten yerself inta some trouble, aye lad? Don'cha worry now, Torden Ironfist is 'ere to put things right."

Grabbing the hatchet lodged beside his neck, the angry pale man tensed up before tugging the weapon from his body in one sharp movement. "Ah... the dwarf. Yes, I *was* a bit curious as to where Talon's **newest batch of failures had scurried off to.**" His voice altered mid-sentence, the man's normal speech twisted into something beyond human.

Glancing down, the dwarf made eye contact with the two humans and, seeing the looks of confusion on their faces, smiled. "Big words comin' from a corpse." Circling around, away from the two humans, Torden and the pale man stared daggers at one another, shifting grips on their weapons.

"You will perish like all the rest, *mortal*." With his volcanic sword, the pale man leapt forward, slicing downward with a speed betraying his size.

Parrying the initial blow and stepping to the side, Torden found himself on the defensive as blow after blow rained down upon him. Cinders flew from his opponent's weapon with every clash, trailing smoke as they drifted to the floor. Overhand, underhand, from left and right, Torden found it not so difficult to parry and dodge the fiery flurry. Clearly, the pale man was not a warrior, though the speed of his strikes, and length of his blade made it far more lethal to try and close the distance.

The two figures danced around the room, the pale man's fiery assault never resting while Torden dodged, ducking and diving from the smouldering blade's path. They trailed around

151

the room, a line of cinder and ash tracking their path, collecting in a wobbling, disconnected circle. As this circuit came to an end, mostly washed away from gusts of wind, Torden braced himself.

With more force than previous strikes, the dwarf slapped the pale man's sword to the side, the head of his ax making a shallow dig into the volcanic blade. The pale man was thrown off balance while Torden released his grip on the mighty ax.

With a sudden rush, Torden grappled the man's leg, twisting at the joint, and using his lower center of gravity to topple the larger man to the ground. Together, they crashed to the shattered marble, the dwarf pushing himself up to jump on the pale man's chest. Doing what he could to keep his opponent down, the dwarf cocked back his right fist, throwing a mighty punch towards the pale man's face.

His arm, fully extended, never found purchase, his fist never landing. Torden, blood dripping from his lips, sailed through the air. The leather covering his torso now crackled with fire, his ears ringing from the explosion that had shot from the pale man's hand, the concussive force enough to launch him across the room.

Hardy as he was, even Torden couldn't fight off the shock of bones cracking, the exposed skin of his face sheared away by shards of marble as gravity took hold, lines of crimson joining the almost-orange of his beard. Stunned, the tangy flavour of copper filled Torden's mouth. A silent curse passed his lips.

Through blurring vision, Torden watched the erratic tip-tapping of black boots, the tattered leather a dusty gray broken only by the blood both old and new that covered them, rusted buckles no longer able to unclasp from the pale man's bloated feet. **"You are a tenacious one, I shall give you that. Unfortunately, swords are neither my specialty, nor the only weapon at my disposal."**

A groan escaped the pale man's throat, his robes rustling at the disturbance, barely noticed by Torden, the dwarf losing consciousness. "There's no way you could have known that, of course." Surprised by the sudden normality of his own voice, the pale man released a sigh that sounded of relief, throwing his sword down, letting it fall within Torden's broken grasp.

He turned from the dwarf, striding to the center of the room. There, he stood before the beaten down adventurers, his arms spread wide. "Alas, our time together is over, ending tonight's evening festivities." A devilish sneer crept across cracking skin, his razor-sharp teeth only accentuated by their near-rotted lips. "I wish we could entertain each other for a while longer, but alas, it appears that dinner has arrived, and my strings are no longer needed."

CHAPTER 17

Scarlett held her breath, the putrid stench threatening to invade her lungs.

A congregation of disease poured through the busted doors, grim parodies of men wearing the red of the new guard stumbling over each other. Flesh sloughed off bone with each step, blood and mucus gurgling from throats coated with disease, their armour straining to contain the bloat.

Groaning in delight, Sepulchre rumbled back to life, its tentacles casually scraping against the walls, whipping the ground around the fetid crowd as they made their way towards the gleeful abomination, spurred on by its sudden movements.

Struggling to move, Scarlett and Rolt could only watch as Sepulchre's fleshy mound of a body split open, revealing gnarled teeth formed from blood-stained bone shards, its gums calloused skin squirming around the jagged fangs.

A discoloured tongue spilled from the boney gorge, spotted with pulsating boils and open wounds bleeding pus, leaving behind a trail of acidic disease as it slithered across the broken tiles of the Citadel. It neared the crowd of shambling warriors, quaking with anticipation, before shooting out. The tongue forked at the tip into a dozen spears of muscle, impaling over fifty from the crowd of Marbleton, easily puncturing through the mortal-made armour. Just as quickly as they'd shot out, the forked tongue retracted, Sepulchre slurping in the massive group like a man in the desert finding water.

In and out the putrid tongue went, shredding through the crowd as quickly as they arrived.

Scarlett gagged, covering her ears against the grating noise of slurping meat.

Behind her, Rolt stirred. Straining, he lifted his knees slowly from the shattered ground. With his legs spread wide, he was able to finally balance himself, then stumbled towards the broken dwarf across the room.

Viktor's maniacal laughter filled the room, relishing each body that Sepulchre devoured. "Yes! Feed! Don't leave a single bite left on your plate!" So engrossed in the abomination's gorging, that he was completely unaware of the giant man dragging himself over to their discarded weapon.

Rolt grabbed the crackling cinder-blade from where it lay, the sword's handle scorching his gloves as he lifted it. His arms trembled as he held it up, muscles struggling to lift even this hollow weapon.

Fire burned in Rolt's eyes as he charged, feet dragging across the short distance to the mage. Muscles screaming, he lifted the smouldering sword over his head.

He wouldn't be able to stop the rampaging monstrosity, but he could at least kill the spellslinger who'd orchestrated its awakening. He closed in, taking one large leap before striking, gripping the sword with both hands.

The blade crumbled on impact, disintegrating into a cloud of gray, black and flickering red, leaving only the barest markings of soot on Viktor's neck. Ash slipped between the giant's fingers, and his eyes met with Viktor's, the mage's face contorted into an uncomfortably welcoming smile.

"You didn't really think that I would be felled by my own magic, did you now?" Pressure gathered within Viktor's hand, shooting out in a concentrated lance of pure force, impacting with the warrior's sculpted chest.

Knocked from his feet, the warrior skid across the ground.

"A valiant effort, my intrepid adventurer, but sadly you just weren't strong enough to beat me. To contain me. To lop off my arms and legs and throw me in a cell, shackled in chains, to spend an eternity in suffering." Viktor glanced over his shoulder at Sepulchre, the beast never hesitating or slowing in its feast. "Oh no, certainly not strong enough to do to me what was once done to my hungry friend over there." The mage sneered down at his beaten opponent, reveling in his inevitable victory.

He had been worried at its awakening, but the psychic leash fueling his body had wiped away his fears, the power creeping through his veins overpowering his doubts. They were connected now, more than they had ever been before. They were one, and together they would seek retribution from the world that had caged them.

"It's time we ended this. Now that Sepulchre has finally caught up on its beauty sleep, it'll need a countrywide feast to fill them up. It'll be quite the show, I've been led to believe." With a few brisk strides, Viktor stood before the large warrior, a crooked finger pointed down. "Too bad you lot won't be there to see it." Muttering an incantation below his breath, crackling magma swirled before his outstretched finger, building up in a quivering mass.

A shadow crossed over Viktor.

Reacting more on instinct, he turned his blast towards the rotting corpse flying towards him, shearing it in half with the blast of magic prepped at his fingertip. Annoyed, his eyes flickered over to the redhead, who was still sprawled on the ground.

"Archmage!" The new voice flanked him, leaving Viktor little time to react. Spinning on his heel, the mage brought up a shield formed of pure energy, an iridescent plane shimmering in its attempt at perfection. Clipping past just the first layer of his barrier, a steel sword, no different from those given to the common guard, flashed towards him in a cold fury of calculated strikes. In moments, Viktor's barrier was shattered, and he panicked, peddling backwards, throwing up hasty shields to avoid losing his head.

A mere man now struck out at him. Rickard, he recalled, having met him early on during his first appearances as Marbleton's Archmage.

Tall and muscular, but not the freak of nature that the warrior before him had been. A regular set of tunic and breeches, stained with sweat and blood, rustled through the clean movements. A grizzled face of brown hair and thick beard sat grim and focused. He was quick with a blade, this was undeniable, his years of training evident in the mastery of his skill as a swordsman. No longer having the boosted reflexes that came from Sepulchre's puppeteering, Viktor struggled to keep up with the assault, the ex-guardsman coming at him markedly faster than what the adventurers were able to muster since Talon had collapsed.

He was not facing glorified mercenaries anymore, their mostly-untrained skills untested on the fields of war. Now he faced a knight. A soldier, a veteran of melee combat, sworn to protect the lands and laws of the Eternal King.

"Archmage!" Rickard yelled, veins popping alongside his bared teeth, the spellslinger turning just in time to block his initial strike. No hesitation, Rickard moved from one attack to the next, his swings seamless in their perfection.

Every strike met resistance, each blow shattering another shield of pearlescent energy, Viktor's defense more frantic with each retreated step from the old soldier's onslaught. With no one else to step up, Rickard's brazen charge continued without rest.

Meanwhile, the creature gorged, devouring the thinning

line of bodies. Leaving only a handful of the rotting guards, it curled into itself.

Scarlett watched as bone and muscle swirled under its skin, changing into an amorphous, pulsating mass.

Sepulchre quivered, satisfied with the appetizers, now ready for the main course.

CHAPTER 18

Veins popped along Sepulchre's body, seven bulging masses gathering along its back. Six of the mounds spread evenly into two columns of three, the last mound pushing directly downwards, extending Sepulchre's already-horrific body as it formed first into a squirming bulb. The one stretched out into a tail, barbed all the way down to the end, ending in a vicious spear-tip.

Like the tentacles that now twirled around each other, forming more rigid appendages, its tail whipped the tower's side with incredible force, the structure quaking with each strike.

Along its back sprouted wings, thin sheets of flesh folding from boney joints, the massive span crashing against the Citadel's walls. The grotesque imitation of bat wings squelched, dripping with sweat, mucus and disease. The abomination's form solidified, its macabre parody of natural lifeforms warping perspective around them. With its new arms, still writhing like the tentacles they'd formed from, Sepulchre began clawing its way into the room, mouth salivating, walls collapsing and shattering against its immense weight.

Scarlett struggled to her feet, stumbling and colliding with the wall, narrowly avoiding Sepulchre's lashing tongue, scooping up what remained of the shambling crowd. She broke out in a cold sweat, watching as Sepulchre devoured the crowd in a single pass, licking its gaping maw as its eye – Rolt's sword still lodged deep within – settled on her.

It sneered, dragging itself across the floor with calloused talons, making a noise between gurgling and cackling. Licking mucus from its body, smearing the fluids around, its acidic saliva left a steaming trail against the marble tiles.

Scarlett's legs trembled, eyes tearing up. Pressing her back against the wall, she squeezed her eyes and mouth shut, turning away.

Look at me.

A faint screeching reverberated from Sepulchre, and Scarlett turned, back arching as she struggled against the psychic compulsion.

You have caused me a great deal of anguish, and humiliation, **little girl.**

Throat dry, Scarlett swallowed hard against the avarice seeping from the creature, its disfigured mouth twisting into a horrendous sneer.

Oh, there is no need to speak. The regret upon your shoulders is **palpable.** *Perhaps you feel bad for the damage you have caused to my great form... oh, but of course not. You feel regret at having let yourself fall into such a position of powerlessness. Regret over your inability to keep hold of your* **friend.** *Regret and* **terror** *that the last thing you will feel is being torn apart from inside me. But worry not, youngling, I will make it as quick as it will be painful.*

With every word spoken, Scarlett reeled, a gong ringing inside her head, her focus dulling as the sounds of the world became muffled before crashing in around her.

Her injuries boiled against the abomination's tongue, Scarlett shrieking, the pain immense. Rearing back, elation spread across its twisting face, Sepulchre threw itself forward.

Meat flew, and Sepulchre's mouth filled with blood.

Talon struggled to breathe, eyes aching as they opened to

the carnage around him, the *thoom thoom thoom* of rubble crashing against the floor waking him. Decaying meat lay strewn across the floor, the stench of death hanging thick amongst the winds straining in through the large cavities smashed into the Citadel's walls. A menagerie of sound blended together, the dissonant mix pounding against Talon's ears.

His vision cleared, familiar black robes pedaling away from a common-dressed assailant, his unremarkable sword a storm of death in his experienced hands. Viktor looks bigger, Talon thought, his head pounding. Struggling to his feet, the hooked claws of his gauntlets scraped against what remained of the wall, leaving deep scars in the otherwise smooth stone.

He *had* to get up. To finish what had been started so long ago. To stop the fifteen-plus-year cycle of cat-and-mouse, the typhoon of destruction left behind them, all for one purpose.

For Master Horace.

Cerulean energy dancing around him, Talon craned his aching neck to survey the room. Instantly, he focused in on Sepulchre, the abomination even more monstrous than before.

Bigger than he'd ever seen it, and more developed than what he thought it could become. It looked like it was on the verge of eating another mortal in its thrall, a woman straining against its hypnotic gaze, her identity hidden behind the beast's squirming mass. Tearing his eyes away, he glared at Viktor, the mage's back turned to him. He took a step, baring his crystalline claws.

Then he saw a flicker of red, and paused.

An illusion, surely.

Scarlett, bruised and bleeding, pushed herself harder against the wall.

Sepulchre's tongue, forked and whip-like, dragged itself against a patch of her skin, leaving a trail of pus mixed with dirt across her alabaster skin. The abomination reared, bleeding malice, the muscles beneath its skin bunching up.

Power surged down into Talon's legs, and he flew across the room, the scorched remains of his cloak billowing around him as the leather of his boots dug into the marble beneath. With no idea where his dagger was anymore, he slashed with the tips of his gauntlets, fluids gushing out as he sliced through the tough meat of Sepulchre's tongue. Standing between Scarlett and her would-be-feaster, Talon thrust with his other hand, his magically-charged fingers straight as his hand dug into the creature's eye.

Sepulchre screeched, shrieking as its severed tongue hit the ground, pitch rising as Talon hooked his fingers around the inside of the bloodshot orb, ripping his hand out with brutal force. A torrent of fluids poured out, splattering against the adventurer's back as he spun around, flipping his singed hood back over his head. His eyes connected with Scarlett's, for the first time in three years. "Wipe that goop off your arm, it'll burn straight through your skin."

She nodded, her perfect face spotted in black and blue. Each contusion another sin that needed to be repented for. "Right." Her voice cracked, straining with pain. Nodding again, she pulled out her dagger, scraping the sludge off with the blunt side of her weapon.

Baring his teeth, Talon once again turned his attention towards Sepulchre, the last few sparks of his magical power dancing around him.

Now blinded and grievously wounded, Sepulchre's elongated body thrashed in circles, its head and tail smashing away what remained of the Citadel's top floor. Craters formed beneath its feet, bricks flying with each shiver of its horrific form, its uneven skin now sharp and jagged, glistening like an ugly jewel.

Sepulchre's tantrum shook the room, throwing everyone still standing off balance, including Viktor's assailant, who lobbed a lopsided swing at the Archmage.

Viktor reeled back, swinging his arms in circles. "Crush this pest, damn you!"

Sepulchre whipped its tail around the room, the barbed appendage dragging across the floor as it swiped through the perimeter. On the edge of its reach, Rickard threw himself back, showered in debris as he rolled. Viktor, caught between the abomination and the soldier, took the brunt of the hit, Sepulchre's barbs catching his side, piercing through his chainmail, before lifting him up and tossing him not-so-gingerly upon its back.

Viktor's screams became muted under Sepulchre's own unrestrained wails.

Skirting just outside of the abomination's reach, Talon watched for an opening amidst its mindless thrashing. All too aware of his own exhaustion, the rogue moved with extra caution.

With its wings now fully formed and Marbleton sufficiently fed upon, the creature had no need to stay within the city any longer. Knowing this, Talon wasn't too surprised to see it spin around, lashing its tail in one final attack, before grappling the edges of the Citadel, and dragging its massive body out into the open. Flesh sludging out over the edges, it didn't take long before Sepulchre was sliding out into the air, Viktor's screams trailing its descent.

As the mass of flesh plummeted into a freefall, Talon lunged forward, jumping out after it. "VIKTOR!"

"What are you doing?!" The soldier yelled after him, his words hollow in the adventurer's pounding ears.

Sepulchre scraped the ground as it pulled up, its new wings struggling to gain ground. As the beast began rising, Talon aimed for the beast's tail. He landed fist-first, the claws of his gauntlets digging deep into the fleshy plates.

Viktor lay before him, on his back, bleeding and pale of face. "By the gods, you are persistent." He spat through gritted teeth. "Ten years of planning, ruined!" Blood stained his side, leaking through his trembling fingers.

Talon gained back strength with each step that he took, the wind whipping against him slowing down his march but reinvigorating his spirit. "I don't give a damn about your plans! You killed my master – *our* master. And with this damnable thing, what plan could you possibly have? World domination? Blind chaos? Nothing good can come of this monster!"

"Monster? Ha! You don't understand even remotely what Sepulchre is. Just like your pathetic *master* before you, only seeing what's on the surface. Sepulchre is a *god*! A blessed being, their power torn away by foolish mortals like *us*. All I've done is return a fraction of power that was once its own." Viktor coughed up blood, now wheezing. "What I'm doing... is worth more than just a few puny lives."

Talon lunged, seeing red as he wrapped his fingers around Viktor's neck. "NOTHING is worth what you took from me!" Viktor's pulse weakened under his grip, scrabbling at Talon's face with broken nails.

Then the two were sliding, Sepulchre's body screeching as the creature keeled to its side. They scrambled, Talon letting go of Viktor's neck to grab for purchase, fingers digging between its fleshy scales.

"What are you doing?" Viktor wheezed. "I was your savior, your salvation! Don't let me die like this!"

But as Sepulchre twisted around, the two humans fell, watching helplessly as the creature righted itself, continuing its flight into the darkness of the night.

Time slowed to a crawl, Talon watching as the light of demented hope flickered from Viktor's eyes, the mage's will dying out before they'd even hit the ground. Still breathing, but lacking any soul left for Talon to strike down. Killing him now, he realized, would avail the adventurer nothing. His revenge had been thwarted by the simple turning of a beast in flight.

A deep emptiness filled Talon, the forest outside of

Marbleton coming ever closer.

In the distance, a familiar voice called his name.

CHAPTER 19

"Talon!"

He jolted awake, cold sweat running down his face. He ran the back of his hand across his forehead, his leather glove soaking up the thick sheen that had gathered overnight. The gloves had been tightly-fitted, and were strangely warm; softer than he remembered.

"Are you finally awake, or am I going to have to dump some water on you to get the horses racing?" The faux smugness within his words was a constant, one that Talon had grown to appreciate over their two years training together.

The silver-haired youth waved the other boy off, "I'm up already, Viktor. No need to get the bucket again." Climbing to his feet, using the trunk of the tree he'd slept by for support, Talon took stock of their situation. The campsite had been neatly hidden away in the thicket of trees a ways off from the main road; just far enough that anyone who found them would have to have been looking.

The remains of smoked beef still hung in the air from the previous night, the campfire nothing more than a pile of cinders and purposefully-placed rocks. The bedrolls had been neatly packed up, and the singular tent with them. Camp had been cleaned up without his help. "Where's master?"

Viktor shrugged, his immaculate robes of red wrinkling from the slight movement. "Said he'd be back soon, but not where he was off to. Probably went to get some water down by the river, or hunt some rabbits or something."

A familiar tale, one that Talon accepted without issue. "I suppose he'll want us ready to go by the time he gets back."

"Undoubtedly so. We're still several hours out from Fallkirk, and he'll want to cover that ground quickly." Viktor swung his pack over his shoulders, tightening the straps so they didn't jostle. He then adjusted the buckle that held his spell tome to the ornate, leather belt cinched around his waist.

"You going to be able to keep up with all that stuff weighing you down, bookworm?" Never able to understand how he functioned with all his equipment, Talon found it easier to poke fun at Viktor for it than try to talk him into downsizing.

The young mage chuckled, "Oh, I'll be quite alright. Though, I may have trouble keeping up with those of us who got their beauty rest last night. Some of us actually stay up through their allotted watch."

"Oh, give me a break. You know I'm a light sleeper. Besides, I was just resting my eyes; I'm always battle-ready."

Viktor stared quietly for a few moments, eyeing the roguish boy. "You know your dagger slipped from its sheathe while you were sleeping, right?" Without thinking, Talon reached for the weapon, still firmly within its place at his belt. For just a moment, his panicked eyes betrayed the calm demeanour he tried so desperately to hold. Viktor tossed Talon his bag. "Battle-ready, right?"

Pressing his lips together so firmly that they lost colour, Talon slipped the bag over his shoulders. "Yeah, right." What followed was an awkward silence as the two adjusted their gear, the young boys unsure of how to proceed with their master still gone. "So..." Talon's voice trailed off, his inadequate social skills serving him poorly.

"You remember the mission details?" Viktor asked, as he

always did during an awkward break in their conversations, bringing Talon back to a point that he could discuss with confidence.

"Oh, uh, yeah. A village recently discovered some old temple nearby, and we're to make sure the area's safe."

"Why?"

"Because the ruins showed up suddenly, where there had been just a hill before, and there could be any number of creatures-"

"Undead or otherwise lurking about, correct."

Still not fully awake, it took Talon a moment to realize the voice speaking to him now was a new one. He spun around, glancing a bemused smirk upon Viktor's face before laying his eyes upon the familiar face of his teacher. "Oh, master Horace! Uh... good morning."

Their master, scratching his scraggly beard of salt-and-pepper, gazed up at the sky for a few moments. "Yes, I suppose it is. Dry for now, though a bit cloudy." He nodded to himself. "Indeed, a good morning to be sure. Astute observation, Talon."

Unsure of whether he was being talked down to, Talon glanced over at his fellow student, who simply shrugged at the unspoken question. "Right, okay. So, Master, should we be heading out then?"

Horace cocked his brow. "Unless there's something else that requires handling. If not, then we head out right away." He didn't wait for an answer, and began making his way towards the road from the open copse. Talon and Viktor tightened up their gear before rushing after their master.

The journey's end took the better half of the day, and the clouds had moved in, water drizzling across the adventurers as they entered within the boundaries of Fallkirk. As a small village that specialized in the production of lumber, the rural settlers were largely uneducated in the ways of magic or historical architecture, offering few details of the ruins, save for where the ancient-looking structure now stood.

With the rolling plains going on for miles amidst the western regions of Udrela, the stone columns and crumbling arches were not immediately visible from the village's edge. It was only after walking another kilometer-or-so that the structure came into view, its purpose suddenly clear to the trio of travelers.

"It's a tomb." Viktor whispered, the thick fog around them threatening to choke out any life that made its presence known. The mage gripped at his collar, pulling the fine silk from his neck, huffing. "It's draped in death, and an unrelenting hunger for life."

"Perfect place to find some undead, it sounds like," Talon added shakily, fingers caressing the fresh leather binding around his dagger.

Horace, ever cautious, drew his sword. "Talon, to my left and two meters behind. Viktor, watch our backs. Whatever's in there hasn't left yet, which means there's a good chance it's bound to the place."

Walking deliberately down the soft slope, the young boys took their positions behind their master.

Two stone figures stood vigil on either side of the tomb's entrance, each with a single wing on its back, pointing away from the somber grave, their carved faces harsh even under the cloud-heavy sky. Each bore a longsword, pointed down into the ground, the weathered crossguards covered in elaborate runes, their crisp forms long faded from heavy rains and whipping winds. Whoever's visage the statues had been carved from was unknowable, but even within the lifeless stone the craftsmanship made clear the power and reverence that was once held for them.

The limestone doors hummed a faint song, immaculate runes alight with ancient magic. Viktor, squinting at the symbols from behind Talon, loosed a frustrated growl. "Well, that's annoying."

"Problem?" Horace glanced back, the shimmer of his brown

eyes hidden beneath the moist air.

A quick nod. "These runes are carved in the tongue of death; a set as dead as the god it originated from."

"Zeichfer, you mean?"

Viktor swallowed hard, his throat dry at just the mentioning of the corpse god. "Just so."

Talon looked between the two, confused. "And that means?"

Wiping sweat from his forehead, the young mage seemed hesitant to answer. "Well, usually that would mean nothing more than for this place to have once been worshiped by his followers, abandoned ages ago. But with the sickly energy hanging around the place, I'd say it's far worse than just some abandoned tomb.

"That said, the magic here has largely faded, the wards keeping it hidden only recently dissipating, which is probably why the people of Fallkirk have only just spotted it."

Talon chuckled, false mirth failing to hide the anxiety pulsing through his body. "Ancient magic from the god of death? Nothing to worry about."

"Just stay sharp, you two." Delaying no longer, Horace put the leathery palm of his glove atop the door.

Feeling the warmth of life, the runes upon the door sparked, green and purple energy drifting from the ancient notes. With an ear-shattering creak, the doors scraped along the ground, opening themselves wide, stopping only when they slammed against the inner hall leading into the cavernous belly of the tomb. Their purpose fulfilled, the magic within the doors faded, leaving only the scratched out letters of Zeichfer's cursed tongue upon them.

Horace lit a torch, and they made their way inside, moss squishing beneath their feet in thick layers. Moisture coated the walls, air whistling through its cracked surface. Deeper down, they heard dripping water, echoing down the cramped passageway.

Talon swallowed hard, sweat stinging his eyes as the light of the torch wrapped around his master's body, fiery tendrils writhing in the darkness. They danced around the walls, flickering claws that threatened to come down upon the trio. The notion struck him as ridiculous, and the young adventurer swatted the thought aside.

"Watch your step." Horace's advice came as he stopped, Viktor bumping into Talon at the sudden stop, the momentum of their fall carrying them to the ground. Their master avoided them by stepping to the side, waiting for the groans of his apprentices to subside before speaking again. "Talon, can you see?"

Helped up by Viktor, the silver-haired boy scanned the hall, the blue tint of his night vision picking up minute details of the old, stone passageway. "It's an empty hall; nothing hostile directly ahead."

Horace nodded, "Good. Let's continue then"

"We're fine, by the way," Viktor muttered.

Talon patted his shoulder before following their master further down the tomb.

Talon's nose wrinkled, the foetid air wisping into his nostrils, slipping through closed fingers as he covered his face. His thoughts lost clarity as they delved deeper, forcing himself to keep his breathing controlled.

"Quite the horrid scent," Viktor noted, his voice muffled, face covered from within the crook of his arm. "Whatever's down here certainly wasn't preserved well, I have no doubt of that."

Talon shook his head. "This tomb is supposedly thousands of years old, right?"

Viktor nodded. "Correct."

"Well, nothing rots for *that* long."

Viktor paused for a moment, face scrunching up at the thought.

"Nothing natural, at least," Horace added.

The black-haired youth groaned with an exaggerated roll

of his eyes. "Well, no one can say our little group isn't optimistic."

Suppressing a chuckle, Talon began scanning the walls. Rune after rune had long ago been scratched into the stone, unreadable to his unscholarly mind, and completely devoid of the magic they must have once held, rendering the former point a moot one. "Any ideas for what kind of spell was woven into this place?"

"I haven't even mastered the *living* languages of spell-crafting, so you'll have to excuse my lack of knowledge for what's largely considered a forbidden tongue." Viktor's voice lacked his usual pride, words sliding out as a listless murmur.

Talon continued, the conversation keeping his mind clear. "Well, you identified it pretty quickly, so I just thought you might be able to decipher some of it."

"I can't read any of it, save for a few basic words and phrases, and that was largely taught to me for the *sole purpose* of identifying it. If you ever bother to study magic languages, you'll find that each one has its own stylization and affectations." Viktor motioned towards the wall with a wave of his arm. "Death runes, as you've probably noticed, look like they've been scratched at with a sharp rock, attempting intricate patterns without the ability to maneuver curves, leading their turns to be sharp and often connecting multiple lines together to make up for it. It's why a lot of them tend to be hexagonal in form."

Cocking his head to the side, glaring more harshly at the runes, Talon started to make sense of the designs, which had seemed almost random to him. "That is... useful information to have."

Horace cleared his throat. "Not as useful as you'd think. The chances of you running into a place that's actively using this type of magic is rare. Even veteran explorers may only see two or three places like this throughout their lifetime."

Viktor ran his fingers along several of the runes as they walked. "It's even more uncommon to find a group or even an

175

individual that still practices this language, as it's been largely banned in most civilized cultures, any evidence actively burned away by the Order of Paladins."

Talon's free hand once again moved to the dagger at his hip. "Is it really that big of a deal? I mean, magic is magic, right?"

Viktor sighed, his patience clearly being tested. "Different languages call upon different magical forces. Death runes gather energy from the land of the dead, *Sol'tel*. It's very good at dealing with, you know, dead stuff. Take for example, a necromancer. While other magical languages can raise and control corpses like puppets, the language of Death can actually implant souls into the bodies, giving them more autonomy and sense of self. It has the distinct downside, however, of opening small rifts to the land of the dead, allowing spirits to come through more freely.

"Though, mastering the language of Death can also allow a necromancer to control spirits such as wraiths and geists, to trap souls, and ultimately leads to a lot of them turning themselves into liches. It certainly has its uses, like most magic." Viktor slowed, eventually coming to a full stop as he scanned several runes that caught his attention.

Talon stopped soon after, turning around to watch as Viktor squinted, chewing on his lip. "Is something wrong?"

"I just... I feel like I've seen this phrase somewhere before, in my readings. 'Souls to be,' or maybe it's 'to those soulful,' or 'with willful souls?' Gah, nevermind! It doesn't matter anyway, the runes are long dead." Viktor started walking again, pushing Talon along. "Come on now, before our dear master leaves us behind again."

CHAPTER 20

The door glowed ominously as they approached, purple and green mist mixing together as the magical energy bled from the scratched-out symbols. Iron chains dangled across the giant slab of earth, rattling and dancing, reaching for the adventurers as if sensing company for their noisome festivities.

"Well, if there was any kind of destination in mind, I think we've reached it." Viktor's ragged voice echoed between the walls, the sickening odour thickening with each step taken. "The rusted chains are a bit much, but I appreciate the lights; really goes well with the whole 'us probably dying today' aesthetic."

Squinting at the entropic dance of intertwining energies, Talon's sense of danger deepened, his pride the only thing stopping him from voicing as much. "Wouldn't it be closer to 'tonight' by now? Feels like we've been walking for hours."

"Are... are you really nitpicking the phrasing of my banter right now?" Viktor's expression was a mix of irritation and pure befuddlement.

Horace stepped forward, tapping one of the lower chains with the edge of his sword. The metal links rippled like a droplet of water falling into a lake, reverberating until they reached the ends of that line of iron. "Interesting. Viktor, what do you suppose would happen if I cut through these chains?"

"As your magical expert? No idea. As a source of common sense? The door will probably open." He waved towards the point of his irritation with bent fingers. "Whether that's a good idea or not will largely depend on what's behind said door."

"Good enough." Their master nodded and raised his sword in a two-handed grip. Stepping into his swing, he cleaved through the chains, splitting a particularly rusty link down the middle. The two split ends hit the ground, scraping as the weight of the iron length settled. Horace stepped back and waited. And waited... And waited.

Talon leaned in towards his fellow apprentice, whispering. "What were the chances of those just being regular chains, by the way?"

Viktor shrugged. "Could have been purely aesthetic, could have exploded on contact, or they could have come to life and strangled us all. It's really hard to say with ancient magic sometimes."

"Your field of knowledge is, at times, unpleasant."

The chains laid upon the ground, unmoving, lacking the vigour they'd previously shown. Talon exhaled at the anticlimactic display, thinking the chains devoid of purpose. Only as if to spite him, they started rattling once more before quickly retracting towards the wall. Zipping through the rungs at the edges of the stone, the chain shortened, seeming to disappear into itself until nothing was left save for the rattling, which continued to echo through the cavernous passageways.

The runes upon the door shined bright for a moment, the slab rising up into the ceiling, opening into a large chamber. What sat inside even Talon couldn't quite make out, the darkness inside impenetrable. He could, however, see Viktor's smirk from his peripheral.

"Common sense wins out again."

"Well, that was certainly something." Horace inspected his blade for any chipping before letting the weapon rest at his side once again. "Talon, do you see anything?"

Squinting in one final attempt to glean some kind of information, Talon saw absolutely nothing. "A lot of black. Not even the colour, but just... darkness. A lack of, well, anything."

Horace nodded his approval. "Checks out so far." His phrasing struck Talon as odd, but he was far more concerned by his master's lackadaisical manner as he strutted into the chamber, disappearing into the darkness.

Talon rushed after his master, hearing the light footfalls of Viktor following him soon after. Together, they slipped through the all-enveloping darkness, learning several things all at once.

First, that the darkness was another source of energy, its swirling force throwing the two off balance.

Second, falling face-first into a stone floor hurt quite a bit.

Their final lesson, as they threw up what remained in their stomachs, that the sight and scent within had been relatively contained behind the magical darkness.

Hunched over, tears dripping down their faces, the insides of the two boys emptied, their senses coming back to them properly only after several minutes. Even the disappearance of the swirling darkness, and the return of their sight, did not break them from the assault on their insides.

Only after their stomachs were rendered desolate, and their minds desensitized to the mephitic gases of the sepulchral chamber, did they look up and realize they could once again see each other. Talon, barely a silhouette to Viktor, made out the young mage in excruciating detail, covered in sweat, the edges of his mouth still layered thinly with vomit. Surely, Talon thought, he must have looked a similar state.

"You two done over there?" Horace stood near the center of the chamber, his sword now sheathed and a pair of crystalline gauntlets over his forearms, which he quickly stuffed away into his pack when realizing that Talon had spotted them.

"Yeah, I... I think we're good now."

"Speak for yourself." Viktor wiped the vomit with his sleeve, struggling to get back on his feet, fighting back the bile that was still trying to force its way out. "Please just tell me that we're almost done here."

The grim frown upon their master's face answered Viktor's question.

Talon watched as Horace began to march, heading towards the back of the chamber where something squirmed amidst the bondage of heavy chains, like those outside. Drawing his sword once more, the older man stepped cautiously. The chained creature began to thrash about, rattling the restraints that kept it held aloft two meters from the ground.

The creature was small, easily held by the hands of an adolescent were it not for the stubby tentacles that writhed around in protest of such an act. A singular, bloodshot eye took up a large portion of its mass, the opposite side completely split agape by a line of slavering, boney fangs, crisscrossed like straightened fingers interlocked.

Standing free of its gnashing mouth, Horace whispered something and, line by line, the runes scratched across the walls began to light up. Unlike the rest of the tomb, these symbols radiated a calming blue, their structure more curved and elegant, less frantic in their creation.

Viktor's face relaxed, fascination taking hold before turning sour. "Ah, elvish... fun."

Squinting, Talon figured out quickly that his understanding of the elven language was just as nonexistent as other magical tongues, and that these languages were far from intuitive. "Can you read *this*?"

"Some of it, sure, but my studies haven't delved too deeply into elvish. That said, I could probably translate most of this with some time." Unclipping the tome at his waist, Viktor flipped through the pages, eyes moving up and down, comparing the writing on the wall with the inscriptions in his book. Then he closed it, hooking the book back into its harness. "But before that, I think I'd like to know what in the gods' names that wriggling little... *thing* is."

Talon had almost forgotten about the creature, being about the only thing he'd expected to find in a magical crypt. "We should probably deal with that problem first, now that you mention it."

Together they walked, watching as their master poked the creature with his sword in one hand, stroking his beard with the other. It swung back and forth with each poke from Horace's sword, the blade unable to penetrate its flesh, regardless of how much pressure was put down.

"Not as big as I imagined," Horace muttered to himself, Talon once again struck by his master's strange wording, but pretending not to have heard him. Stepping away from the creature, he examined the lines of runes surrounding them. "Viktor, you said you could translate these, correct?"

"With enough time, sure. This is a lot of work, though, and it could honestly take weeks to accurately get through it all."

"Well, we're not in a hurry, so get to work." Horace sheathed his weapon, glancing over at the fleshy creature. "Just try not to stare at... whatever that thing is for too long."

"Trust me, that won't be a problem. Thing creeps me out."

Horace nodded, his expression softening. "As it should. Come, Talon. We'll set up our bedrolls and a fire, and then you can head back up to get some supplies, preferably some incense from Fallkirk's church. We'll be down here for a while, and that smell is pungent."

Two weeks passed in a blink. In that time, Talon made several trips between the tomb and Fallkirk for supplies, always rushing right back to set up the incense and restock food. His master, on the other hand, tended to take his time up top, talking to the villagers and reading the small selection of books available at the modest chapel.

This left the younger adventurers alone, Viktor spending hour after hour transcribing the runes upon the wall, piecing together the spells cast upon the room at an excruciating pace, while Talon was left to simply wait. Watching. Listening. Whispers in the back of his head, always strongest when he looked upon the chained creature. He felt drawn to its gaze, the hints of words that he didn't understand sweet and indulgent.

Repugnant as it was, Talon found his mind at ease – though lacking clarity – when staring at the creature, his focus only torn away when Viktor or Horace distracted him. As in the current moment, where the fellow apprentice sat grumbling, cursing under his breath, face buried within his palms. Pushing himself to his feet, Talon made his way over to his frustrated friend, crouching next to him as Viktor continued trying to read the walls between his fingers. "Everything going wrong over here?"

Viktor sighed, letting his hands fall atop his crossed legs. "Yes! My mind is being fried here, I've not seen the sky in two weeks, and that *thing* smells like a month-old latrine." He pointed accusations at the flesh ball, which made a noise comparable to a cat's hissing, though drowning in its own phlegm. "And just glancing at it makes my head hurt, which I wouldn't doubt is just pure, undiluted revulsion that I'm feeling."

"Is it really that difficult to just translate these?"

Shaking his head, Viktor motioned towards the wall with a casual wave of his hand. "It's not that simple. Sure, it's nothing more than time-consuming to change one set of symbols into another, and if that's all there was, I'd probably be done by now."

"Then what's the problem?"

A bunch of parchment was spread in front of Viktor, shifting around further as he picked up a single sheet from the pile, holding it up to Talon. In crisp ink, there was note upon note, translating, breaking down, and grouping up different symbols, deciphering their meanings. Talon took it gingerly, scanning its contents. Translating the runes into a more basic form of mortal spellcraft, Viktor then seemed to be able to more accurately figure out how the elvish symbols fit together. "Okay, so spells are the manifestation of magical energies into a physical form. That's about the basic understanding that everyone has, correct?"

Talon nodded, slow, comprehending only half of Viktor's words. "Right?"

"Right, but what most people don't understand is how spells are formed. I'm not going to waste time trying to explain it in-depth, but basically, symbols within magical languages conjure effects; the more complicated a spell, the more runes are required to bring it to fruition." The wariness that had plagued Viktor's face began to fade as he spoke. "Actually, calling them languages is a bit misleading, in terms of spell-crafting. They're closer to mathematical formulas, each symbol affecting every other symbol both before and after it in different ways. You following me?"

Talon nodded again. "I think. So, this is similar to breaking down a math problem?" A foul taste filled Talon's mouth at the thought of his master's education, and the mental strain that came from that particular subject.

"Correct, though it's far more complex than simple arithmetic. It's even more difficult when you consider that each symbol is still technically representing a word or phrase, which is hard for most people to disconnect from. Elvish is probably the worst, because it's both a magical *and* spoken language."

Still examining the sheet, Talon spotted an untranslated group of symbols, his head becoming foggy as he tried to decipher them. "I don't understand this."

"Yeah, I know, that's why you're not helping me with this nightmare." The young mage chuckled, taking some modicum of joy in his superiority.

"No, I mean, doesn't this read more like a warning than what a spell should be?"

Viktor ripped the sheet from Talon's hand, quickly scanning through it. "Can you read this?" His tone was almost accusatory, though hidden under audible disbelief.

Hearing the question, Talon's mind cleared, and his face soon held the same confused expression as Viktor's. "I... shouldn't. I can't." He shot to his full height, scanning the walls, seeing words and phrases where there had only been scribbled lines before. "This isn't right. Viktor, something has gone wrong."

"That is a severe understatement." Viktor pushed himself to his feet, placing his hand upon Talon's shoulder. "We may need to discuss this with Master."

"Yeah, right. He'll know what's going on, or at least what needs to be done about it." Talon looked over at the creature again, sweat trickling down his neck.

Horace's face paled as his apprentices explained the situation to him. They all sat cross legged on the ground, Horace stroking his beard. "And you're sure you're accurately reading what's on the wall?"

"I double checked, it was flawless." Viktor's pile of notes had been neatly stacked and bound with several clips, the only missing sheet held firmly within his hands, having translated several phrases he'd had Talon speak out before Horace had returned.

Staring intensely into Talon's eyes, Horace resembled a wolf eyeing its prey, solely focused on his roguish apprentice, watching his every movement. "Talon, I'm going to need you to be *very* honest with me: have you been staring at the creature?"

Flinching at the accusation, his master knew the answer before he answered. "I sometimes... find my eyes drawn to it, and when that happens, I... it's hard to tear myself away."

"How bad has it gotten?"

Talon glanced over at Viktor, the young mage just as

confused as he was. "What do you mean, 'how bad?'"

Horace's jaw clenched, a vein rippling at his temple, his voice strained. "Does your vision go blurry when you look at it? Do you hear whispering in the back of your mind? Do you ever find your head filled with thoughts not your own?"

Almost instinctively, Talon tried to back away, uncomfortable with the depths of his master's knowledge, and the accuracy at which he unleashed it. "How did you know about the whispers?"

For a man of his age, edging into his fifties, Horace moved quickly. His swordsmanship was matched by few people, and his ability to throw away mercy for the sake of completing a job could be seen by many people as heartless. Talon had always admired these aspects of his master, even now as his collar was tightly gripped, the blade of Horace's sword pressed against his neck. "What have you heard? What *lies* has that thing tried to tempt you with?"

Viktor shot to his feet, looking back and forth between his two companions, panic taking hold. "Wait, hold on, what's going on?" Their master gave no answer, simply staring daggers into Talon, waiting for an answer.

"I haven't been told *anything*. The whispers, they're just... noise." Talon shivered, his master's eyes boring into his.

Horace let go of his student, sheathing his sword as he took a step back. "Then it's not too late for you."

"What is even going on right now?" Viktor reiterated.

Rubbing his temples, Horace plopped back down to the ground. "In short, Talon's been compromised." He eyed his students, both waiting in silence for him to continue. With an uncharacteristic exasperation, he did. "Okay, so you two have probably noticed my extended leaves during supply runs. Well, during that time, I've been at the chapel, reading from their – admittedly small – library.

"I was hoping to find some information on that creature over there," Horace indicated vaguely towards the back of the

185

cavern, "and for the most part, there was nothing, save for some bare-bone mentioning of what it does to people. Mainly of which," he pointed at Talon, "is mind control. Well, it's more accurately described as 'suggestive manipulation', but it's basically the same thing. It's especially effective against weaker minded individuals."

Feeling a wave of shame wash over him, Talon couldn't help but hang his head low, avoiding eye contact. "Am I really that weak?"

"On the contrary, the fact that you haven't stabbed us in our sleep yet, after two whole weeks, goes to show just how strong your mental fortitude is." Horace waved away the self-pity, and continued. "But, like I said, you're compromised. The longer you're down here, the deeper it's going to drill into your subconscious, and you just don't have the training yet to fight it off indefinitely."

Viktor gently rested his hand on Talon's shoulder, grimacing. "I think we know where this is going, and quite frankly, I don't agree. I've been down here the longest and hear nothing from it."

Scowling, their master tapped his sword's hilt, the leather-bound grip muffling the clicking of his fingernails. "Your agreement in this matter is irrelevant. And as for you, Viktor, it's possible that the creature can influence only one person at a time, in its... weakened state. I'm sorry to say this, Talon, but you'll have to leave, and keep yourself busy in Fallkirk until Viktor and I finish the job." There was no room for debate. Horace had made his decision, and Talon was to follow it.

Knowing that it was for his own good, but still feeling the weight of failure upon his shoulders, Talon collected his gear, and made ready to leave the company of his master and friend.

"Don't worry, I'll make sure you don't have to wait for us too long." These were the last words Talon would hear from Viktor as he knew him.

CHAPTER 21

Flipping the crusty page, its crinkling reverberating through the small library, Talon continued scanning the faded script of another tome. Horace had said his information on the creature had come from the church's library, but as far as Talon could find, there was nothing. Most of the volumes available were simply scripture about the gods and the Age of Strife before the birth of magic, and the Eternal King's exploits during the Age of Heroes shortly thereafter.

There were some biographical works of other prominent historical figures, and even a journal that documented the history of Fallkirk itself. There was a book describing the major sights of the country, *Udrela's Two-Hundred Sights of Deificness*, and even fairytales such as *The Ent of Evergrove* and *Lockmoore, the Castle of Dreams*. All interesting reads to someone, Talon thought, but none held significance to him.

Brain fried, he closed his latest choice of reading. Leather-bound, and without any markings, he'd hoped for something more exciting than a collection of local recipes. Looking for clues where there had been none, he'd consumed a substantial amount of the information to be had before concluding his reading for the day. Slipping from the small desk, Talon returned the cookbook to its rightful place on the shelf and stepped out into the nave.

The church was small, barely holding eight benches, split into two lines before the altar. Behind that altar stood a single depiction of O'deus, the god of light and master of forges, hammering the mortal plane of Gaea into existence. It was beautifully crafted, the god a giant, his hammer gilded with gold, Gaea barely a large rock in comparison.

"A magnificent sight, isn't it, my child?"

Talon continued staring at the mural, the now-familiar voice of Father Martin coming from the opposite direction of the window. "Must have been very expensive and time-consuming to have made, Father."

The priest chuckled, his two chins bouncing with the effort. "Perhaps. I wouldn't quite know, as it was commissioned well over a hundred years ago, from an artist that I imagine is no longer among us. Not quite sure how we got the gold to pay for it, but my ancestors managed it somehow; quite well that they did, for Fallkirk now holds a unique piece of history. It's quite the attraction for pilgrims who wish to see such things. And for some, such imagery inspires faith."

"Excuse me for saying so, Father, but it sounds like you don't take much stock in such things." Talon pulled his attention from the mural, the sun setting too low for light to properly shine through. Father Martin's robes were a creamy white trimmed with gold, held at his waist by a knotted rope, decorated with a circular buckle of bronze. His face was that of a man who had experienced much joy in his forty years of living, his skin creased with laugh lines, far more evident due to the utter lack of hair covering the priest's head.

"What you see there is nothing more than some pretty glass, my child. Just as books are nothing more than parchment and ink." The priest pointed at Talon, playfully wagging his finger. "But you didn't hear that from me."

A smirk played at the adventurer's face, the young boy crossing his arms and shrugging. "I don't know, sounds pretty heretical to me."

"Maybe it is." Father Martin laughed. "But I doubt that

matters much to you."

"Would it be a problem to you, were that the case?"

"Oh, not at all. I'm not so insecure in my beliefs that everyone around me must worship the same figure, regardless of what those boys in the capital say. Besides, your life of adventure would be much more suited to the Lady of Shadows." Father Martin took a seat upon the nearest bench, bending down to rub his ankles. "Speaking of which, have you finished your research for the day?"

"If you could call it that, sure. Too dark to read now, unless there's some secret stash of oil lamps I could borrow from. Why?"

"Oh, just an old priest curious as to the comings and goings of the youth. Also, I find it interesting that you're now spending so much time within the library. Did you, perhaps, get into a fight with your fellow adventurers?"

Was it morally okay to lie to a priest? Talon wondered. "Just wasn't much I could do, so my master thought I would benefit from some studying."

Father Martin nodded along, "Indeed you would. Now, you say there's not much for you to do in those ruins, but I'm not even sure what's down there."

"The Guild was paid to search and make sure the ruins were safe. Any specifics are unnecessary information for the townsfolk." Talon turned from the priest, making his way towards the exit. "It's getting late, Father. You'd best retire for the night."

"The same could be said for you, my child."

Unease keeping him from sleep, Talon walked the village's perimeter as he had the past several nights, thinking how it would leave a sour taste in his mouth if it were attacked while he was all cozy within the chapel's guest room. As he had every other night, Talon spent about an hour circling Fallkirk, one rotation taking roughly thirteen minutes.

Each time, he'd pass both the southern and eastern

entrances, greeting both pairs of men that guarded the two ends as he walked by. After the first few nights, of which they were incredibly skeptical during, they grew to appreciate the extra protection that the adventurer's presence promised, even if it were from someone they saw as just a boy. As far as he'd been able to tell, his efforts were wasted, the area devoid of any real threats.

Bored, and with his rounds finished, Talon spent the rest of his time awake stargazing, lying in the grass just a little ways from Fallkirk. As always, the twin moons were out in all their glory; Elysium shimmering a calming blue, Tartarus an aggressive red. The stars never changed position, simply disappearing as the sun's light overpowered their flickering glare, painted backdrops to the rock forms as they drifted across the sky.

Enjoying the peace, yet anxious at the lack of action, Talon's mind drifted to thoughts of Horace and Viktor. Of his failure to his master, and the reliance of which Viktor could be depended on. He thought of how he could better himself, needing to train not only his body, but his mind, as well. These were all nice end goals, Talon thought, but all pointless in the short-term. No matter how much he wanted it, improvement always came slow, and nothing could change him so severely in such a short time.

Forcing himself to sit up, yet unable to suppress a yawn, Talon tried and failed to muffle the sound with his mouth. He rubbed his eyes, red-rimmed and heavy, muttering to himself. "Time for bed."

The chapel's guest room, while small, provided far more comfort than might be expected in such a rural town, the mattress soft and the sheets warm. And unlike many inns he'd spent his nights within, there was no one else to disturb, as even Father Martin had his own cabin to return to. For all of this, he was glad.

Even so, dread draped over him like a cloak. This wasn't strange, as he'd been weighed down by such feelings since leaving the tomb, but somehow it was less ephemeral than previous nights. Now he tossed and turned, anxiety gnawing at him, pushing him out of bed. For a while, he paced, his bare feet padding against the wooden floorboards.

Forcing himself to stay within the confines of the small room, Talon found his mind wandering back to his thoughts of Horace, Viktor, and the creature that now watched them. He'd conversed shortly with his master just two days ago, when he'd stopped in for supplies, but he'd not seen hide nor hair of him since. This also wasn't strange, and Talon tried to convince himself that everything was fine, but something beyond reason told him otherwise. Telling him to go back to the tomb, that only he could fix what was to soon be broken, sweet words whispered in his ears.

Come to me.

It was a clear thought amongst the rumbling of raw noise, but one not born of his own mind. This realization terrified Talon, and soon he was slipping his boots on. He grabbed his cloak, throwing it over his shoulders, stepping outside where his boots met the dirt path connecting the church to the rest of Fallkirk.

Then the rumbling began.

At first, it was nothing more than a gentle vibration underfoot; strange, but otherwise nothing to worry about. Then things began to shake. Small things, dangling from straps or small chains, as though hit by a strong gust of wind. Glass began to crack, and Talon was thrown to the ground, the shaking quickly shifting to violent tremors.

Panic ensued outside, screaming and yelling adding to the earthquake's chaos.

Unsteady, Talon pushed off the floorboards, running for the door before slamming into it. Groaning, he threw the door open, stumbling the whole way as he fled the chapel.

Several minutes passed until the vicious quaking subsided, Talon passing through the eastern gate. Huffing, he broke into a sprint, the guardsmen doubled over as he passed them.

Come to me.

Invisible chains dragged behind Talon, chest heaving with each step he took across the plains. Even so, covered in sweat and out of breath, the green came and went, replaced by the dull stone of the old tomb.

Death spilled from the open doors, the one-winged angels staring to the heavens, blood seeping from their eyes.

Trembling, Talon stepped inside the tomb, chest tightening as he descended. Drawing his dagger, he dragged the broad blade through the air, frost forming along the walls as a cold mist left his lips.

A sharp pain stabbed at Talon's throat as he breathed in the arctic air, his hand instinctually covering his mouth, breathing into his palm to contain the heat.

Come to me.

Pushing through the cold and the fear, Talon continued his march into the tomb's depths, devoid of the wriggling shadows that he'd seen during the first journey through the anathematized corridors. Though as before, every minute dragged on, feeling like hours, the confined halls threatening to close in at any moment, forcing a feeling of claustrophobia onto the boy.

Come to me.

He ran, trying to escape the sense of dread and the whispers threatening to drive away his sanity. His mad dash carried him to the depths of oblivion, to the room that no longer swirled with dark energies, to the room that held the abomination in chains.

Come to me.

To the room where his master lay in a pool of his own blood, a huge gash over his left collarbone.

Talon rushed over to Horace, nearly sliding as he came to a stop before him. "Master!"

The old adventurer groaned, his eyes hazy, cheeks pale.

What looked like a nasty cut at first, Talon realized was just missing flesh, like something had taken a bite out of him, the edges uneven and the sinewy muscle scooped out. The bone had been fractured, but overall was intact. In addition, his left arm was horribly burned.

"MASTER!"

"Talon..." Voice cracking and short of breath, Horace struggled to raise his hand, managing it just long enough for his student to take it within his own.

"What happened?" Talon grit his teeth, eyes watering.

"Listen... Viktor-"

"Viktor did this?!" Even through the pain, Horace's look of disapproval was clear, and Talon quieted himself.

"Viktor... took the creature," He fought through a coughing fit, blood and pus spurting from the hole in his chest. "Sepulchre." His hand tightened around Talon's, a fiery passion dancing within his smouldering eyes. "I was foolish... arrogant. Thought he would be... immune. Safe. Thought we could... seal it back up. I was wrong. Kill them all. Order must... be kept. Do you under... stand me... Talon?"

More confused than he'd ever been before, but not wanting his master's final moments to be of disappointment, he nodded.

"Good... don't let my– *our* mission... go to waste." His eyes fluttered shut, his message relayed, breath slowing to shallow gasps. He was alive, barely, needing immediate medical attention.

Slinging his master's bag over his shoulders, Talon slipped his arms under Horace, his eyes flaring as energy flowed through his muscles, giving him enough strength to lift the sleeping man from the ground. This would be his greatest mistake, as a large band of symbols lit up, a glowing blend of orange and yellow. For the split second that Talon saw the symbols, he recognized Viktor's handwriting.

Then the room was engulfed in flames, the large explosion

searing the walls in a devastating barrage of fire.

Singed and charred, Talon's clothes clung tightly to his body, cinders dusting his limbs with every jostling step. Reacting faster than even he'd thought possible, the boy had turned and leapt from the rune-covered chamber, the explosion hitting his back and carrying him out into the halls of the tomb. His body had begun healing on impact, but the fire burned away at his clothing for several minutes, the boy all but ignoring the pain as he scrambled to get his dying master back to Fallkirk.

Exhaustion hit him hard as he reached the final step out into the open, the moons the first thing to greet him, almost mocking in their splendour. Shaking off the distractions, he continued his march back to town, every step threatening to be his last moment of consciousness. Yet, he persevered, stomping over the rolling plains, moving purely on instinct.

The torchlights of Fallkirk flickered into sight, and Talon snapped back to reality. He'd made it. *"We've* made it, master." A genuine smile crossed his face, and he looked down, his eyes going wide as he saw his master.

No longer breathing, Horace's wound had festered unnaturally fast, nothing but rotting flesh and boils spewing pus. Taken by disease and rot instead of blood loss, he'd died within Talon's arms, unnoticed by his student, who had been too preoccupied with getting him back to town.

Talon looked back up, tears running down his cheeks, blurring his vision. A small group made its way towards him, led by a figure in white carrying a lantern.

Talon fell to his knees and collapsed.

CHAPTER 22

Marbleton greeted Talon as he jolted awake, pain thrumming through his body, now covered in bruises and blotted with dried blood. Moving slow, he scooted his legs out from the fur-lined sheet he'd been placed under. Cold stone met his bare feet, a comfort to his sore soles. He was bare, save for a pair of trousers he didn't remember owning, and a not-so-conservative number of bandages wrapped taut around his upper-body.

He sat within a jail cell; not a particularly alien place for the rogue, but always an annoying situation that needed solving. He pushed himself off the cot, pressing down on his ribs to try and dull the pain that assaulted them. He stumbled over to the gate, gripping one of the iron bars for stability.

Pressing his face between the rods, trying to angle himself for a better look around, he found that his cell was alongside only three others in a square formation, a wooden door leading out of the area.

As far as he could tell, the other cells were empty, and no one was watching over him. Under most circumstances, this would be the perfect time to escape, but with his body battered and his reserves of mana depleted to the point that his body was no longer even regenerating, it would be a nigh impossible task. Talon lumbered back to the cot, sliding down into a comfortable position, too tired to feel much past his injuries.

This was, of course, when the clanking footsteps of

armoured men descended into the dungeon, the wooden door swinging on well-oiled hinges. Two guards, dressed in their city's combination of leather and iron, marched before Talon's cell. One was young, still filled with energy, though his eyes were rimmed with heavy bags. The other man, gray-in-the-beard-soldier type, had a much harsher look to his face, glaring at Talon with an unspoken accusation.

"You're awake." The old soldier's voice, which was as gruff as his appearance, spoke the obvious. His hand rested on the grip of his sword, fingers twitching in an expectation that his tone lacked.

"So I am." Talon, very intimate with this brand of guardsman, knew that nine out of ten times, the curmudgeonly soldier wasn't the one making the final call of his fate. "What happens now?"

"You're going to have to come with us, unfortunately." The younger man interjected, struggling to raise the atmosphere between the more serious men in the room. "The captain is very interested in hearing what you have to say, as I've been told." The older guard gave his partner a fierce sideways look, which the latter made a visible effort to ignore.

"I see." Pondering his situation for a moment, Talon pushed himself back to his feet, once again his bones aching in protest. "You'd best lead the way then, before my body crumples in on itself."

Turning to his superior, the young guard cracked a smile. "See, Lieutenant? No need to worry, he understands the situation he's in."

Grumbling, the lieutenant pulled out a set of keys, unlocking Talon's cell and sliding the door open. "Fine, but *you're* helping him, Private."

"Yessir! Wouldn't want to strain your brace, after all." The look the private received as he saluted was somewhere between mild irritation and murderous rage, and even Talon was unsure of the boy's future state of being. Eventually, the lieutenant limped past the boy, grumbling all the while. The private stood stock still for several seconds before letting out an exaggerated sigh, "Well, I suppose we'd best be getting on then. I'm Goddard, by the way. And the curmudgeony one is Lieutenant Sigurd. Do you need any help walking? There're stairs, just so you know."

Talon could have sworn the boy's teeth sparkled when he smiled.

The climb was uncomfortable for the three men, Goddard clearly not appreciating the bloodied and sweating body staining his leathers, leaving his metal plates slick with a thin film of perspiration. Each step aggravated the already-thrumming pain throughout Talon's body, and for the first time since he'd entered Marbleton, he felt relief, reaching ground level.

What Talon thought was a sectioned-off part of the guard barracks was in fact just a small building on its own, a single room with a table and two chairs sat opposite a small window. An isolated jail, placed within Marbleton's inner circle to separate the rich from the poor. Glancing down at the older guard's limp, it didn't take too much thought for him to figure out who'd been watching over the place the past few days.

"Stay close, and follow me." The lieutenant headed for the exit without pause, far too eager to leave, given his injury. Talon and the private followed nonetheless, neither being in any particular mood to act the fool.

Clouds covered the sky, mirroring the somber feeling that pervaded the damaged city. People strode with purpose, either downtrodden by the bodies they carted around, or resolute within their efforts to rebuild what had been destroyed. Some did nothing, sat atop the dirt, curled in balls or staring blankly at those that remained autonomous. Where there should have been mindless jubilation, Talon saw grim and confused faces all about.

Most buildings now sported some type of damage, most of which was superficial, though some were severely burned or broken through, requiring more serious repairs. Shattered windows and doors knocked from their hinges became a common sight, blood splattered across the inner walls and floors of these structures. Talon, relieved to see the damage was all man-made, nodded to himself. Sepulchre hadn't come back to ravage the town, at least.

"People went crazy and started rioting." Goddard's voice surprised Talon, jumping slightly as the silence was broken. "Soon as that giant creature showed up, the city turned into chaos. You know why, don't you?"

Talon huffed, indignant. "I thought we were going to leave the questioning to your captain."

The private shrugged, jostling Talon as he did so. "It was worth a shot. You seemed pretty relaxed, so I thought I might catch you off guard. Guess not."

"You should be more subtle about it then, if that's what you're trying for. Besides, talking about this in the open might not be the greatest idea. Your citizens are-"

"They'll be just fine, don't you worry about that." Goddard smiled, this one more genuine than any prior. "The people of Marbleton might be a bit more pampered than most, but they're strong, just like any other Udrelian out there. Honestly, while we lost plenty of people, most were part of the new guard regiment. Can't say I'm sad to see them gone, especially since they were the ones doing most of the killing during the Harvest."

Talon's brow furrowed. "The Harvest? Pretty grim name you lot decided on."

The private's grin fell. "It's not what the citizens know it as, certainly. That's what the Archmage called it... in his journal."

"*Silence.* We're almost there." Sigurd spun his head around, glaring at his protégé for an awkward amount of time before turning back and speeding up, his limp ever more evident as he accelerated.

Against Talon's expectations, their destination had not been the guard barracks, but the duke's estate. It was untouched, save for a broken window on the top floor, which looked as though a bull had been slingshotted through, the wooden framing nothing more than splinters clinging to the bricks they'd been fitted between.

Taking little notice of the destruction of property, the pair of guards led Talon into the duke's manor. The squeaky entrance swung open to reveal a bevy of guards searching the place. Some were examining the floorboards, while others tore apart the furniture, a select few flipping through books in the duke's private library, intensely reading each word they scrolled past.

"I see you're all still at it," the lieutenant mused.

Goddard glanced around, unsurprised by the progress on display. "Well, it's not like we've found much besides the journal that woman told us about."

Seeing no sign of the captain, the trio moved on, up to the second floor, once again overcoming the dreaded stairs attacking Talon's ribs. More guards mulled about, standing watch more than searching, having most likely flipped the entire top floor by now. Passing several rooms, the lieutenant led them to the only one with an open door, a deep grumbling breaking through the monotony surrounding them.

"This is ridiculous. Seven mages and a dozen apothecaries, and not a single one of them can figure out what's wrong with him!" Before even seeing him, Talon knew they'd found the captain. Being the only one fully covered in steel-plated armour, and a short cape draped over his shoulders bearing Marbleton's crest, the man screamed *important*.

Sigurd stepped forward, unfazed at his superior's outburst. "Captain Evrich. We've brought the last adventurer. As of now, he's been... compliant."

"You sound almost disappointed by that, Sigurd." Tired, but

visibly eased at the return of his lieutenant, the captain pinched the bridge of his nose, trying to rub away the exhaustion plaguing his haggard face. "So, adventurer, what's your name?"

Talon raised an eyebrow. "Strange question to start an interrogation off with."

Evrich rolled his eyes. "What, would you prefer I take a knife to your leg to start things off?"

"I would have," the lieutenant muttered.

The adventurer ignored the old guard. "Fair enough, I suppose. My name is Talon."

"Of course it is." The captain stepped forward, leaning in to stare Talon in the face. "It is to my understanding that you played a not so insignificant role in the chaos that ensued several nights ago."

Talon grit his teeth, used to such accusations being thrown at him, but still chagrined by such. "Far less than your *Archmage*, I can assure you of that."

"*Former* Archmage," the lieutenant corrected. "And trust me, we're well aware of his *involvement*." He glanced over his shoulder at the hallway, cautious in his wording. Taking a few steps back, he pushed the door until it latched, now whispering. "We found a journal on his body, the contents now known exclusively to the people in this room."

"Assuming a bit much there." Talon spun his index finger in a circle as he raised his hand, stopping only to point straight at his own face. "I know of no such journal."

"You may not have known the existence of the journal, but it references you on multiple occasions." From his satchel, tucked just behind the sheath of his sword, Evrich pulled out a small, leather-bound journal. It was kept closed by a dull, copper button over a triangular flap. With a flick of his finger, the guard captain unsnapped the button, beginning to flip through the crusty pages, stopping only a fraction into the bound parchment.

"This first entry comes from about three years ago," Evrich stated. "*He finally found me. Talon, as tenacious as he is foolish. So merciful was I, to leave him alive, yet he dogs me at my feet even still. Well, I suppose this was to be expected. I will have to find a better place to prepare.*"

Evrich flipped to the middle of the journal and continued.

"Roughly three months ago: *Fifteen* years. *Fifteen bloody years, and I'd thought I was rid of him. However, I got word from my spies just moments ago that someone matching Talon's description has been snooping around town. Another problem to deal with.*"

Several more pages turned, Evrich picking up pace in his reading.

"Same month as the prior: *Black Hollow is on fire. Forced to burn it after Talon infiltrated the keep and attacked me. He's bigger now, faster and just as stubborn. Never seen someone carry such a fiery intent to kill within their eyes before. I must keep my distance. Relocate to somewhere more obscure. Sepulchre is too big to carry much farther.*"

"And finally, the most recent passages" The guard captain turned one final set of pages.

"*Talon's arrived in Marbleton, and he's not alone this time. I suppose it was only a question of time. No matter. My time here is almost done. Just a few more days for Sepulchre to rest and regain its strength. Bloody thing gets real tired after eating. No matter, I'll just have that pompous little brat go after him. No doubt he'll check up on the duke, and follow the crumb trail up to me.*"

With a soft clapping of parchment against parchment, Evrich closed the journal, clasping the button down, and shoving it back into his satchel. "Quite an interesting read. I especially like the odd few pages where he goes on mad rambles, and my favourite parts are where our dear Archmage admits to all the atrocities he's committed. Makes the paperwork a lot easier."

Talon shoved his anger down at Viktor's apparent tabs on

him, "Then why am I here, if you know all of that? Unless you plan on offering me up as a scapegoat to appease the people of your dear city?"

"Quite the dramatic one, aren't you?" The lieutenant remarked sourly, scratching at his limp leg.

"Nothing so barbaric, we assure you." The private jumped in, his manner placating. "We just have a certain, uh... problem that, of course, needs solving."

Evrich nodded along. "Private Goddard speaks true." Stepping to the side, finally out of Talon's immediate vision, the captain revealed a regal-looking man sitting atop the bed. Short and stocky, his hair unkempt and pajamas wrinkled, the Duke of Marbleton's stare was a blank one, eyes void of any awareness or spark of intelligence. "He's alive, but that's where the positive talking points end for our duke, given his current state."

Talon shook his head. "Well, you've stumped me on this one. Never seen someone get it this badly before."

"But you do know what *this* is?" Evrich's tone lightened, the barest slip of hope slipping through.

"That vacant look is something I know very well, yeah. He's completely catatonic, though, and that's new to me. Everyone else I've met under Sepulchre's mind-control has at least held some minor level of consciousness. Your duke, on the other hand, just had a fly crawl into his mouth and didn't even flinch." There had been no fly, but the sudden panic amongst the guards' faces made it clear to Talon that it had been the right choice of words for his own entertainment.

The lieutenant swallowed down the lump in his throat. "So, you're saying our duke is under the influence of-"

"That abomination of flesh that flew from the Citadel, yes. Usually, an overload of sensations – mainly pain – can disturb the flow of magic that keeps them under the spell."

"Why do I feel as though there's a 'but' coming?" Goddard

shrugged Talon back up, the adventurer slipping from the private's shoulder.

"*But* I'm not even sure the duke can feel, well, anything right now." His bones continued to ache, and Talon wished for nothing more than a bed to rest upon. "You could try smacking him a bit, but I doubt that would do anything."

"I would also have to arrest myself for assaulting our governing official, and that sounds like a paperwork-filled nightmare." Evrich cupped his chin. "Is there another option, perhaps?"

Talon took only a moment to consider his next words. "Well, yeah... two, actually."

CHAPTER 23

Scarlett tapped her foot in time with the bard's strumming, staring into the rippling wine within her cup. Her purse jingled as her leg bounced, the fine incurred by the city guard – for breaking and entering, not the slaughter of several guardsmen, oddly enough – relieving it of some weight. They have bigger problems to deal with right now, Scarlett thought.

This, however, did not ease the redhead's mind. In some ways, she even wished to have been locked up, alongside Talon. Together, they could have easily escaped their cells and found a way out of town, just like they'd done so many times before.

She glanced over at Rolt, sitting calm and relaxed, his demeanour failing to betray his thoughts. Even so, she knew what left him so glum. While her weapons had been collected and returned to her, Sepulchre had flown off with Rolt's blade stuck firmly within its eye. The best replacement he'd been able to buy from the remaining stock of a blacksmith was a regular claymore. It was a well-made blade, sure, but nothing compared to the monstrous sword he'd carried since before she had ever even met him. It was irreplaceable.

Then there was the dwarf, who'd made fast company with them after their release. Deeming him far too big of an annoyance to keep watch over, he'd simply been released. Over the two days, Torden had explained the situation with Talon to the best of his abilities, the information of which had been largely known to

Scarlett and Rolt. Still, his upbeat and bombastic personality had helped to soften the mood, and any adventurer worth their salt could appreciate that.

"-an' ya wouldn't believe da gall o' dem! Scaled up a bloody wall dey did, wit' me strapped to 'em by a blasted rope. I, o' course, was fearless in dis, but dey wouldn't stop yammerin' on da whole time. Big babies, da lot o' dem." Lifting his large tankard from the table, the dwarf downed his sixth serving of ale in a single stream of gulps, plopping it down with a thunderous thud before demanding another.

Scarlett barely registered what he was saying.

Save for the stout man's yammering, the tavern was quiet, most of its patrons just there to drink away the memories.

Rolt tapped the wooden top, gaining the attention of his tablemates, though he was looking at Scarlett. With a flick of his finger, he directed her over to the bar, where the owner was glaring at them, wiping down the inside of a mug.

Scarlett gave her friend a weak smile, being the most she could muster given her own spirits. "Don't worry about him, big guy. He's just upset that we're disturbing the mood of his establishment... well, what's left of it anyway. He doesn't have any reason to cause us trouble, and we have no reason to give him one. We'll just stay out of trouble until the guards come and fetch us." Not knowing if the adventurers would provide more information, the guards had forbidden them from leaving town, though they were held more by the promise of Talon's return than any legal punishment.

As if by fate, which had never been the kindest of forces to the young woman, the inn's entrance flung open, a pair of helmeted guards stamping their way into the building. Spotting the conspicuous party of adventurers almost at once, they made a beeline towards their somewhat-crowded table, stopping before them with a raucous clank of their metal boots.

"Scarlett, Rolt, and Torden, I presume?" The guard asked only out of courtesy, clearly already having a description of them within his steel-encased head. None of them answered, simply waiting for him to continue. "We have orders to bring you to-"

Scarlett's chair screeched as it scraped the roughly-sanded boards below. "Just lead the way already. I'd rather not waste any more time right now." The men at the table followed her lead, finishing off their drinks before collecting their items and standing on either side of their crimson-haired leader.

The guards, unfazed by Scarlett's outburst, turned on their heels. The talkative one looked casually over his shoulder. "Follow me then."

Marching down the ruined streets once again, Scarlett couldn't help but think of Sepulchre as they passed burned-out huts and hacked-apart stalls. She thought of the creature's quick escape, and how lucky Marbleton was – how lucky *all* of them had been – to still be alive. Maybe the abomination had deemed the area too dangerous to take the risk of sticking around? Maybe it simply had what it needed? Or maybe it required rest before going on another rampage?

"Hey, dwarf?"

"Finally up fer sum talkin', are ya?" Torden grinned at her, his joviality infectious in all but the most somber of occasions.

She smiled back, the first genuine one in quite some time. "Just... thanks. For keeping Talon alive, I mean. The idiot means a lot to me, and sometimes I have trouble keeping him out of... trouble." Rolt's stare was an accusatory one, and Scarlett couldn't help but chuckle at the irony. She looked back at Torden, and saw a distinct look of confusion adorning his face. "Did I say something strange?"

"Aye, ya did, lass. Not ta be, urgh, *intrusive*, but the lad don't seem so carin' 'bout things like friends. Speakin' frankly, I'm not sure 'ow he's gonna be now that his mage is, well, dead."

Scarlett bit her lip, considering Torden's words. Talon had abandoned her and Rolt just over three years prior, without a note or even a hint of where he'd disappeared off to. In that time, she'd seen him for a total of two minutes where he was conscious, and he'd carried the same cool demeanour he always had. "Up in the Citadel, just as he'd awoken, he jumped to my rescue. You said before that he'd been tracking down the Archmage, correct?"

"Wit' da drive of a madman."

Scarlett nodded. "Well, he chose protecting my life over killing that bastard, so I definitely think you've missed something about him. Sure, he can be rough, but he cares."

Torden huffed, "S'pose I'll just have ta keep me eyes on 'im."

"Please do. He would've died a hundred times before, had someone not been watching his back."

"I could say the same, lass. Our travels are fraught wit' dangers. Only fair we keep an eye out fer others."

"Just don't expect everyone to see things the same way you do; that's a pretty good way of getting yourself killed." Scarlett responded immediately, more bite in her tone than intended.

Torden puffed out his chest with his usual bravado, his yellowed teeth somehow gleaming through the thick beard layered over his tough features. "Lass, I seen plenty in me time up-top. I ain't goin' down ta sum lowly back-stabbin'."

Glancing between Torden and Rolt, Scarlett couldn't help but think that her group needed someone less averse to tempting fate than her current bunch of hooligans.

They reached the guard barracks in record time, Scarlett only slightly surprised that the captain had moved from the duke's estate.

Inside, the barracks rang with a cacophony of stamping feet and clanking armour, a small retinue of guards adjusting their equipment near the entrance while half-a-dozen more rushed around in a panic, still looking for needed items. The ones hanging near the entrance murmured to each other, their whispers light yet hurried. Excitement ran through their ranks, though whether that excitement was tinged with fear or anticipation, Scarlett wasn't exactly sure.

The guards led the adventurers to the back of the complex. Past new trainees shuffling by with hands full of parchment, more guards in the middle of combat practice, and a single carpenter hammering in new floorboards next to a stone wall that had been sprayed with blood.

They reached the captain's office, and their escort knocked on the doors three times before stepping back. Several moments passed in silence before a response finally came. "Enter." Evrich called, his tough but not-so-harsh voice easily picked out even when muffled through the heavyset doors. Their escort motioned for them to enter before they turned and walked off.

Scarlett turned to Rolt and Torden, motioning for them to enter, parodying the guard's same movement.

Rolt rolled his eyes before pushing the door open, its handle turning with well-oiled ease, the latch making a noise so small that it almost went unheard.

She followed her friend in, regretting the decision as Rolt came to a halt, barely through the frame he'd needed to duck under. Bumping into his back, Scarlett got a full whiff of his odour, which had been over-saturated in sweat from the day's heat.

While Scarlett gagged, Rolt lunged across the room, Torden walking past her with a shrug.

Talon struggled to breathe within Rolt's tight embrace.

Muscles still exhausted, and body struggling to regain what little strength that it could, Rolt's embrace became more pain-filled than Talon remembered. Wheezing, patting his friend's side, his words came out in hurried gasps. "Okay, yeah... good to see you too… crushing me here, big guy." His lungs expanded only as Rolt released and dropped him to the ground, chest burning as air rushed back in. "There wasn't any malice in that hug now, was there?" Looking up, he was greeted by the warrior's steely gaze, the barest upturn of his lip betraying the serious façade. The two chuckled, Rolt's silent trembling against Talon's barely audible huffing.

Glancing at the guardsmen watching the affair, Talon appreciated the understanding looks they gave him, their posture relaxing as the somber air became more jubilant. The clanking of Torden's armour tore his attention back to his companions, the dwarf strutting into the room with a wrinkling of his nose. "Seems yer still standin' in one piece, Lad."

Talon nodded, tucking a few shimmering strands of silver back behind his ear. "I'm alive, at the very least. You seem perfectly fine, everything considered."

"Aye, most of me damage is under me steel." The dwarf pounded his chest, the polished metal unmarred by the duress of combat. "A few scratches an' bruises ain't gonna keep me down long."

"Good to hear. Hopefully you're in form to keep up the—" Talon cut himself off as the bundle of crimson that was his greatest friend walked into the room, Scarlett watching him with an uncomfortable amount of focus. "Ah…"

Now that she stood before him, Scarlett had no idea what to do, her desire to track Talon down having superseded any thought as to what she would do afterwards. Was she supposed to hit him, or cry in his arms like all those poems she'd scoffed at as a child? Deciding that none of that mattered now, she fell into old routine. "I hope you realize how many party nights you've missed out on, and the number of drinks you owe me when we get back."

For just an instance, gone so quickly that another might

have thought it a trick of the eye, Talon's expression softened. He strode deftly past the dwarf, gently slapping his palm against Scarlett's shoulder as he glided to her side. "I look forward to it."

Captain Evrich cleared his throat from behind his large, oaken desk. Scarlett remembered the desk well, along with the elf she'd found rifling through the papers stacked around it, of which almost none remained now. Less than a week prior, and a simple break-in felt as though it had happened ages ago. The elf's fate crossed her mind for a moment, but Scarlett waved the matter away, refocusing on the situation at hand.

"Thank you all for coming." Evrich scanned the faces of both adventurer and guard, Goddard and Sigurd watching with knowing anticipation. "I know these last few days of inaction have been stressful for all of us, as we all no doubt have some desire to track down the beast that thrashed about Marbleton, and eliminate it."

Scarlett thought little of Marbleton's fate, but kept her thoughts to herself as she spotted the conviction of every other soul within the room. All except for Talon, whose eyes were filled with a baleful sadness, his actions fueled by a desire unbeknownst to her.

Evrich continued, "That's why, with the help of Talon here, we've devised a plan of action to track down the beast, kill it, and hopefully rid the duke of whatever curse has left him as dumb as a dead mule." With a sharp wave of his hand, the captain gave the floor to Talon, who stepped forward, away from Scarlett.

"As most of the people in this room already know, the Adventurers' Guild within Brimlux has a powerful mage whose focus is steeped within the art of curses – both casting and dispersing them."

Talon's face belied his thoughts, but Scarlett knew from past experiences that the silver-haired adventurer dreaded the idea of asking any mage – even one so respected by the Guild – for help.

"Our hope is that he will be able to rid the duke of his curse, and with the help of the Guild as a whole, lead us to the whereabouts of Sepulchre."

Scarlett shivered at the idea of meeting the abomination again, the ghosting touch of its tongue still haunting her. "Not to be the bringer of bad news, but I think we'll need a pretty major force to take that thing down."

"Just so." Evrich picked up a scroll bound with a wax seal from his desk, casually holding it up, presenting the enclosed parchment to the room. "Which is why I've reserved a stock of gold to be transferred over to Brimlux's guildhall, in exchange for the support of some of its more skilled members."

Scarlett crossed her arms. "You've set up a job, you mean."

Talon shook his head. "A job request can take days to process, and could be picked up by any group of idiots once it's posted."

Evrich nodded along. "The Guild's rules and bureaucracy won't cut it here, so we've decided to expedite the process with a... hefty donation, in exchange for a favour."

Talon indicated the scroll with his thumb. "Such things are done on rare occasion, as are plain mercenary contracts, when speed is required."

"And just in case such a tactic is insufficient, I will personally be leading a contingent of guardsmen to accompany you all on the hunt." Evrich's words took the room by surprise, all but Talon whose expression remained neutral. The lieutenant looked especially taken aback, mouth hung agape. "In my stead, Lieutenant Sigurd will lead Marbleton's repairs." This last bit stopped the lieutenant's protests before he could voice them.

Sigurd grit his teeth, scratching at the bum leg that still caused him to limp. No one else had the experience required for such a task, but even so, his feelings were obvious.

Evrich pocketed the scroll, giving one last look to the rest of the room. "Go collect your belongings, and head towards the

Southern Gate. We leave in three hours."

CHAPTER 24

Scarlett tightened Ruby's saddle, the mare snorting in Scarlett's face. "I know it's shameful, girl, but we wouldn't want me falling off, now would we?"

The mare stared down at her master with a blank look in her eyes, the answer hanging between them.

"Okay, well that's just not nice."

Rolt and Obsidian acted with far less noise in their preparations, though the former of the two smiled at his friend's playful banter, seemingly disregarding how weird it was that she could understand the red-maned mare.

"Ya sure it's safe fer me ta be ridin' like dis, lad?" Torden clung within a strange-looking arrangement of leather patches and iron buckles to the front of Private Goddard's own saddle, who had accepted the task of riding double with a characteristic eagerness.

The private smiled wide, looking up at Torden as he buckled the final straps. "As safe as riding any horse is, really. Just don't fuss around too much, and it'll be fine; we wouldn't want to upset dear Snapper here." The brown gelding was aptly-named, requiring a muzzle for anything resembling a humanoid to safely get within reach. "He's one of the fastest horses in all of Marbleton, and he knows it. He can cause a bit of trouble here and there, but that's what you get when dealing with people who know they're worth something."

Snapper smacked his head into Goddard, its snout straining

against the muzzle around.

Scarlett scoffed. "Sounds more like a child throwing a tantrum to me."

Laughing, Goddard patted Snapper's muzzle, though the adventurers struggled to find anything humourous about what had been said. "I suppose it does! It's better if you don't tell people that, though. They can tend to lose their tempers when insulted in such a way."

"If they don't want to be insulted, then they shouldn't do stuff that warrants being insulted." She couldn't explain why, but Scarlett found her patience thin when dealing with the young guardsman. Maybe it was his overly cheerful demeanour, which oftentimes came off as a façade, or perhaps it had more to do with how he tried to avoid conflict through said humour. Disregarding the thought for the moment, feeling Goddard's beaming eyes upon her, she kept her back to him.

"I suppose that's one way to look at things," he continued. "But I think it's more important to encourage good behaviour than simply stirring up trouble for the sake of it."

"It's not *just* for the sake of it," Scarlett retorted. "It can also be for fun, depending on who you're riling up." The faint bruises upon her face were perfect evidence against her logic, but Goddard made a point of not directing any attention to them.

"To each their own." Goddard redid a few final straps before patting Torden's shoulder. "Alright, you're all set. Once the captain and your friend return, we'll be all ready to go."

Scarlett perked up, her back straightening, glancing over her shoulder. "Where did they head off to, anyway?"

Goddard's head titled to the side, mimicking the expression of a puppy, which annoyed the redhead greatly. "Didn't he tell you? Talon asked the captain to let him see the Archmage's body."

The crypt was dark, and damp, detailing on stone

colonnades faint, weathered from centuries of decay. Where once they had depicted clear the grim visage of Zeichfer, master of necromancy and sole ruler of the plane of death – all acting as a macabre reminder of the fate that awaited the living – the crypt's pillars now stood as nothing more than unremarkable support beams.

Every major city had a Hallowed Hall, a place to hold their dead; sprawling complexes that wound around like mazes, pathways intersecting one another below their respective towns. More than anything, they were religious symbols, larger than regular cemeteries that dotted the lands and smaller villages, but with the same utilitarian purpose of storing the dead.

Talon thought of Horace, buried within Fallkirk's humble cemetery, feeling that ever-faint regret that toiled away in the back of his mind. His master had deserved more, but it was the best that could be done.

Evrich led the way with torch in hand, illuminating coffins both plain and opulent, some bodies left out to the open, mummified, either requested by the individual before death or by their family after. All of those preserved had been given proper respect and honour in their handling. These were not the bodies that Talon wished to see.

Down each hall, new turnoffs and crevasses were being worked on by workers swinging iron pickaxes, Marbleton's streets needing to be cleared of the unfortunate souls who had perished in Sepulchre's chaos. The older bodies smelled stale, but the incense and fresh flowers laid for the newer corpses staved off the smell. As the captain led the adventurer down another flight of steps, the pleasant smell of incense and flowers disappeared, replaced by the stench of decay.

They reached the bottom of the final flight, and Talon couldn't help but sneer in disgust at the display of bodies put forth before him. Tucked within the deepest bowels of every Hallowed

Hall was a place not of respect and reverence, but one fueled by contemptuous hatred. The two men now stood within Marbleton's Chamber of the Damned, where those deemed too irredeemable are strung up to rot, buried so deep that their only destiny is to be forgotten by the lands above, their tales wasted away to the annals of history.

The captain's quiet voice echoed throughout the chamber. "I present to you, Marbleton's Archmage, Viktor, and Marbleton's Prime of Law, Sarah Hawse. Both found guilty of perfidy within the walls of the city they'd sworn to protect and act only within the best interests of, now stripped of their ranks and strung up to bare their sins to any who wish to see them.

"Viktor has also been found guilty of mass murder, with the beast Sepulchre as his weapon, Sarah Hawse acting as a knowing accomplice. With this knowledge, may they now serve Zeichfer as the lowest of his refuse, never to rise again upon Gaea's supple earth."

The speech was a practiced one, given to all escorted to the depths of the cavern, though usually ministered by the Hall's Watcher – the tomb's keeper, of sorts.

Upon one of a pair of crucifixes, Viktor dangled, hanging next to a woman, her body too mangled to identify. The mage's neck was twisted in an impossible angle, his pale skin already wasted away, sloughing off to reveal the rotting muscle and bone beneath. The woman was somehow in an even worse state, her body broken and flattened by the mass of people that had stomped the life from her unconscious body.

Scanning the room, Talon saw several more bodies strung about, all much older than the two he'd been introduced to, and infinitely less recognizable. Some were nothing more than a collection of bones held together by thinning strings of meat. This cursory inspection was just that, and he turned his attention back to the man who had once been his friend.

Viktor's lifeless eyes were crossed above a slack, lipless mouth, the once-maniacal features now nothing more than a dark mockery of the dangerous killer he had been only days prior. "He was like this when you found him?" Talon's words slipped out as barely a whisper, a deep void filling up within his stomach.

If Evrich noticed Talon's change in mood, he didn't show it. "Well, he still had most of his skin, but for the most part, yes, he was the same. His neck snapped against a tree branch, far as we can tell, and his eyes were wide with shock... or terror. We aren't quite sure." The captain spun on his heel, heading for the stairway behind them. "I'll be just outside, when you're ready. Take any frustrations or misgivings you have on him now, if you wish; he'll be far too withered to do so within the next few weeks."

Left alone, Talon allowed himself to relax his posture, shoulders slacking as a sudden realization came to him. "I failed." His hands balled into fists, his teeth clamping hard, body trembling with anger and self-loathing. "You're dead now, but what does that matter? It was supposed to be by *my* hands that you perished, not from some asinine fall. Now all that's left is your damned schemes! Was this your plan, as one final spiteful act against me?"

Viktor remained silent.

"No, of course not. That look in your eyes, when you fell... they were the same as when I saw master die, his body as lifeless as yours."

Viktor's jaw moved around slightly, and for a moment, Talon thought that he might speak, dread and excitement pooling in his chest. Then a centipede slithered out from the dead mage's mouth, crawling over his face and down the crucifix, scurrying away as it touched the cold floor beneath.

"What was I expecting to accomplish by coming here?" Talon gripped at his chest, feeling a weight that should have been lifted only fatten, a void forming where before there had been passion and a sense of conviction. "I'll kill Sepulchre, and destroy the last

219

shred of whatever plan you had for this world. It's all I can do – the only thing that might appease for my failure and bring peace to our master's soul."

Without another word, Talon turned towards the stairs, leaving behind what remained of his old friend and lifelong enemy.

Talon jostled behind Scarlett, hands on her waist for stability, Ruby's canter unaffected by the extra weight. Rolt rode on one side, Goddard and Torden on the other, following behind Evrich in an arrow-shaped formation, the rest of the half-dozen guardsmen following in two lines of three. They rode a moderate distance behind the vanguard, watching for bandits and other dangers found within the woods south of Marbleton.

No one spoke, not even Torden, all listening for sounds of danger. A twig snapping, a peculiar rustling of leaves, anything that could be heard over the soft clip-clopping of hooves or shifting of cloth and metal. This was another reason the guards kept their distance, the less grouped up together the horses were, the less noise they made, and the easier it would be to parse out abnormalities.

The better part of a day had passed on saddle, the party making their way into the Wildlands only an hour prior, the forest south of Marbleton they had all passed through only a week prior.

The bodies of the hobgoblin, Krük, and his shorter followers were all gone now, the carrion devoured by wolf and crow. He thought of the jennet, and how similar one of the horses in the backline looked, before letting his thoughts drift back to more important matters.

"What's on your mind?" Scarlett's voice, spoken so softly that he'd barely heard it, took Talon from his thoughts. She was looking over her shoulder, her expression neutral.

"Why do you assume anything is?" He made sure to keep to a whisper, restricting their conversation to the two of them.

Then she smiled. "Because your hands just tightened up, and that usually means you're worried about something."

Talon turned his eyes from hers, huffing. "There's a lot to worry about."

Reaching back a bit to pat his forearm, she nodded. "So there is. Nothing we can't handle, though."

We. The word sounded strange to Talon, having taken every effort the past three years to keep her and Rolt from his affairs, to keep them away from Viktor and Sepulchre. To keep them safe. But it was too late for that now. Now it was a job, and she wouldn't let go of such a matter while he remained involved. The thought was a calming one and, unbeknownst to him, his grip around Scarlett softened, the redhead smiling to herself as they road onward.

Selora watched as they snuffed out their campfire, the twin moons hanging high above the shifting clouds and lifting smoke, both waning. Following had been hard on her legs, but they had ridden with only a fair amount of haste, her preternatural speed allowing her to keep pace. She hadn't made a sound, the forest speaking to her as it always had, directing her along the most straightforward path.

Selora's legs still ached, however, and she was glad for the rest. High above the ground, hidden within the thick brush of tall trees, she absently traced her finger along the clan markings that wrapped around her skin, the tattoos barely darker than her natural skin colour. Chewing on her bottom lip, eyes darting around in a manic state, she had never fully calmed since her underground escape back in Marbleton.

Her anxiety had been a constant, low thrum, only spiking further as she realized that they meant to hunt the abomination. She would have gladly rejoined Talon and Torden, and even the two new adventurers, had they simply left the city, leaving the beast to its own devices. But the thought of confronting it again made her heart pound, leaving her throat dry, hands covered in sweat.

So now she followed from a distance, not wanting to abandon the only link she had to the outside world. She couldn't return to her clan. Not yet. But could she even face the creature again? She battled her fear with the thought of lost honour; how could she face her clan again if she was willing to run when people needed her? They would sneer and mock her, just as they had when she'd left camp, banished by the elders for her transgressions. The thought was too much to handle, and the thought of facing such treatment again halted her.

And so she followed, as she almost always had, hoping that the right choice would be forced upon her when the time to decide came.

CHAPTER 25

Their return trip, smooth and uneventful, finally ended.

For this, Talon sent his thanks to any god that was listening. He was also thankful for the several extra days to patch himself up. Aside from some bruises, and a withering exhaustion, he was back in fighting form. Leaning over the saddle, he looked over Scarlett's shoulder.

In the distance, Brimlux stood before them. Its luster a different kind from Marbleton's, Udrela's central city stood as the beacon from where all roads start.

"Welcome home, big shot." Scarlett turned in her saddle to look straight on at Talon, her smile bright and welcoming. "Or, at least, I hope you still consider this place your home."

A smile pulled at Talon's lips, small and reverent as he laid eyes upon the circular wall, broken up by eight watchtowers spread equilaterally around the city. The large tower in the middle – the *Divine's Spear* – housed Brimlux's sect of the Sons of the Eternal, as well as the Order of Paladins, and all the clerics and serfs that worked under them. The Sons of the Eternal were the main governing force over the city and wider lands, working cohesively as the Eternal King's left hand, collecting taxes and enforcing his laws.

Talon smiled gently at Scarlett. "Home is where the plunder lies, as a young woman once said to me."

Scarlett nearly choked on her spit, "By Los, I said that when

I was like fifteen!" She turned back, her cheeks taking on a slight shade of pink. "Forget I said anything." She urged Ruby forward, not seeming to realize that Talon was still sharing a saddle with her. He exchanged an amused look with Rolt as the two rogues trailed ahead, the giant chuckling to himself as his old friends fell back into familiar routines.

The streets were as he remembered them, crowded with buildings, and people of every caste and character. Rugged warriors mingled with froofy nobles, street magicians entertained children with simple parlour tricks, all the while nondescript pickpockets slipped coins from the pouches of merchants. Every store bustled with activity, from smithy to bakery, run by everything from human to dwarf to minotaur.

Brimlux was a melting pot, in part due to the uncommonly high number of guilds and organizations that operated within the city, the Adventurers' Guild only one of dozens. The Wardens, the Order of Demon Hunters, the Mages' Guild; every brand of organization could be found amongst the streets of Udrela's second-largest city, all except the Thieves' Guild, which had been driven out decades prior. Largest amongst all these groups, however, was the Order of Paladins, acting as the Sons of the Eternals' private military, their authority unquestioned by even the city guard.

Talon glanced around, their party going largely unnoticed as they rode through the wide road, their mottled and mismatched kind dotting the city streets. Now riding in the front, Scarlett leading as it became clear just how unfamiliar Evrich was with the city, he saw the few disinterested glances that came their way. There was more interest in the guards, dressed in another city's heraldry, than the adventurers, who were just a handful of the hundreds of unique-looking mercenaries that prowled the streets, looking for a good deal on supplies, or rumours of a potential job.

"Brings back memories, huh?" Once again, Scarlett broke

the silence.

Talon nodded, taking in the names of stores, studying their structures and the carved signs that hung loosely on chains and rope. "I see some of the old shops have changed hands."

She shrugged, the change being wholly less obvious to her. "Things come and go. Shoddy blacksmiths are run out by the good ones, potion shops go down when their favourite ingredients become harder to obtain, novice mages get too fancy and set some buildings on fire. You know how it is."

Talon raised an eyebrow. "That last one is a bit more specific than the others. You thinking of someone specific?"

Scarlett let out a quick bark of laughter. "You'd think so, but it's happened several times now in the past year, and it's always someone different from the last."

Evrich cleared his throat, having pulled up next to the adventurers, a sour look under his iron halfhelm. "I'm relieved to see your spirits haven't been diminished by the task at hand, but I feel I must remind you of our business here."

The redhead rolled her eyes, motioning ahead of them. "Yeah, yeah, we'll be at the guildhall in about... now." Ruby jerked to a stop, Evrich's horse pulling several meters ahead of them before the captain was able to rein her in.

A titan compared to the buildings that surrounded it, the Adventurers' Guild's guildhall was three stories of solid oak and mahogany that towered over the street. Every piece of metal, down to the nails and screws holding it together, were crafted from the highest quality steel, the Guild never passing up a chance to show off. For this very reason, bright banners threaded with gold and crimson silk hung from either side of the entrance, a golden fist gripping a sword splayed over the blood-red background. A large flag fluttered gently atop the roof, the symbol prominently displayed for even the birds overhead to see.

"Quite a place," Torden mused. "Much, eh... *grander* than

anythin' in Shadowfen."

"A shack with a pretty door knocker would be grander than Shadowfen," Talon muttered, slipping from Ruby's saddle.

Scarlett and Rolt led their horses around the corner, disappearing into the attached stables.

Goddard helped the dwarf from his own saddle, plopping Torden back on solid ground. "I s'pose dis is where I'll be gettin' more o' dat adventure I was wantin'."

"Well, stick around here, and you'll find that there's more work to do than there are swords in the world." Talon indicated vaguely towards the guildhall. "Never enough people for the coin being handed out."

"Sounds promisin'. I look forward to da work. *After* we hunt yer beasty, o' course." Torden crossed his arms, grinning.

"Of course," Talon said flatly.

Scarlett and Rolt reappeared from beside the building, the redhead jaunting back over to the party. "Alright, me and the big guy are all checked in. You ready to head inside?"

"To see this Jacques of yours, yes." Evrich dismounted from his horse, handing the reins to Goddard. "My men will wait out front."

"Wouldn't want to cause any more of a commotion than we're already bound to," Talon agreed, motioning an up-ended palm towards Scarlett. "Ladies first."

"What a gentleman," Scarlett said, her tone playful and mocking, sticking out her tongue at him before turning and striding for the entrance.

A bewildered gnome watched them enter from the porch, a lacquered pipe hanging from dry lips.

An explosion of noise hit them like a hammer, mixing with the sounds of the city outside. Talon grabbed his head as the familiar experience played out. Shutting the door behind them shut off the noise of the outside world completely, intricately woven runes lighting up around the doorframe as the latch clicked. All that remained were clanking tankards, the senseless noise from dozens of conversations, and a bard's lute being strummed.

Talon stopped just a few steps inside, taking a moment to smell the brew of steam-cooked meat, alcohol, and sweat that swirled through the open air. Basically a tavern, the guildhall's crowded first floor acted as a place of rest for its adventurers. Agile barmaids moved between tables, trays filled with food and drink swirling above their heads.

Cork boards filled with job requests lined the eastern and western walls, bounties and miscellaneous busywork packed so tightly together that the actual cork beneath became a distant memory. Each piece of parchment had a stamp of approval in the bottom right, next to the signature of the clerk that had approved the job, each stamp a different colour that indicated the minimum rank an adventurer had to hold before their inquiry would be accepted. Most of the stamps were either dull bronze or glittering silver, a rare gold peeking out in the ocean of lower-ranked – and lesser-paying – work.

A pair of stairs, leading to the administrative floor, bordered the bar stretching across the back wall, four bartenders attending to several dozen adventurers at once.

Sometimes spending your money was harder than earning it, Talon thought.

"Hey, Scarlett! Rolt! Over here!" A strong and hearty voice broke through the haze of sound.

Scarlett immediately jaunted towards the voice, Rolt following close behind.

Talon turned towards Evrich and Torden, shrugging off their questioning looks. "Give them a minute. A quick detour won't hurt anything."

Clearly unhappy with the delay, Evrich kept his thoughts to himself only due to ingrained professionalism, and followed, staying slightly behind the adventurers.

Wood clacked as the woman's chair emptied, the amazon shooting to her feet like a spooked bird taking flight, her arms wrapped tight around the redhead's torso, lifting Scarlett from the ground with ease.

"Nice to see you too, Amelia," Scarlett croaked. Gasping for air as her feet hit the ground, she grinned up at another familiar face.

"By Be'luun, it's been far too long!" Amelia laughed, slapping Scarlett's back, throwing her off balance. Standing just half-a-head under Rolt, the amazon's copper skin pulled taut around corded muscle, pulling at scars new and old that she wore with pride, as though they were each a treasure to be coveted. With her pitch-black hair bundled in a loose tail, Amelia's handsome face was on full display, her strong chin and high cheekbones leading up to a pair of rounded eyes, the softness of which belied just how dangerous a hunter she was.

Nervous laughter slipped from Scarlett's lips, her voice weak as she spoke. "Well, you're always out on some kind of job, so it's difficult."

Ignoring the comment, Amelia stepped towards Rolt. "Hey there, big guy! How you doing?"

The two giants clasped hands as if preparing to arm wrestle, squeezing for several extended moments, staring one another down.

Letting go, the Amazon threw a light jab at Rolt's shoulder. "Good, it seems, though I see you lost your fancy sword." She kept smiling, broad and toothy.

Rolt returned a much softer one in response, eyebrows dropping slightly.

Rolt appreciated Amelia's directness and friendly demeanour, Talon remembered, himself preferring her tendency for extreme violence when called upon. Glancing past her, the rogue spotted Amelia's claymore, the large, two-handed blade plain and nondescript, standing against the edge of her table. Across from the weapon was another adventurer, sipping on a mug of cider, his immaculate face undisturbed by the noise around him.

Opposed to Amelia, who dressed lightly, preferring the mobility of leather over the protection of standard platemail, Glaive covered himself head-to-toe in burnished steel edged with bronze. A surcoat dyed in the Guild's crimson and gold hung over his armour, the golden fist emblazoned on his chest.

The knightly figure turned, his gray eyes locking with the rogue's. "Talon. So, you're alive after all. I took you for a dead man a few years ago."

Talon sneered. "You look healthy as ever, Glaive. Still hiding behind your tin s-" He gasped, Amelia knocking the wind out of him as she wrapped him in a tight hug. He wondered momentarily why this kept happening.

"Talon! By the gods, it's been *years* since I've seen your mug round these parts." After a moment, she loosened her grip, but kept Talon's ribs constricted. "You *really* should stop by more often."

Unfocused as he was, the rogue was still able to pick out the implications of her tone, sucking in air between his teeth until she finally released him.

"Well, come on and sit down. We'll get you all some drinks."

Scarlett held her hands up in a placating manner. "Sorry, but we'll have to do that later. For now, we have to see Jacques."

Amelia's expression fell like a stone, and she glanced back at Glaive, his taciturn look disturbed, clearly going down the same line of thought. She directed her attention back to Scarlett, eyeing the rest of the party one at a time, finally noticing Torden, and then Evrich. "This must be pretty big, to involve him."

Scarlett's smile was a strained one. "You have no idea."

Amelia turned to go set her chair upright, having clattered to the floor in her sudden rush to greet them. "Well, you best go talk to Jacques then."

"That decision isn't up to your discretion, Amelia."

The room fell quiet, compelled to silence as a new voice entered the cacophony of the guildhall. Boots of supple, brown leather made their way down the steps, neither foot disturbing the boards below as the figure's translucent robes fluttered just above, a perpetual updraft keeping the fine chiffon from touching the ground, rippling above the dark green tune like smoke.

Gale, master of Brimlux's branch of the Adventurers' Guild, made landfall, and even Talon's jaded and weathered heart couldn't help but skip a beat. Every adventurer, from warrior to thief to magician, collectively held their breaths as their guild master glided across the floor, stopping just a breath away from the silver-haired rogue.

His eyes, green as emeralds, radiated magic, the sparks flying from them causing the air around to shimmer and distort for several seconds at a time, the guild master's brown hair resembling a shade of orange when seen through these ripples. "Talon, in my office. We have much to discuss."

Intense pressure held Talon down in the cedar chair, sweat soaking through his clothes and into the cushion below, suspense and foreboding holding him captive. He glanced to his side where Evrich sat, the guardsman in a similar state.

Across from them Gale sat, examining Evrich's scroll, his fingers dancing atop its surface. "You came here to make a request." Talon released the breath he'd been holding, Evrich stabilizing with a surprising elegance. Gale's attention was solely focused on Talon. "You, who disappeared for three years, leaving nothing behind but a trail of trouble for me, come asking for assistance."

Talon swallowed hard, his throat dry. "Apologies, Master Gale, but I... fail to see how my disappearance could cause you any trouble."

Gale took a deep breath, exhaling slowly, dragging the motion out.

It was one of his favourite tactics, Talon knew, yet its effect was no less palpable upon him.

"Paperwork, Talon. You, as an official member of the Guild, act under the jurisdiction granted to the Guild, and *only* the jurisdiction granted to the Guild." The guild master's volume didn't rise, yet his voice filled the dark room. "But you have been acting on your own, regulations be damned. And while this isn't usually an issue, most of my renegades don't go off on a three-year revenge quest that ends up lighting an *entire city on fire*!"

Evrich cleared his throat. "In his defense, Marbleton's fires were minor."

"You think this is about bloody *Marbleton*?" Gale shot to his feet, his chair tipping over but not falling, righting itself before hitting the ground, pointing a finger accusingly at Talon. "Let me tell you a little story about a city to the east: it was once called the city of iron, could be found on every map under the name of 'Black Hollow', and housed a thousand of Udrela's best-trained knights. It was a bastion of safety for the people around, as it staved off the encroaching threat of dark elves that had been pushing at the fringes of Udrela for centuries. That is, until it was *burned to the ground*, just a few months ago."

The captain watched Talon in his peripheral, looking for any kind of reaction, but getting none. He turned back to Gale, hesitantly. "I heard that it was overwhelmed by the dark elves while the fire raged, and that it's currently being inhabited by several clans of the twisted knife-ears."

Gale nodded solemnly. "All of that is true. However, some crucial information was kept hidden, at no small cost to myself, the main point being who actually set Black Hollow aflame." He motioned towards the captain with a vague wave of his hand, sitting back down in his chair, which scooted forward to catch his weight. "You already know the perpetrator was Viktor, of course. Your dear *Archmage.*" He said the last word with no small amount of venom. "But had Talon not forced the whelp's hand, Black Hollow would have stood a while longer, and the workload I had to take to hide his mistake never would have happened."

Gale took a deep breath, centering himself. "Now, Marbleton." Gale waved his hand, as if swatting away a bug. "The fact that you rode here, requesting the Guild's help with Sepulchre, means that anything any of my adventurers *might* have been guilty of has been dismissed, you being Marbleton's highest authority at the moment. And if you haven't done so, you will, or this discussion of help ends here."

Talon and Evrich shared a strained look, neither sure where the guild master's point was going. They did, however, latch onto the abomination's name, of which neither had yet spoken.

"You already knew why we came here," Talon said.

Gale grit his teeth, insulted. "Of course I knew. I've had Jacques keep tabs on you since you first went rogue. Had this mission of yours been any less important, I would've had him drag you back here by the scruff."

Talon's mouth opened, but he kept his silence as he heard the door to the office creak open.

"Ah, speak of the devil."

Master of the Vault, and the right hand to Gale, Jacques stood as no less imposing a figure, though in stark contrast to the guild master. Where Gale was harsh, Jacques was gentle. Where Gale eschewed formality with harsh casualness, Jacques' every movement was controlled and elegant, every word chosen carefully. Opposed to Gale's robes, which shimmered like smoke, Jacques's were a rich black trimmed with dark purple. Gale's eyes blazed with magic, while Jacques stared out with orbs of abyssal black, absorbing all light that touched them. Even their beards were polar opposites, Gale's uneven and roughly cut, while Jacques's was professionally trimmed and oiled.

Compared to the maelstrom of chaos that was the guild master, Jacques was a small blade, honed to perfection. And now these two masters of magic were focused on Talon, Jacques giving him only the barest nod of greeting.

Gale pushed himself to his feet, standing only a few centimeters over his second-in-command. "Jacques will help you locate Sepulchre, kill it, and restore Duke Giles' wits. Captain, I will personally handpick some extra help for you, and give you my best wishes in dealing with this certain abomination. I want this matter put to rest, once and for all. And then, Talon, we will speak of your punishment for causing me so great a headache."

CHAPTER 26

In the near twenty-five years that he'd been associated with the Guild, Talon had stood within the confines of its vault only twice before. The first time he had still been a boy at twelve years of age, already four years into his training with Horace, and had been allowed to follow his master inside.

The second time had been twelve years later, eight years ago now, when he needed a dagger that could trap souls, as a hamlet several days east of Brimlux had found itself overrun with angry wraiths. Apparently, some bandits had pillaged the place a few days prior, leaving the survivors to die by the hand of the hamlet's vengeful spirits.

This time, Talon felt a larger sense of import, Scarlett, Torden, and Evrich at his sides, forming a small half-circle around Jacques. All around the gilded room, the tile walls alternating between malachite and onyx, sat shelves upon shelves. Each was filled to the brim with ancient, magical, or cursed items, Jacques the master of it all.

The Master of the Vault held a skull, blackened from age, its eyes white flames that shimmered and danced within the scorched sockets. "This," Jacques began slowly, always a fan of theatrics, "is a skull of soul-sight. Trapped within this ancient cranium is the soul of a powerful seer, sealed before it could pass through the realm of death."

"That's really gross," Scarlett remarked, physically shrinking away from the rotted skull.

"Indeed," Jacques agreed. "Which is why I highly recommend you all wash your hands with water, fresh from the well, after this is done."

Talon's lips thinned. "You say that as if we're going to touch the damned thing."

Jacques met Talon's stare with his own black orbs, unblinking.

"Shit."

Jacques nodded. "I'm afraid so. You see, by touching it, you can direct thoughts of something or someone into the skull, and in return it will give you visions of whatever you seek, as long as your target has a soul. The more familiar you are with the target, and the more accurately you can visualize it, the greater the clarity of these visions will be. Thus, soul-sight." He slid his hand horizontally through the room, palm up. "It works best with multiple people, and I'll be here to regulate, just to make sure that none of you end up going insane, or worse."

"Or worse?" Evrich couldn't hold back the bitter tone that entered his voice.

"Ah, yes. Sometimes, if the seer's soul is strong enough, it will try to switch its soul with another, trapping someone – that isn't a seer, annoyingly – into the skull." Jacques tapped a knuckle against the skull's temple for emphasis.

"And what do we do if that happens?" Talon asked.

"Oh, then we just destroy the skull to release the newly-captured soul, and kill whoever the seer took over. Things are a lot less complicated that way." Jacques said this in the same tone that one might remark upon the weather. "As you can imagine, me not having met Sepulchre myself, I can't do this myself. Otherwise, I wouldn't risk putting you all in danger." He shrugged. "Oh well, no sense in wasting any more time. Let's begin. First, I'll need you all to strip your gloves off; there'll be no effect if your skin doesn't make contact."

Slowly, cautiously, they all obeyed, each stripping off a single glove.

"I don't like dis business, lad," Torden muttered. "Disrespectful ta go messin' 'bout wit' corpses."

"Technically speaking, the skull would still have to be attached to a body for it to be considered a corpse." Jacques waggled the skull around, as if to parade around the lack of appendages. "Now..." He held the skull out in front of him, the upper row of teeth – the only remaining row of teeth – gently nestled in his bare palm. "...rest your hands atop the skull."

The four shared a tentative look, all nodding to one another, too deep in to back out now. Talon put his hand on it first, Scarlett placing her palm down next, fingers caressing Talon's. Evrich followed a second later, and finally Torden relented, only able to place the tips of his fingers on the seer's temple.

"Good." Jacques closed his eyes. "Now close your eyes as I do, and think deeply of Sepulchre. Focus in on the creature, from the broadest form to the most minute of details. Let your memories of the abomination flow into the seer's soul."

They closed their eyes in unison, bodies tensing.

Talon concentrated on the writhing skin and its singular eye, tracing out every vein and blemish that he could remember, letting only hints of his loathing seep through.

Scarlett focused in on the creature's tongue, and the infectious saliva it had lapped onto her arm, letting her fear and disgust fill out the rest.

Torden thought only of battle; of how it moved, and thrashed about, about the wings that it had sprouted and used to flee. Its tactics, or lack thereof, and how he planned to fight the abomination when next he met it.

Evrich, Captain of Marbleton, once again felt the anxiety that he and his men had shared riding through their city, the relief he had felt as it had taken flight and disappeared, and then the guilt that had sprung from his inability to save his home. What he gave the seer were only flashes of Sepulchre's form, seen briefly from a distance, but also the hatred he felt for it, and the desire to redeem himself by facing it head-on.

These memories melded together into a near-flawless replica of the abomination's writhing form, the image swirling through the seer's entrapped soul, now ablaze with the familiar pattern of divination. Below their fingers, the skull began to warm until it was scalding, the white flames within the eyeless sockets dancing with increased intensity.

All at once, the living minds that filled the vault mixed into a stew of thought, and together they became witnesses to the barrage of information shooting through them. They saw through the seer, experiencing soul-sight.

Bodies. The chamber. Stone. Flesh. Pulsating, squelching flesh armour. Armour. Crunched between boney teeth.

Come to me.

Sepulchre. Feeding, then sleeping, then feeding. All dead, still dying, about to die.

Come to me.

Stairs now. Up, up, and further up. Sunlight. Relief, fear. A town. A village. Now a graveyard, all dead within and without.

Come to me.

A church. Light beamed between the pews. A window. Stained glass. A god, wielding a hammer. O'deus. Cracked, blood dripping from the golden tool.

COME TO ME.

Dark now. Gnashing teeth. A blood-shot eye. A grating voice, shivering with death and decay.

"COME TO ME!"

———•———

Talon wrenched his hand away, throwing Scarlett and Evrich out of their own reverie. Heaving, Talon leaned against Scarlett, the redhead helping him stand upright. Behind them, Evrich heaved, hands gripping his knees.

Jacques watched them, eyes fluttering. In a single motion, he placed the skull back on its designated place upon the shelves, the flames within the eye sockets dwindling to embers. "So, that was an interesting experience."

Scarlett grit her teeth, forcing words out with effort. "That thing *talked* to us. You didn't say it would do that."

"Speaking honestly, I didn't think it could." Jacques locked eyes with Talon, his stare a knowing one, the others too absorbed in their own suffering to notice. "It's an anomaly, really, but anything can happen when you deal with cursed artefacts."

Evrich's head snapped up. "That thing is *cursed*?"

Looking almost insulted, Jacques's hand came to the center of his chest. "Of *course* it's cursed, it's a two-hundred-year-old skull with a soul trapped inside; anything with a soul trapped inside is immediately considered as such. Did you think it would be anything else?"

"I just-"

"Enough," Talon growled. "We got the information we needed. We'll rest tonight and head out tomorrow morning to kill the damned thing."

Torden fell into a coughing fit, forced to clear his throat before speaking. "Lad, if ya could make anythin' from dat mess, I would be impressed."

"Best get that praise at the ready then, because it sounds like he understands what we saw." Scarlett let go of Talon, the two back on their own feet.

"I do." Looking down at his bare hand covered in soot and ash, the memory playing out in such clarity that he could swear it happened just moments ago. "The darkness, the stairs... the church and the mural. Sepulchre has gone back to where it first awoke. Whether to hide or to feed, it's flown back to Fallkirk."

CHAPTER 27

"Thank you for waiting." The clerk's voice, sweet like honey, danced across Torden's ears as she finished filing his paperwork. "You are now an official member of the Adventurers' Guild. Please be safe in your work, Torden Ironfist, and make sure to look for a job that best fits your abilities." A practiced speech, given to every new adventurer who joined the Guild, as was the copper dog tag the young woman passed to the dwarf. "This is your identification tag. You'll need it when you file for a job, and it will help people identify you if you perish while out on the field, so make sure to keep it on you at all times."

Torden turned the dog tag between his fingers, humming as he examined the smooth metal. "A li'l more official than I was expectin' fer a bunch o' mercenaries."

"You'll get used to it," Talon assured the dwarf, waving to the clerk as the two adventurers walked away from the line of counters. "It's a lot more paperwork than you'd think, but the clerks tend to take care of most of it, as long as there aren't too many complications on a job."

"Aye, I'm not one fer such things, but I'll learn ta deal with it." Torden pursed his lips as he continued examining the tag. "Why copper? Surely steel or iron would do the job just fine."

Talon nodded. "If it was just for identifying your corpse, you'd be right. The main purpose of these tags are to let others know what your rank within the Guild is. Copper is the lowest rank, and is given out to anyone willing to sign up."

Seeing Torden simply nodding along, he continued. "Silver is the next one up, and usually denotes that you can get a job done without dying. Above that is gold." Talon slipped his fingers into one of his pouches, pulling from it a similar tag to Torden's, but made of glittering gold. "To get to this point, the guild master will decide when you're ready to ascend, and task you with a special job; finish it successfully and live, and ta-dah."

Torden slipped the dog tag into his pocket. "Aye, so three ranks, is it?"

Talon shook his head. "No, there's two more, though achieving these are more than rare. Above gold is platinum, but to even be considered for that rank, guild masters from three different branches of the Guild have to recommend you, and that often requires you to be a pretty well-known hero working a pretty wide net."

The two began making their way down the stairs leading back to the first floor, the noise of drunken adventurers and excited music flooding back into their senses. "A noble goal, helpin' people. And the last?"

"Orichalcum." Without noticing that he was doing it, Talon began rubbing the back of his gauntlets, made from the mythical, nearly indestructible material. "Only two people currently hold this rank, though I've only seen one, and from a distance." Talon's face scrunched up, the ethereal figure appearing in his mind. "To carry a tag made of this stuff, five of the Guild's masters have to come together. As one, in whole agreement, they all sign this thing known as a Writ of Heroism – a petition, of sorts – that's then presented to the Eternal King himself. If he sponsors it, then it goes through, and the adventurer's rank is raised to orichalcum."

Torden huffed, "Sounds ta me like a lot a trouble fer some title."

"It's not just a title." Talon stopped as they reached the

bottom of the stairs, Torden almost tripping as he halted his descent. "Orichalcum-ranked adventurers are given special privileges when it comes to how they interpret the laws. They act not just as a member of the Guild, but are also at the beck and call of the Eternal King. If he needs something dealt with that the Order of Paladins simply can't handle, then these special adventurers will be sent in to clean up, may the gods be merciful upon those at the wrong end of their ire."

"Lad, ya seem... scared o' them."

The human stood silent for a long moment, breathing deep. Then he started walking, making his way for the exit. "If you ever meet one of them, you'll understand."

Sun barely above the horizon, the stables shook with activity. Adventurers came and went, cleaning and preparing their horses. Rolt and Obsidian stood out in the street, Scarlett and Ruby staying back, waiting for Talon, waving excitedly as he turned the corner. "Hey, you get Torden all set up?"

He nodded. "He's officially one of us. He's getting strapped up in the guard's saddle at the moment. Now, what did you want to show me?"

His straightforwardness hadn't changed at all, Scarlett bemoaned. "Well, I thought that it was a tad unfair to have Ruby haul both of us around, and that you would also appreciate being in control of the saddle again."

"You got me a horse." The fact was stated in near monotone.

"Wrong!" Scarlett threw her shoulders back, putting thumb and index in her mouth, whistling. It was a short tone that started low but quickly rose, followed with two quick sharp chirps.

Talon's ears twitched, watching in silence as a pitch-black horse clopped around the corner, amber eyes meeting his cerulean. "Shadow," Talon whispered. The horse's ears pricked, walking slowly towards him. "How? I lost him months ago, near

Black Hollow." After the fires scared him away, he thought drily.

"Yeah, well, he just kind of showed up here one day. I've been paying for his care for the past few months; there were also some maps tucked away into his saddle bags, which is what gave me my first leads into tracking you down." She smiled as Shadow nuzzled his snout into Talon's palms. "He was really depressed the first few weeks, you know. It took a lot to cheer him up."

Talon smiled, small and barely imperceptible. "I guess I should apologize, to both of you." He placed his head against Shadow's. "Sorry for not finding you sooner... and thank you, Scarlett." With his horse already saddled up, Talon swung up onto its back, grabbing the reins in one smooth motion. "I feel as though I've gained back a piece of myself."

With a grin, Scarlett hopped up onto Ruby, pulling her up next to Shadow and Talon. "Glad to hear it. Now, let's go kill that ball of flesh, and be done with this."

Urging their steeds forward, they entered the streets, the rest of their hunting party watching as they approached.

"It's been a great many years since we've worked together." Glaive's sudden comment broke the group's silence. "Hopefully your senses haven't dulled during your absence."

Talon sneered at the warrior, baring his teeth for all to see. "Don't worry, I still know how to make use of a human shield. Speaking of which, how good is your new armour?"

Glaive grunted. "Enough to deflect your bottlewash, at the very least."

"Pretty low bar you set for your blacksmith. It any good at deflecting blades too, or was that out of your budget?"

"It's certainly nice to see them showing some enthusiasm, that's for sure." Amelia muttered to Scarlett, the redhead grinning at her in response. "Still, I do wish you two would get along better!" The amazon called over her shoulder.

"We get along just fine," Glaive countered, peering at Amelia through the slits in his helmet. "Sure, Talon would be better suited to scrubbing the filth from under a beggar's nails, but I don't mind fighting next to him."

"What about in front of me?" Talon asked drily.

Glaive snorted. "Not in a million years. Never again."

Talon glanced over his shoulder, catching Evrich's stern glare. The captain and his retinue trailed half a furlong behind the adventurers, keeping an arrow-headed formation with Evrich at the front. Next to him sat Private Goddard, Torden riding in the jury-rigged saddle. Turning back to the other adventurers, Talon shrugged. "Oh well, I'm sure I can find a replacement."

Their journey continued in this manner, the nights passing in quiet respite, opposing their daytime merriment.

He couldn't see. An abyss stretched before him, devoid of light or life.

Talon tried to move, the heavy nails digging into his palms, pinning his outstretched arms. His legs dangled under him, numb and useless. He tried to lick his dry lips, but found he had no tongue, nor teeth. His throat itching and lungs empty, he tried to swallow, to suck in air, but those too became a pointless effort.

A light flickered in the distance, bobbing as it approached, two figures outlined in shades of red and orange. One cloaked, the other in armour.

They approached, staring up at him, features hazy, changing under the shifting light. Their lips moved, but Talon heard nothing, his ears rotting stumps on the ground, peeled from his head by gravity. The figure in armour disappeared, there one second, then gone the next, the torch gone with them.

The hooded one continued talking, emerald eyes glowing in the darkness. He took a step towards Talon, craning their head up, hood slipping to reveal Viktor's gaunt features. Their mangy black hair crawled in the darkness, inky tendrils reaching for the dead that surrounded them.

Talon's throat wriggled and bulged, mouth opening against his will. The centipede slithered around his ribs, pushing its way up through his throat before skittering across his face, legs catching against his lips. Struggling, it pulled against Talon's head, snapping it to the side before disappearing from sight.

A woman hung next to him, trampled and rotted, her crimson hair draped across her face. Scarlett's head rose slowly, twitching into place centimeters at a time before snapping up, her singular, bloodshot eye staring him down. A rictus grin spread across her face, stretching thin. Wider and wider, straining against her own bindings, the crucifix rattling from the effort. Her mouth opened, bugs pouring out from between dagger-like teeth, a torrent of black carapaces flooding the room.

A grim parody of her voice screamed inside his head.

"Come to me."

CHAPTER 28

"Talon!"

He snapped from his daymare, Scarlett leaning into his line of sight, her crimson curls bouncing in the midday sun.

"You feeling alright?

He stared blankly at her for a few moments, blinking as he came back to the present. "Huh? Oh, yeah. I was just... thinking."

Though she clearly wasn't assuaged by his half-hearted explanation, the redhead sat up, pushing the matter no further. "Well, you might want to start paying attention, because we're almost there."

Looking up, long past the densely-populated forests, Fallkirk crested over the horizon. The small village Talon remembered had grown, its church sporting a new bell tower and an additional wing that had not been there during his last visit. All around the chapel, the huts and hovels stood tightly packed alongside slightly larger cots. The settlement, almost doubled in size, lead Talon to think back to the priest, and the pilgrimage to O'deus' mural that he'd spoken so fondly of.

The party stopped, staring down at the thatched rooftops and dirt road sketching out the mismatched grid between buildings. Holes peppered every building, flesh-toned lines tracing around the settlement, snaking down the streets. Even from a distance, these tendrils looked as large as tree roots.

"Where is everyone?" Amelia stood in her stirrups, leaning

from side to side as if she'd see some of the villagers playing hide and seek.

"Dead, I imagine," Glaive said. Pulling up to the front, his nose wrinkled. "I smell a lot of blood."

"I've smelled worse in recent history." Scarlett leaned back in her saddle, exchanging a look with Talon, a gentle smile crossing her face as he urged Shadow down the sloping hill towards Fallkirk.

Without prompting, the rest followed him down, the muffled clopping of hooves becoming suddenly violent as healthy green turned to crunchy brown, the grass as affected by Sepulchre's corruption as any other living organism. By the time they passed through the small town's outer wall, all that remained of the lush nature outside was dirt fit only for corpses and a few, sparse trees, so decayed they were liquefying, becoming warped, sludgy obelisks.

The buildings were even worse up close. The tentacles slithering from earth and home jerked and jumped, bright red boils bulging to the point of near bursting before then deflating, another pulsating lump soon gathering along the winding flesh roots. Nevertheless, the pungent scent of rot permeated the air, seeping into the riders' clothes, noses burning as their horses snuffled and whimpered. The houses creaked and whined as they rode down the main street, windows and doors warping to follow their path, nails screeching as they bent, struggling to keep the once comely domiciles intact.

"Creepy," Scarlett muttered, her eyes snapping forward each time she deigned to look around. Her hands trembled, knuckles white.

Talon didn't respond, teeth clenched too tight to speak. Sweat dripped down his brow, stinging his eyes, unable to force them shut. Pressure built up within his skull, an aching presence wailing to be free, scraping along his ear canals.

From all around came the tickling whispers of people who

had once been. Voices full of merriment twisted into a cacophonic chorus; the *put put put* of a rubber ball bouncing, accompanied by the strangled cries of children; the town bellman chiming alongside Fallkirk's final, bloody hymns. *Ring ring. Ring ring.*

Bong! Bong!

The belltower rang, overtaking the false whispers of the dead, its booming clang calling the town's intruders to its holy abode. Then it was silent, the oversized chime swaying in the gentle breeze, not even an echo of the golden alarm left. Talon pulled his hands away, unsure when he had even covered his ears. Looking next to him, he met Scarlett's worried gaze, her brow knitted together.

"Hey," she started, cutting herself off as Talon shook his head.

"I'm fine," Talon said more sharply than he'd intended. "It's just... just a headache. I'll be fine, really. Come on, let's go check out the chapel." Spurring Shadow on, Talon tried to ignore the emerald eyes burning a hole into his back, and the conspiratorial whispers coming from further beyond. He stopped in front of the church and waited for the others to join him.

The muttered concerns of the guardsmen gave form to the shared unease spread amidst the large party. Though not pristine by any definition, the holy building stood unmarred by rot and corruption, its stone and wood so plain it was jarring in contrast to the veritable wasteland surrounding them. The stained-glass windows, though in need of cleaning, reflected the light with their usual effulgence. Holy idolatry seemed to ward off real beasts just as efficiently as they did spiritual ones.

But even with this apparent purity, a haze hung over the place. An invisible but not ephemeral weight baring down on the mortals sat before the church. Dragged by the subtle tugging of psychic hands, Talon's feet hit the ground without memory of dismounting. It must have looked natural enough, for Scarlett and Glaive dismounted, as did Evrich, keeping close to the rogue as his feet dragged him to the chapel doors. His hands, cold and numb, reached up, pushing against the hard wood that barred entry to the consecrated sanctuary.

The hinges ground together as Talon pushed the doors inward, rust flaking from the unseen corners of the large entrance. Any sense of untaintedness left soon after, the sight and smell of corpses, dozens piled high up, greeted the advancing group. Flayed to a bright red, the bodies intermingled into a senseless mass, arms and legs poking out at random amidst screaming faces, silent in their final display of agony. Blood pooled around the pile, a crimson moat around the meaty monolith.

Scarlett pedaled away, covering her mouth as she gagged.

Glaive turned his head, cursing under his breath, his great helm likely staving off the worst of the pile's effects.

Evrich simply stood there, frozen, his open-faced armour giving no protection nor hiding how his face twisted and grimaced.

Even those still mounted, farthest from the pile, audibly gasped and cursed. One guardswoman, the youngest of the bunch, puked, nearly falling from horseback.

Talon ignored all of this, his eye drawn not to the blood-soaked orgy, but the figure hanging above it. A man barely into his adult years dangled over the piled bodies, his own entrails corded tight around his neck, the excess drooping from a large gash in his abdomen, the priest's vestments defiled by grime and ichor. O'deus's mural, the god's striking figure blotted out by dried blood and taut flesh, worked as a grim backdrop for the holy man strung from the rafters.

His head light, Talon stepped inside, beyond the safety of the outside world. Passing toppled pews and braziers, he stood before the pile, staring up at the priest's corpse, swaying gently. They look *peaceful*, Talon thought, taking in the dead man's slack jaw and empty eye sockets.

Like they're taking a long nap.

I could use a nap, he thought, eyelids suddenly heavy.

Rest your eyes, just for a moment.

Just a moment...

Eyes close to shutting, Talon threw his hand up to his chest, digging the sharp claws of his gauntlets deep into his flesh. The pain dispelled the exhaustion, and Talon growled at the body swaying above him. "So that's your game now? Petty tricks? Show yourself, Sepulchre!"

The priest stopped swaying, his body freezing midair. Then with a violent snap, the corpse's eyeless face looked down at the adventurer, his smile too wide to fit his face. The dual voices echoed in Talon's head, one just as new as the other was familiar.

"A shame. I was hoping to make this easier."

All at once, the pile came to life, arms shooting out and grabbing Talon. Though bereft of skin, their blackened nails punctured through his limbs, dragging him forward with a collective iron will.

"What are you–" Talon struggled against the grasping paws, but couldn't muster the strength to resist, his limbs suddenly filled with lead. Head thrashing, his vision became enveloped by red, flayed bodies surrounding him as the pile fully enveloped him.

"Come to me."

"Talon!"

He was once again sat atop Shadow, the pale gray steed looking at him over its shoulder. Mind still hazy, Talon looked up, the desecrated chapel no longer before him. Instead stood the familiar pair of one-winged soldiers, the statues standing vigil either side of the tomb's open entrance, their swords pointed downwards, bloody tears running down their faces.

"Talon!" Scarlett called again, breaking the silver-haired rogue from his stupefaction. "What happened? Why did you run off like that?"

"I..." His mouth felt like it was filled with sand, his tongue struggling to form syllables. He simply shook his head, gathering his thoughts. "The chapel. What happened?" Each word came out forced and sluggish, Talon scrunching his eyes as he struggled to push out the now-strange sounds.

Scarlett's left eye twitched. Her lips parted for a moment before shutting. She glanced over her shoulder, towards the rest of the group, still in the distance and riding at a much less harried pace than she must have been. Tightening her grip on Ruby's reins, she leaned towards Talon, hissing. "Talon, after you opened the doors to the chapel... you just stood there, all spaced out for a minute. Then out of nowhere you jumped on Shadow and ran off, full speed."

Lazily turning his head back towards the tomb, Talon nodded. "Right," he said, not remembering anything but agreeing anyway. "Yeah, sorry. Was just... freaked out."

Grabbing his collar, Scarlett pulled Talon in close, her words barely above a snarl in their intensity. "Do *not* play that game with me. I saw your face, and even though it's been a while, I still know you well enough to know what you're feeling. You weren't *freaked out*. You weren't even angry. You were just... gone. Expressionless." Letting him go, she backed off, her tone shifting into something less feral, but still stern. "Listen. If something is wrong, you *need* to tell me. Okay?"

Talon nodded, staring into the cavernous darkness before him. "Right. Okay." He could still feel Scarlett's displeasure; could still see her scowl and the way her shoulders bunched up in his peripheral. Whatever she had to say next, however, was kept to herself, the rest of the group finally joining them.

Evrich stared daggers at the pair. "Would one of you like to explain what happened back there?" His scowl was more intense than Scarlett's, more practiced with deeper lines giving him a harsher appearance.

Ignoring the captain's question, Talon slid from Shadow, feet barely disturbing the dead grass surrounding the colossal crypt. "We go inside."

Jaw tightening as his grimace deepened, Evrich looked towards the open doors, peering into the darkness beyond the one-winged angels. "And you're sure about this?"

Again, Talon ignored the captain, letting go of Shadow's reins and distancing himself from the appraising looks of his traveling companions. "I feel it. At the bottom." And saying no more, he entered, the cavernous shadows enveloping him.

Evrich cursed under his breath and ordered his men to follow, while the other adventurers scrambled, dismounting to follow their silver-haired friend into the abyss.

CHAPTER 29

Selora stepped tentatively through the abandoned streets, avoiding the snaking tendrils and puckering pustules. Fallkirk, like most of the outside world, was strange to her.

Opposing the extensive cities and their titanic towers she'd come to know, this little town felt lacking, spacious roads lined by buildings that each held their own hold on the now-dead greenery surrounding them. That wasn't to say it was small, as there were clear signs of expansion, told mostly through the remnants of what used to be. Closest to the center, the smallest abodes were king, finely cut boards creating tight boxes with bare furnishings. The further out the town went, the more complex the buildings became, stone walls replacing wood while locks became a more prevalent feature amidst the higher-quality doors.

It was a simple, practical layout, the minimalism now ruined by the invasive organisms laced throughout like weeds.

Stepping around a tentacle thick as a tree trunk, Selora peeked her head into one of the houses, its door blown off its hinges. Toppled furniture littered the floor, dents covering the table and walls, flies buzzing around spilt food. Blood stained the corners of a broken table leg, but the humble abode was otherwise free of the telltale signs of a struggle. Selora stepped away from the house, the rotting food itching her nostrils.

Meandering back to the center of the road, she slowly took in the damage. The trees and grass were silent, dead to their roots and cut off from the elf's preternatural senses. She tried to focus in on anything nearby that still lived, but only heard the distant warning cries of the trees from the forest she'd passed through to get here. They were screaming for her to leave, nature echoing her own desires.

She ignored them and herself, pushing away the psychic wails of nature for her more primitive senses. Disease infested the town, boils and unwashed flesh all-encompassing. Unescapable as it was, smell became almost useless as a point of reference. But the scent of death? Of rotting bodies and festering blood pools? That was strong, and singular. Following it was like being lead on a leash, a one-way track that became impossible to detour from, standing out from even the worst that Sepulchre's infestation had to offer.

The chapel reeked, its open doors letting out the festering mildew and congealing blood. Even before she looked inside, she knew what she would see, the familiar dread of her earliest mistake enveloping her senses. It was perhaps this familiarity then that allowed her to stare at the crimson pile, feeling only self-indulgent guilt. The crucified human dangling from the rafters spun slowly, his noosed insides stretched taut.

Disgusted, Selora closed the chapel doors, sealing the stench back within the modest temple. Stepping back, her feet sunk slightly into the ground, pulling her eyes downwards. Tracks, both human and horse, so obvious now that it was absurd that she had missed them before. Given her knowledge of Talon's group, and the fact that these were the only tracks leading away from the town, she followed them.

Her pace was slow and forced.

CHAPTER 30

The clattering of a near-dozen metal boots echoed unerringly throughout the steep stairway, the passage tighter and the steps shorter than Talon remembered. Have I grown so much since then? he wondered, hand tracing along the stone walls, worn smooth by the passage of time. Every breath and creaking joint echoed in the cramped corridor, the party's own mortality beaten into their ears with each passing second. Talon wiped away a bead of sweat sliding down his cheek, the humidity rising.

"The air is stale," Glaive said, his traditionally noble voice distorted into something strange, words bouncing off the walls and overlapping.

"It's a tomb." Talon's voice was distorted in a similar manner.

Between them there was an unspoken desire to break the silence, but a force beyond their conscious understanding made every syllable feel dangerous, as though something were stalking them. This feeling only deepened as the walls around them turned from stone to flesh, shades of gray suddenly enveloped by pallid beige and ivory. Talon jerked his hand away, fighting back bile as the fatty meat squirmed and jiggled in response to his touch.

"It knows we're here then?" Scarlett braced herself against the last few inches of stone, grimacing at the veiny walls.

Talon nodded, unsure if she could even see the movement, the dim torchlight grasped within Glaive's hand barely reaching their shoulders. "Most likely, yeah." Staring down, his mood soured further. A few more steps and they would be at the bottom of the stairway, and from there every tile and grain of dust was enveloped by Sepulchre's malevolent incursion. Sucking in air through his teeth, Talon continued, his soles sinking into the pulpy ground. The others followed him soon after, announcing their landing with separate curses and words catalyzing their revulsion.

Ignoring their cries, Talon moved on, forcing the others to follow. Whether they did or not wasn't his problem, he decided. Only he needed to reach *the end*; to see out his *destiny*. Destiny? A curious word. One he had always scoffed at in the past. So why should it find substance in his mind now? He shook off the thought, focusing on the path ahead, barely glancing at the dead runes inscribed along the tomb, their imprint somehow still peeking out from the veiny canvas smothering the dead language. A dead language, or the language of the dead?

Talon grabbed his head, knuckles digging into his temple. His feet plodded along while his mind wandered, thoughts that weren't his own tugging him along asinine threads. He trudged along, vision blurring and refocusing as unfamiliar sounds danced along his ears. Was someone murmuring in the distance, or was there an underground spring burbling just around the next bend? There was no such thing, of course. He turned the corner and there was simply more hallway, more tomb. An endless array of tunnels that bent and twisted, a singular path that still managed to disorient.

The passing of decades had twisted his memory of the place, thinking the journey a much shorter one than it was turning out to be. Were there truly this many turns? Though it felt like only minutes had passed, surely, he had taken a few hundred or even thousand steps by now. Hadn't he? Slowing, Talon began counting his steps.

One, two, three, four, five...

Twelve...

Sixty-eight...

Three-hundred and-

Talon stopped, rubbing his eyes. Had he lost count somewhere? Was he blacking out? Something wet touched his lips, and out of instinct he wiped it on the palm of his glove. Blood stained the supple leather, dripping from his nose in a thin stream. He opened his mouth, a witty dismissal only moments away, when his tongue refused to move, throat tightening against the desired ignorance. Grabbing his neck, he squeezed, wheezing and gasping, each breath becoming shallower than the last.

Something was wrong.

His hand kept tightening, choking him, the points of his gauntlet drawing blood. His knees buckled, and he collapsed onto them, his other hand struggling to pry away the first from his throat. Then both were wound together in unison, interlocking fingers pushing his trachea shut. Tears welled up, and he was cursed.

So weak. So worthless. Better off dead.

Then he began to sink, deep into the floor. Hands formed from the meaty ground, clawing and scraping at his battered clothes, stripping the skin from his face.

A waste of flesh. Better given to the dead.

Bare muscle screamed, blood seeping from the fibers, dirt and dust digging deep into the tendons. He tried to scream, but even that was taken from him as hundreds of fingers wormed their way down his throat, fighting through the bile that tried to free his lungs.

Relax. Death is better than living. It will be peaceful.

He melted, every second spent in agony, until he was barely a puddle on the floor. A meaningless existence.

"Talon!"

And then he awoke, standing at the base of the stairs, Scarlett shaking him by the shoulder.

"Hey, why'd you stop so suddenly?" Her voice was trembling, eyes wide and panicked. Her hand felt cold against Talon's shoulder even through her gloves, and her lips were dry and cracked.

An odd thing for her, Talon thought, licking his own lips. "Sorry, I was... just listening." He looked over his shoulder where the rest of his hunting party waited, concerned faces filling the cramped chamber. Waiting for him amidst flesh-covered walls, the pulsating cylinder resembling a throat.

"Listening for what?" Scarlett pressed, leaning in, her brow scrunching.

"For Sepulchre," he lied, regaining his sense of self. Shaking his head, Talon pushed Scarlett's hand from his shoulder. "Don't worry about it, we just need to keep going." Once again, he moved away from her without hearing her out, the redhead's mouth hanging open while she decided whether to push or pull back.

And as before, she tightened her lips and followed her friend.

Talon followed the path laid out before him, this trip going by far quicker than the hallucinatory one. The halls went on longer, fewer bends allowing him to see the end of each corridor. He counted his steps and found no evidence of lost time, his confidence rising as reality cemented itself. He saw no glowing runes, nor bodiless hands, and heard no thoughts besides his own. Every time he looked over his shoulder, Scarlett smiled weakly at him, the others just as tense. Tense, but sure.

Uncountable minutes went by with this surety, and they reached the end.

The large double doors, once held shut by ancient magic and abnormal chains, stood wide open. The darkness beyond greeted the adventurers and guardsmen, waiting patiently for them to enter. And yet they hesitated, filtering slowly into the square antechamber.

"I don't like this," Evrich stated plainly, hand grasped tightly around his sheathed sword.

Amelia snorted, the amazon's large arms crossing over her scarred chest. "Can't say I disagree with you, though it brings me shame to shy away from something just because of the dark."

Glaive took a step towards the darkness, waving his torch around, but not daring to stray too close.

"Don't bother," Talon said, motioning for the knightly adventurer to step away. "I can't see anything either, which means the darkness is magical, or at the very least a mass hallucination."

Evrich drew his sword, limbs stiff, movements unrefined. "Hallucination, magic, or whatever else it might be, our options are limited to blade and brawn."

Torden unslung his ax, the dwarf having been strangely quiet. "Right you are! I say we charge in and suhprise the damned beast." His voice trembled, eyes focused and sobered. The flask at his hip had gone dry during the trip, and he'd had no way to replenish it, the consequences of this fact showing themselves in his white-knuckle grip.

Talon leaned forward, trying to peer deeper into the darkness. The stagnant abyss, unmoving, contrasted the swirling black that had blanketed the chamber upon his first arrival. "It knows we're here already." Though maybe charging in isn't the worst idea, he thought. Because for all the group's banter and bluster, no one took another step towards the chamber draped in darkness.

Not that they had to, as only moments later, a shadow burst out. An inky tentacle shot across the antechamber, wrapping around Talon's leg, and jerked back, throwing the rogue to the ground and dragging him along the rough tiles.

"Talon!" Scarlett's shouts went unnoticed, dust billowing up, blinding and deafening the rogue as he passed through the open doors, wholly enveloped in the drowning abyss.

He couldn't breathe, the darkness thick like tar, giving way to his flailing limbs but not allowing oxygen to fill his lungs. His

261

head hurt, the pain gifting him a sensation akin to being crushed under the weight of a deep ocean. Eyes swimming, Talon quickly stopped struggling, vague shapes twisting in the hazy void, flashes of detail coming to light as the adventurer's body sparked with magic.

Somewhere, Sepulchre was watching him. Grinning and cackling, licking its lipless mouth, enjoying every second of Talon's powerlessness. Pride and malice, centuries old, seeped into its vile concoction, driving its presence deeper into Talon's mind.

I knew you would come. You could not resist. Just like all the others.

Talon struggled to listen, grasping for the final vestiges of his fading mind.

You are not special. There was once a time where many like you walked the earth. Haughty and full of themselves. I devoured many of them. Gained their mass. Became strong.

Talon curled fingers into fists, teeth clenching so tightly his jaw ached. The abomination's voice slithered between his own thoughts, breaking them apart so he could focus only on it.

But of course, that was taken from me. By those that were greater than you. But they were mortal too, and have passed through the veil between worlds. As you will, and many others. Perhaps I will as well, one day. Or maybe I shall live forever, in the ruins of your cruel world.

A great maw widened. A thousand teeth like splintered bone twitched and ground from pustulent gums. Flesh cracked and oozed as it stretched impossibly wide, fetid flaps folding over themselves as the inhuman jaws cracked shut.

The impossible darkness disappeared, replaced by Sepulchre's riveted innards, and Talon tumbled down the beast's esophagus. Acid burned away leather and wool, smoke rising in their place. His skin bubbled against the toxic walls, his body fighting to stitch the damage and repair itself, cobalt energy dancing around him like lightning.

Pain drove his every action, every flailing limb and failed attempt to grasp the caustic lining, every scream and grunt accenting his descent. His vision focused only enough to see the boiling pond beneath, rapidly approaching and ready to devour him whole.

Talon scrambled, panic taking over his oxygen-starved brain. His hands scraped against the red and gray walls, tearing away diseased flesh as he plummeted further down. His palms boiled, skin and muscle seared away in moments, pain unescapable as his fall finally came to its end.

CHAPTER 31

"Talon!" Scarlett's shout died amidst the rumbling corridors, the ancient walls surrounding them beginning to shift and contract. The floor wobbled, shaking beneath their feet, Scarlett and Amelia losing their balance alongside several guardsmen.

"We have to go!" Evrich shouted, pulling Goddard to his feet.

"What about Talon?" Glaive yelled back, keeping his balance by digging his halberd into the floor.

"Little late for that, I think." Amelia got to her knee, the amazon pointing towards the room Talon had been dragged into, the impenetrable darkness fading, lifting to be replaced by the glare of a single, massive eye.

Sepulchre roared, its mouth in a pained rictus. All at once, the warbling walls and uneven flooring began to constrict around itself, stone twisting and grinding against the flesh infesting the ancient architecture. The antechamber sunk into itself, threatening to crush its inhabitants into pulp.

"Run! Now!" Evrich's voice cut through the cacophony, his commanding tone spurring both guard and adventurer to their feet.

All except Scarlett, who froze, the desire to save Talon battling against her own survival instincts. She had no time to come to her own decision though, as Rolt's bearish arm wrapped around her waist, dragging her away from the chamber and its fading darkness. She wanted to scream, to tell Rolt to go back, but the giant's maneuver had left her winded, fetid air clogging her gasping lungs.

And so, she watched, helpless, as the cramped halls became even tighter behind them, every step taken matched by the crumbling flesh. They were the last in the trailing line of fleeing dungeoneers, Rolt forced to slow himself while behind the dozen others running for their lives, armour and weapons rattling all the way.

Then the hands began to rise, grasping paws stretching out from the throat-like passage, decrepit fingers clawing and scraping, digits too long and with too many joints to be human. Sick parodies of mortal anatomy, yet no less real. Caught unawares, the guard heading the escape tripped against a pair of interlocked hands, falling face-first into the grasp of a dozen more. His screams, filled with agony, gave the others pause. A brief pause, too short to thwart their escape, but too long to save the man. He died in moments, curling fingers pushing deep into his eyes and ears, a whole hand crawling down his throat, suffocating him.

"Don't stop!" Evrich shouted, pain accentuating each word.

No one argued, boots trampling over the man's corpse, too little space to do otherwise. His features died in the stomping parade, his name unknown to Scarlett, maggots already crawling from his orifices as the crypt's tightening walls crushed the body to pulp.

Every second, more hands appeared, fingers pulling at loose cloth or slipping between metal plates. Weapons were drawn without command, and bodyless hands hacked away, replaced by two more. Every meter gained was arduous, the horde surrounding them requiring three times the energy to keep speed.

The guardsmen's' one-handed swords and Torden's shorter throwing axes were the most effective weapons in the cramped confines, most of the adventurers stuck using their fists. Even without weapons, and one of his arms taken by Scarlett, Rolt bludgeoned his way through, his massive fist crushing or tearing the alien hands from their curse-borne perches. Glaive and Amelia supported each other, gauntlets and amazonian brutality keeping the other safe.

Marbleton's soldiers fared well, but most lacked the animalistic strength that drove the adventurers. A man with a burly moustache and hooked nose was pulled against the wall, a hundred twisted hands holding him prisoner, snapping his neck before crushing his bones, body devoured by the fleshy enclosure. Goddard tried to help the man, but there were too many of Sepulchre's mockeries, hands folding over one another to block sword strikes. The private was forced to give up and keep running.

Then another, barely older than Goddard, was plucked from the ground, two powerful arms slamming his head into the ceiling so hard that his skull imploded.

Evrich cut the arms as he passed, dropping the guard's body to the floor, but had no choice but to leave it behind as well.

Glaive picked up the dead man's sword as he passed, putting the blade to good use immediately as a similar pair of arms tried to grab him. Ducking under the thick fingers, he spun on his heel, cutting the hands straight from their too-thin wrists. Pus dripped from the severed stumps in thick clumps, the adventurers gagging at the stench.

They continued in this manner, each bend bringing another surprise, another death. Scarlett barely registered any of it, staring over Rolt's shoulder as Sepulchre upended the ground, the fetid pathways rising like roots being pulled from soft dirt. Runes briefly flashed along the walls, burning through the tanned canopy covering them, before the stone they were etched into cracked and crumbled, and the last of the tomb's magic evaporated.

"There! Up ahead!" Goddard cried out, pointing his sword at the staircase as it finally came into view. The group's speed and fervour increased, the hands beginning to dwindle as Sepulchre's influence became stretched, bare walls once again within sight.

They abandoned caution and fled, the vestiges of the midday light covered by rolling black clouds.

Selora pinwheeled her arms, balancing against the sudden earthquake rumbling beneath her. Battered houses rattled alongside her, the town's crumbling walls finally toppling. She'd barely made it to Fallkirk's edge when it began, and she wouldn't be leaving until it was over, bent over and legs wide, body flailing as she struggled to keep her feet.

The rumbling's intensity continued to increase, knocking the elf to her knees, hands digging deep into the hard dirt. Her fingers traced each tremor, her preternatural senses guiding her along the vibrations, tracing a path to the earthquake's center. She snapped her head around just as it reached peak magnitude, and Fallkirk's chapel disappeared in an explosion of earth and stone, brick and glass shooting up into the sky to rain down upon the destroyed homes.

Selora, dumbfounded, watched as a colossal worm burst from the cloud of dust, reaching towards the sky and roaring. Sepulchre's eye spun and whizzed around in its socket, frantic and unfocused as the bloodshot orb danced from one end to another, a black sword imbedded in it like a needle. Pale scales covered its body, squealing against each other as its massive body stretched and contorted, pus leaking from the thin gaps. Its face had remained vaguely the same, its gaping jaw opening to reveal lines of teeth that looked like shattered bone.

She caught a glint of gold forming from the geysering debris, growing larger within her sight as it soared towards her before striking the ground only inches away from where she kneeled. The impact sent her flying, skin cut and dirtied, into the stump of a dead tree. Groaning, her back bruised and aching, she crawled back up to see the chapel's bell dug into the ground, earth lipped around, cradling the dead instrument. Then a brick smashed against the tree she huddled against, spraying her in shale, and she flinched, knocked out of her stupor.

She sprinted for the line of houses, ducking behind the bell before a sliver of stained glass could impale her, the blue fragment shattering into a dozen shards and dusting the golden shell in its azure. Then she was on her way again, unable to look directly at Sepulchre, its disfigured form almost touching the clouds. The ground continued to rumble, however, and she had no choice but to face the abomination's form, tentacle after tentacle bursting out from the ground. The few homes still standing went airborne, coming apart midfall before smashing back down.

"Why me, why me, why me?" Selora whined, hands covering her head, feet beating in rhythm with the rising tremors. Sepulchre's roars echoed across the land, drilling deeper into her head, pain searing away her thoughts. There was only instinct, a will to survive, to run and hide and never be found.

Anxiety and fear washed over her, enveloping all that she was. More debris crashed along her path, forcing her to careen and wind, the elf coughing and crying as more dust and powdered clay entered her mouth and eyes. She flew forward, a massive wall exploding behind her, tumbling over herself. She bounced – once, twice, thrice – hitting the ground and toppling onto her back, disoriented.

Numb, she stared into the sky, dark clouds rolling over Fallkirk, painting a deep gray behind Sepulchre. It was just like a painting, Selora thought, made ugly and twisted by the cruel gods that no longer watched over them.

Fresh air brightened their spirits for but a moment, quickly washed away by the fleshy towers pooling from the nearby town, and the deep dread the sight brought with it. Fallkirk was obliterated in seconds, the destruction wrought more a side effect of Sepulchre's appearance than through deliberate action.

Their horses whinnied and cried, stomping the ground.

"By Aggoth's beard," Torden whispered.

"How are we supposed to kill that thing?" Glaive asked, dropping the sword he'd picked up during their escape. His armour rattled, the warrior unable or unwilling to stop his body from shaking.

Scarlett swallowed hard, her mouth suddenly dry. "I don't..."

The guardsmen were similarly shaken, some sobbing quietly to themselves.

"Enough!" Evrich yelled, bringing everyone's attention to himself. The old soldier's teeth were clamped hard, lips snarling. His eyes burned with anger beyond description, yet his sword was held steady. "We came here to kill that thing, and that's what we're going to do. Understand?"

"Easy enough to say, but you got a plan to actually make that happen?" Amelia shifted the large sword from her back, seemingly unfazed by Sepulchre's titanic size.

Swinging onto his horse, Evrich held his sword high. "I have experienced many things in my life, adventurer. And one thing that has always rung true is that flesh bleeds. Saddle up, men! Whether by one decisive blow or by a thousand cuts, that beast dies today."

The rest of the guardsmen did as their captain ordered, none pleased, but all willing.

"To our deaths, then," Scarlett muttered.

Evrich snorted. "I will not ask you to follow me, if cowardice drives you, and honour means nothing to your ilk."

Rolt hopped on Obsidian, his sword drawn and ready to strike. He nodded to Scarlett, the meaning unknown even to her.

Amelia saddled up as well, cantering next to Glaive. "Come on, pretty boy. Sooner we strike, the sooner that thing dies." Her broad smile was invigorating, yet it could not hide the doubts hidden just beneath her quivering lips.

Glaive pulled his halberd free, arms shaking but moving nonetheless. "Damn it all, fine! If I die today, then let it be as a warrior." His own horse, Skipper, whinnied as his armoured bulk pressed down on the animal's broad back.

"Well, aren't we all just a bunch of heroes?" Scarlett groaned. Looking up at Sepulchre, she couldn't help but focus in on the malevolent eye raking the clouds, its beige colouring blotting out the sky's blues and grays. Only the thought of Talon, and the man's stubbornness, kept her feet steady. Ruby didn't make a sound as Scarlett slid into her saddle, and the woman patted the horse's red mane.

"Haha!" Torden roared with raised fist, Goddard struggling to get the dwarf back into the strange collection of belts keeping him tied to Snapper's saddle. "A true fight! Worthy a song or two, eh?" Strapped in, he loosened his ax until it was firmly within his burly hands. "Come on now, no sour faces! Aggoth may favour ya, but only if ya lot put yer whole back inta each swing."

Everyone grumbled at the dwarf's enthusiasm, except for Evrich who roared along with him. "To arms, men! Death comes for us all, but I'll be damned if we don't take that monster down with us!" The captain spurred his horse into action, roaring a bestial cry, taking point as the other riders followed.

Their pounding march deafened those within it. The passing minutes felt like only moments, adrenaline warping how they processed time, and before they knew it, they were approaching Fallkirk's toppled walls. The chapel's bell sat snug in the dead earth, an annoyance to dash around as the riders entered Sepulchre's newest hunting ground.

"There!" Evrich pointed his sword at the central mass holding Sepulchre's eye, the body swinging itself around, taunting them. "We'll aim for the main body and see if we can't get a lucky hit on it."

Debris exploded around them, the *boom crack* leaving

Scarlett in a constant daze.

A guard she didn't know screamed, a large chunk of stone spearing through man and horse, leaving behind bloody mist. No one looked back, needing every moment to weave around the meteoric onslaught, the whipping tendrils sending buildings, stalls, and wagons flying from their precarious footholds, each leaving behind their own wood- and stone-filled craters.

Another guard went flying as a tentacle burst from the ground beneath them, his screams dying out as dirt and blood battered the other riders.

"Don't stop!" Evrich screamed, his face contorting in rage with each man lost, his sword held high as they closed in on the center. Just as the captain neared Sepulchre, ready to strike, the abomination attacked first, twisting its gargantuan carapace and diving towards them. Evrich's horse reacted without its rider's input, veering just in time to dodge the boney fangs that raced past.

Scarlett jerked Ruby's reins, twisting the other direction, missed by mere centimeters as Sepulchre's head dragged through destroyed roads, eating up another two guards before shooting back up.

Multiple blades hit its fleshy shell in return, none able to break through, bouncing off with quiet *twangs*.

"Shit!' Glaive cried out, his halberd throwing him off balance and unsaddling him. The warrior crashed to the ground, his heavy armour clanking and rattling as he rolled, throwing up short dust clouds. Panicked, Skipper fled, paying no mind to his grounded rider.

Cursing under her breath, Scarlett snapped Ruby's reins, pushing her into a dash. The redhead stuck her arm out, slowing enough that Glaive, still clambering to his feet, was able to grab it and jump up into her saddle.

"We're not going to break its shell," the warrior said between coughs, his visor caked with dirt.

"Well, it's not like we have many other options!' Scarlett's voice was hoarse, her throat dry and sore. Her legs ached, pressed too hard against Ruby's sides, her body too tense to do anything but hold on and pray. "Its eye is the damned thing's only weak spot, and I don't know how we're gonna reach it without wings."

As if hearing her, Sepulchre came down for another blow, too far away for Scarlett to see the results of this attack but hearing the screams and shouts of yet more people.

"Spread out!" Evrich commanded from somewhere beyond her sight, his voice punctuated by Sepulchre's delighted shrieks.

"Scarlett!" Amelia called out, rounding towards them, having flanked around the beast. She pulled up short of the other two adventurers, turning her horse around and spurring her back into a run just as Scarlett caught up, staying in sync. "Hey, darling. Good to see you're alive still too." Her smile was thin, not a single tooth showing through tight lips.

Face hidden behind his helm, Glaive's expression was hidden to all, but the tremor in his voice betrayed his image. "Pure luck, that's all. Where's Rolt?"

Scarlett furrowed her brow as Amelia shrugged.

"Disappeared," the amazon said. "Thought he was with you."

Rolt had done many crazy things in his life, most for the good of others or to put food in his belly. Rarely did he risk his life over something personal, especially when others were at risk. But his sword, the black blade still stuck within Sepulchre's sclera, was the exception. It was worth the risk.

Or so he told himself, thick fingers clinging to the edges of the abomination's plated skin, dragging himself up its serpentine form. Having narrowly avoided Sepulchre's second lunge, he had abandoned Obsidian for his suicidal climb. Pushing back his fear and regret, and the memory of solid ground, he continued, every meter gained a small victory.

The wind lashed against his face, growing stronger the closer he got to the clouds. Even standing upright, Sepulchre swung from side-to-side, shaking and roaring between attacks. Clinging tight, Rolt pressed himself flat as the abomination stirred, diving down for its third assault.

Goddard didn't have time to turn, Snapper's aggressive but ultimately weak temperament leaving the horse in a frenzy, bucking and kicking and fighting against the reins.

"Come at me then!" Torden roared, his ax held high, as Sepulchre rushed them down, the foolhardy dwarf hoping to face the beast's gaping maw head on.

With his few remaining seconds, Goddard slashed the belts keeping Torden saddled and shoved him aside, sending the dwarf tumbling out of the beast's path before its massive jaws cast a shadow over him mere moments after.

Raising his sword high, a final act of defiance, the private roared: "FOR MARBLETON!"

Captain Evrich yelled something in the distance, but Goddard could make out none of the words as a thousand teeth clamped around him, his final thoughts of his sister and his home.

Selora struggled to her knees, a powerful roar bringing her back to reality. The sky was completely dark now, the rain and thunder to come a matter of when, opposed to if. Groaning, she pushed off the ground, unsteady feet supporting an unready mind. Sepulchre still raged, diving to the ground before rising back up to touch the sky, rippling veins growing to the edge of bursting. People screamed with anger and pain, a new melody slamming into the elf, rocking her back.

She kept her feet barely, teeth clamped as her ears rang. The numbness was gone, replaced by the desire for quiet, to silence the shrieking and the dying. Her senses sharpening as her focus tightened, she felt the horse's presence before she saw it, its dirty-brown coat lacking the perfect sheen of finer steeds. Selora nodded at the horse, greeting it as she had been taught, invoking the name of her mother-goddess. "Hello, son of *Ma'tura*. May I ask your name?"

The horse neighed, stomping a hoof. *Am Skipper. Master fell from back. Need help.*

Selora nodded, this time in acknowledgement. Sweat ran cold down her back, but a request had been made of her, and so she bit her cheek and fought through the fear. "I too could use some help, from you. Will you assist me, so that I may help you?"

Skipper snorted, turning its broadside to her. *We go together.*

With a third and final nod, Selora took up the reins and swung into the saddle, unslinging her bow in one fluid movement. Clicking her heels, the pair rode towards the battle raging before them.

CHAPTER 32

Screams rose and fell behind him, Talon refusing to look at those plummeting to their deaths, lest pity push him to abandon his climb. The toes of his boots boiled to char, his skin bubbling and smoking with each grasping claw and forced step up Sepulchre's acidic lining. Cotton, wool and even leather disintegrated from the merest touch of the caustic fluids. Magic buzzed around him in a constant hum, body fighting to stave off the lethal damage, lungs burning. Each time Sepulchre bucked and dived, he slammed against the beast's innards, the full-body shock causing him to black out, seconds disappearing each time.

He squeezed his eyes shut, lips tight, the pain pushing away any thought besides that of escape. The shuddering came to a stop once more, and he allowed his eyes to open, just in time to hear more screaming. This new voice mixed with the bellowing squeal of a horse, the animal's outline cast in blue amidst the dark pit. Hidden behind the standard attire of Marbleton's guard, the rider's identity was lost to Talon, the man's mangled war cry transformed into incomprehensible agony as he plummeted into the stomach acid below.

Adding another tally to the count of people he'd failed to save, Talon continued his climb, praying for an end to his pain to whichever gods would listen.

Evrich's cry drowned his sensibilities, spurring his horse

to its limits, disposing of his one-handed sword in favour of the claymore strapped to his back. Raising it high above his head with both hands, he rode to Sepulchre's base, and swung. The blade smacked against the hard flesh before bouncing off, a solid hit that rattled and numbed Evrich's arms. Off balance, he struggled to right himself, horse taking him out of harm's reach as Sepulchre trembled, the abomination's massive bulk throwing up dirt and stone around it.

The debris dinged his armour, forcing him to grab hold of the reins to sit upright again. "Kill it! KILL THE BEAST!" He shouted, rage blinding him, no longer aware of anything but his sword and the monster he intended to kill with it. Pulling the reins in tight, he directed his mount back around in a semi-circle, sword poised against his shoulder for another strike.

He felt, or at least believed he did, the beast's animosity towards them. It hated them, taking pleasure in their struggles, their pain. It *laughed* at him, spurring the captain on, pushing forward faster and faster. Raising his sword again, he swung, putting the entirety of his body into the attack.

Steel bit through flesh, barely chipping the first layer, but it was enough. Enough for the sword to catch, the plated exoskeleton gripping the weapon tight in bubbling secretions, pulling Evrich back. Tugged from the saddle, while at the same time the momentum too much for him to keep a grip on his weapon, Evrich flew. He hit the ground almost instantly, bouncing several times before skidding to a stop, the bulk of his armour bruising him with each tumbling impact.

A constant, throbbing pain scrambled his brain, bruised fingers digging trails into the dead earth, his muscles and joints screaming. Evrich slid his knees under himself, feet slipping as he slowly pushed himself up, forehead pressed against the dirt. His body refused to listen, his legs slipping and kicking out, undoing his attempts at righting himself. He ached everywhere, every action, no matter how slight, causing him to seize. Adrenaline did little more than dull the agony.

Taking rasping breaths, Evrich tore helm from head, tossing it to the side. Freed from its constraints, his ears ringing, the captain gasped as water hit his balled fist. The rain came suddenly, the sudden downpour strong, a god's tears to wash away the filth covering the land. Thunder boomed, flashes of lightning accentuating the boils and pus lathering Sepulchre's weeping hide. The noise muffled the beast's roars, an unexpected reprieve from its gurgling laughter. Struggling to his knees, Evrich stared up, Marbleton's killer a titanic tower leering over him, giving him no attention as it lashed out, screaming.

He screamed along with it.

Scarlett groaned in Ruby's saddle, blood dripping down her temple where the ancient stone had struck.

Glaive struggled with the mare's reins, directing her away from Sepulchre and its chaotic rage. With the rain, the abomination's thrashing became wilder, uprooting more of itself from the earth, and more debris with it. Hard dirt and old stone bounced off steel, Glaive left undisturbed by the assault, using his body to cover and defend the unconscious redhead laying against his chest.

He glanced over his shoulder, Amelia still strafing around Sepulchre, her two-handed sword doing little but creating sparks against its thick carapace. She'd sent him away a moment after Scarlett was struck, only to return when he'd found a safe place for her. But as his eyes strayed up, the dark clouds overhead a swirling vortex over the creature, he wondered how far he would need to ride to find such a luxury. Pulling his gaze from the unfolding catastrophe, he spurred Ruby further onwards.

Scarlett moaned, her breathing heavy. He would need to bandage her wound before anything else.

—— • ——

Sepulchre screamed at the storm above, bristling against nature's rising anger.

Rolt neared the top, his sword within sight. His hands itched to feel its supple grip once more, comfortable and kind, not like the rough and uncaring leather wrapped around the mass-produced sword still strapped to his back. Able to stand upright now but not wanting to risk being thrown off, he stayed low, loping like a four-legged beast, bounding past the edge of Sepulchre's lipless mouth towards its bloodshot eye. Towards the black blade Scarlett had wedged within it.

Rain and thunder masked his approach, lightning giving him sight only when he needed it, using the split-second of illumination to judge distance, and leap. Preternatural strength carried him the whole way, arresting his speed by gripping the black sword with both hands. His weight dragged the weapon along with him, tearing through the misty cornea.

Sepulchre reacted immediately, tossing its head and thrashing, anguished cries filling the rumbling sky.

Rolt tried to ground in his heels, sword twisting and slicing with each throw of Sepulchre's serpentine head. Given no traction and nothing to dig into, he went with the beast's rhythm, boots sliding against the eye's slick surface and turbulent curves, more rheum discharging as the wound sealed and reopened.

Thunder and lightning exploded alongside the abomination's anguished dance, a grim play to entertain the dead lands surrounding them. Within the ghastly ensemble Rolt saw hands reaching from the beast's mouth, its jaws constantly agape alongside its cries. Two hands only, clad in cerulean, bringing forth Talon's blackened skin, his azure orbs meeting with Rolt's. His fingers, still steaming, dug deep into Sepulchre's pustulent flesh, his tattered soles pushing against boney teeth.

Pain drove the rogue forward, his eyes watering from the

steam, his body trembling. His lips tried to fuse, staying separated only by the constant snarl etched from his face, teeth clamped tight as his nostrils flared. The only thing that escaped his lungs was a pitiful moan, and a growl that would have once been beastly but was now more akin to an injured animal's mewling.

Spurred into action, as he always was, Rolt charged, dragging his obsidian blade beside him, keeping him upright during his lopsided gait. Lightning struck in quick succession, in time with every third step he took, each electrical lance coming in closer than the last. Nearing the edge of Sepulchre's eye, where the hardened flesh began, Rolt braced. Doubting he could so easily slice through the leathery carapace, he bunched up his legs, and once again leaped through the air.

His arms flung upwards, bearing his sword high over his head. For a moment, his flight was done in silence, shrouded in darkness. Then a bolt the colour of gold struck, meeting the tip of his blade, arcing down the obsidian, wrapping under his arms and to the tips of his toes. Rolt's feet hit moments after, the lightning spreading through him to set aflame the stolen flesh and corrupted veins beneath.

The rain was solemn, the clouds angry, yet the lightning had no voice of its own, the booming of thunder merely a natural side effect. Unlike the slaughtered earth, the lightning was very much alive, a golden hammer striking Sepulchre at its highest peak. Electricity crawled over its body, bursting boils and spasming plates, its scales flaring out uncontrollably.

Skipper hopped over a fallen tree without prompting, Selora too distracted by Sepulchre and the aberrant storm to lead, her bow bouncing at her side, forgotten in her loose grip. More flashes of light erupted all around, golden bolts striking each writhing tentacle in a sustained assault, deafening *booms* announcing their arrival. The smaller appendages burst almost instantaneously, too little mass to sustain themselves against the overwhelming force of impact. The larger limbs survived the initial blasts, chunks blown from their sides, burning to a crisp in short order anyway. These pyres burned for minutes, their lightning leashes present the whole time, never letting Sepulchre escape their electric burn.

Skipper had slowed without Selora noticing, her eyes fixated on the diminishing appendages, the disgusting creature twisting into a bright and strangely beautiful art piece. Dark clouds lashing out with golden rays, taming fire to strike the titanic beast down. Were I a painter, she thought, I might be inspired. But instead, she was relieved, the pain in her head gone completely, her limbs no longer heavy and numb. Her fingers traced the grip of her bow and felt joy at the rough leather, her vision no longer losing focus when staring into the beast. She was right again, yet still the lightning spoke with no voice, the rain receding and the clouds parting as their work finished.

They were falling, he and Rolt. Tumbling really, but with burned nerves and pain overloading his mind, Talon couldn't rightly tell the difference. Scorched eyes perceived only flashes of colour: shades of gold, reds, oranges, yellows, and the flash of blue when his own body rolled into his vision. Jumbled noise unraveled into crackling flames and piercing shrieks as his ears popped and acid burns scabbed over, splitting once more as he bounced off Sepulchre's serpentine form.

Stronger still than any of those sensations was Sepulchre's horrifying voice, booming echoes in his head. No longer were there any words, mocking or genuine, only the anguished screaming of a dying thing. It followed him down, a noisome, pestering cacophony that refused to leave him. Bruised and battered, the contusions no worse than the burns or singed lungs, Talon landed with a splash in muddy water.

He blinked, unable to move, or even speak. Barely breathing, he watched the flames swallowing up the sky, the inferno blocking in his vision. Steam rose from his own body, disappearing quickly in the hard rain, the weather doing little to evaporate the bitter tang crawling along his tongue. Slowly, feeling returned to his hands, the cold, wet earth sloshing between his fingers and into the creases of his palms; it was soothing. He had little time to enjoy it before being jerked from the mud, jostling painfully against Skipper's armoured back, a pair of leather-wrapped thighs jerking up into his ribs.

Sepulchre shrank by the second, too fast to be the simple illusion of distance. Rolt's replacement sword lay sheathed near the beast, the holding strap broken, while a hunched figure limped towards it. Talon saw all this through fluttering eyes, then blacked out.

Selora kept a hand on Talon, his wounds steaming as they sealed themselves shut, turning her fingers black with soot. Though not a pleasant smell, the wisping smoke was natural, not the putrefied stench of Sepulchre's decaying influence. Her heart pounded in her chest, Skipper looking around as it dashed at an angle from the carnage.

Master. Do not see. Skipper's voice reverberated in the elf's head, a pleasant song dancing along the edges of her mind.

She patted the horse's neck, the reins loosely wrapped over her hand. "We'll find him, don't worry! But first let's get Talon to safety!" She had to yell to be heard over the wind, which had picked up intensity, becoming a howling shriek.

Very well. Skipper snorted, accepting Selora's task but never staring straight for too long, eyes always straying.

Torden huffed, ax held high with both hands, his shorter legs and stouter frame failing his charge. He had spent the last few minutes on foot, thrown through the air after the young guard's sacrifice, desiring only to strike a blow against the beast before it burned to a crisp. His flask emptied two days before reaching the destroyed village, he faced sobriety for the first time in many moons, and he despised it.

His mind wandered to failures and regrets best forgotten, soon pondering the possibility of another. At not avenging the boy who had given their life for his, and leaving a debt never repaid. Redoubling his efforts, Torden sped up, breaking into a teetering waddle that few would consider a sprint. He made for the beast, where three other warriors awaited its fall, the dwarf bolstering their number to four.

"FOR AGGOTH!" He bellowed, intent on being heard over the storm.

CHAPTER 33

Barely deigning to acknowledge Torden's battle cry, Evrich unsheathed Rolt's substitute sword. Discarded on the ground, and no longer needed by the giant, who wielded his obsidian blade with focus, the guard captain examined the claymore in his hands. The flames, quickly decreasing in size, cast shades of orange along the bare steel in a coruscating collage, its edge sharp and unused. It would do.

Glancing around him, he noted the adventurers positioning themselves around Sepulchre, creating an uneven half-circle around the diminishing creature. To his left, Rolt, the giant grim and stolid in his mission, his bare arms covered in bruises and slight burns. To Evrich's right, the dwarf, who heaved and huffed, his beard a windswept mess. Beyond him, stood the amazon, Amelia, her dark skin and rippling muscles accentuated by the rain slicking down her body. All wielding mighty two-handed weapons, they surrounded the abomination.

Evrich tightened his grip, the soaked leather squelching beneath his fingers, excess water squeezed from the strips of hide. Widening his stance, he evened his breathing. Rage filled him, but he would not allow it to control him, to lose himself in his fury. He would butcher the beast, and be aware of every cut.

The fire finally puttered out, the sustained lightning disappearing into pinpricks of gold light, leaving Sepulchre severely reduced. It was by no means small, a half-dozen horses worth of writhing tentacles, gnashing teeth and that horrid, bloodshot eye, but it was a manageable threat now.

It wriggled on the edges of its hole, the walls of which still burned with the miraculous flames, a sure death sentence for the beast, if it tried to flee. Its eye panned over them, flesh blackened, the myriad of pustules and disease seared away. Boney fangs spread wide as Sepulchre sighed, or maybe yawned; Evrich didn't care to try and figure out which. A slight shift in posture, and Sepulchre pounced at Torden, its bestial roar high-pitched and ringing.

The dwarf sidestepped the attack, swinging his ax in turn, catching the beast between two tentacles, the weight of the weapon crunching into Sepulchre's mass. Too big to be thrown off balance, it lashed out, slamming the trunk-like appendage into Torden's side. His armour crumpled beneath the impact, leaving him winded and unprepared for Sepulchre's next attack.

Evrich and Amelia lunged in unison, parrying and chopping away the flurry of other appendages. The amazon, lacking any real protection, kept her distance, using the length of her greatsword to slice and stab. Evrich, on the other hand, charged in, relying on the strength of his armour to stave off the abomination's mighty blows, his every swing powered by righteous fury. Swords bit into flesh, Sepulchre's hide weak and unable to fully stop the weapons from penetrating.

Screaming, Sepulchre leapt just as Rolt appeared, his obsidian blade whistling through empty air. Water splashed up, mud clogging Torden's helm, Amelia lifting her arms instinctually, protecting her face. Evrich stepped back, craning his head skyward, watching as the beast soared high overhead. He and Rolt split from the tight circle, running to where the beast would land, swords raised and ready at either side of it.

In seconds it landed, crashing to the earth in a slimy explosion of sludge and detritus. Retreating before the thick wave, captain and adventurer dug into the ground, swinging as a pair of barbed tentacles shot out, each one barely parried before they turned into seven sharp talons and began swiping.

Spinning his blade in an overhead arc, Evrich put his whole body into the next swing, slicing off one of the elongated claws before meeting substantial resistance. The mutilated paw retreated at his assault. The captain caught a glimpse of Rolt opposite him, standing over another of Sepulchre's arms, severed and sinking into the dirty pool at the adventurer's feet.

Backing away, Sepulchre's arms returned to featureless tentacles, thinner than before. Behind it, Amelia and Torden renewed their own assault, charging from behind. Though its eye was not directed at them, Sepulchre must have sensed them, for it spun like a top, whipping an octuplet of its now-thorny appendages.

Amelia braced, digging her heels into the dirt, and angling her sword so the limbs skidded up and over her, blood trickling from the minor cuts she made.

Rolt braced himself as well, but instead of holding his sword at an angle, he held it straight up, letting Sepulchre beat and shred itself against his razor-sharp blade.

Torden barely needed to crouch, Sepulchre not accounting for the dwarf's shorter stature. Even so, he couldn't help himself shouting at the top of his lungs and swinging, his ax pinging off the spinning flesh whips.

Only Evrich fell, blocking the first blow in time to save himself, but lacking the strength to keep his feet on the uneven ground. Pain reverberated up his arms, side bruising as he fell hard, ribs banging against platemail. Keeping his senses, the captain rolled moments before a tentacle smashed into him, reclaiming his footing and cutting the attacking limb. The combined momentum of the creature's spin and his roll allowed the captain a solid cut, shearing off a chunk of Sepulchre's scorched flesh.

The four warriors, adapting to Sepulchre's rhythm, pressed

in with renewed ferocity, butchering their way through the battering tentacles. Wailing, panicking, Sepulchre leapt again, clearing Torden in a quick but shallow arc. Tumbling, rolling, its body quickly morphed, shrinking, tentacles fusing into bestial limbs. A head resembling a canine's sprouted from the mass of flesh, the skin taut around its faux skull, crooked teeth taking up its entirety. Sepulchre's singular eye looked out from its arched back, unevenly distributed and lacking uniformity. The cornered beast hunched down, ready to leap again, but held.

Rolt strode forth like an automaton, sword held stock steady, a silent challenge to the abomination. The other mortals, heaving and struggling to hold their weapons upright, walked at his sides. Evrich refused to miss out on this hunt.

Sepulchre screamed, a migraine-inducing buzz erupting in their subconsciouses. The captain knew this by the way they all staggered in unison, his hand reaching for his temple, sword lowering by just a fraction. A fraction was enough for the beast, who skirted to his side and swiped. With barely a moment to react, he lifted his sword, taking the brunt of Sepulchre's attack on the broad side of the blade. Pain arced up his arm and he retreated under its assault, claws beating against his armour.

Then Sepulchre scurried back, Amelia whirling in front of Evrich, her blade singing through the air. Rolt came from the other side and the two adventurers pushed back, giving their foe no quarter.

The buzzing became stronger in Evrich's mind, but he pushed it away, rejoining the assault alongside Torden, the formless noise not meant for him.

Talon squirmed, watching helplessly through eyes that were not his own as his non-self was slaughtered piecemeal by others. Every slash bit deeper into muscle, bone crunching beneath the weighty ax slamming haphazardly into it. In such a crowded melee, there was no finesse, no fancy shows of prowess or practiced moves, only the wild butchery of animals.

Through his not-eyes Talon ducked and weaved, elongated limbs lashing out only to be hacked away in return. Claws scraped indents into armour, missing flesh by mere hairs, deflected by blade and brawn. Talon felt no pain himself, only the mild discomfort of another's, pleading cries digging deep.

They will kill me, the voice said. **They will end me, that is for certain.**

They will. So what? Talon asked. *You are no mystery to me. A beast, nothing more. I feel no pity for you, my only regret that I will not be the one to strike you down. The world will be bettered with your death.*

My death, a boon? No, the opposite. For, if I perish, what will you do, oh hunter of mine? The voice fluctuated, words a serene calm before turning into sharp notes, punctuated in time with each hit perceived through Sepulchre's eyes. **My death will mean an end to your purpose. You may live, but without reason. Surely you wish to be more than a husk?**

I am more than you. He growled, or perhaps it was Sepulchre who did?

You are a hunter, soon to be without prey. We are alike in that way.

A blade, too fast to tell its origins, sliced deep into their shoulder. Sepulchre screamed, the psychic backlash rocking through and disrupting the pair's mental connection.

Talon believed himself to be smiling. *Perhaps we are. But I don't hold myself to any great standards. I am no saint, nor do I ever wish to be. You have harmed me the greatest, but I will find other prey to hunt, man or beast.*

Sepulchre's pain became more pronounced, retreating before the adventurers and captain closing in. The abomination's words picked up speed in its urgency. **You hold my existence in** *such contempt, as all your kind have, and I do not blame you. I was born to be your undoing, and so I have done so for ten thousand years. But watch yourself, lest you lose sight of what little humanity you have and become a beast yourself, oh hunter. Oh adventurer.*

Talon took a moment to answer, watching through Sepulchre's eyes as it stopped retreating, bunching its legs. *If I become a beast myself, then so be it. As I said, I am no saint.* Though his thoughts were strong, regret underlined every word. What hunter could not even slay their own prey?

And somewhere, hidden within the depths of his own mind, something small and malevolent settled in, and smiled with crooked fangs.

Then so be it. Sepulchre leapt, readily falling onto Rolt's sword, the black blade greeting it in an explosion of gore.

Talon reeled, pain alighting his nerves, before quickly settling and dissipating. Still, it left him unbalanced, his vision blurring as he watched Rolt march the speared Sepulchre over to the still-flaming pit, heat rising as the abomination came closer. Screaming, Sepulchre helplessly waved its distended arms, claws inches from the giant's face.

Rolt braced and heaved, raising his sword high before tossing the abomination down into the pit.

Searing pain erased all other senses and thoughts, until Sepulchre burned away, and Talon fell back into the darkness of his own dreamless sleep.

CHAPTER 34

The sky was clear when he awoke, the dark clouds that had swept over the dead plains wiped away in the evening's dying light. The air smelled of ash and blood, smoke rising from somewhere he couldn't see, his cushioned head unable to rise. Taking a deep breath, Talon sighed. Then Selora leaned into sight, her slender face upside down from his perspective, cradled within her soft lap.

"You're awake," she said, her lips twitching into a failing smile. "I'm glad."

Talon let his eyes shut, his other senses leading. Other voices trailed in from a distance, mostly shouting and too many to decipher meaning from. "It's dead then."

"It is." She fiddled with his hair, thumb and finger pinching the black ends of his silvery mop. "The others are taking stock of the injured and trying to get the horses in order. They're also... burning what remains. Don't want to take any chances, I suppose."

Humming his response, Talon lifted his hands together, numb fingers running along the sharp edges of his crystalline gauntlets, magic humming through them. A dull pain thrummed throughout his whole body, contusions and burnt skin still patching themselves. "How long have I been out?" He opened his eyes to see the elf shrug.

"A few hours. Hard to tell exactly, with the storm and all the chaos surrounding today. Doesn't matter, really. You're going to have to stay down for a few more hours anyway. Might as well use that time to relax and clear your head." Her touch was soft, fingers dancing along his scalp, scraping away soot and ash.

He let himself sink into Selora's body, her voice like music when compared to the dying screams that still echoed around him. "How many dead?

Selora's smile fell at the question. "Too many," she whispered. "Though all your friends are... still alive."

Talon scowled, the dour expression a familiar one. "Why the pause?"

She hesitated but for a moment. "Your redhead took a nasty hit to the head, from what I saw. She's breathing though."

Groaning, Talon tried to sit up. "I need to see her."

"No." Selora pushed down on his shoulders, holding him against her body. "You need to rest. She'll be fine... I promise. Rest now and you'll see her when you wake up."

"You can be annoyingly stubborn, you know that?" Squirming against her grip, he settled in, closing his eyes and muttering. Weaker than he initially thought, Talon passed out quickly, Selora's firm words breaking into sweet, unrecognizable sounds.

"I know," were the last words he heard before the darkness took him once again.

Two days passed in a flash, Talon waking for minutes at a time before his injuries wore him down and consciousness fled. Flashes of colour were all he perceived, a sultry voice whispering to him through his moments of awareness. On the third day, he felt well enough to sit, finding himself in the back of a straw-covered cart.

Scarlett and Selora flanked him, their faces lighting up when he rose, while Torden swung stubby legs over the wagon's edge, facing the road behind them. Scarlett's head was wrapped tight in bandages, though they were bereft of any blood. Recently changed, perhaps? Ignoring a few scrapes and bruises, she looked fine.

"When did we get a wagon?" Talon asked, struggling to focus through a thick haze.

"One survived all the chaos back at Fallkirk," Scarlett answered, placing a hand on his forehead. "We took it before leaving. Hmm... Still got a fever, but you're lucid, so that's an improvement."

Selora smiled when he looked over at her. "See? She's fine."

"Your definition of fine is severely different from mine." Scarlett rubbed the side of her head with the flat of her palm. "Head's still killing me."

"You're fine enough to complain," Selora retorted, poking a finger at the redhead.

Swiping the prodding digit away, Scarlett snorted. "What can I say? I'm vocal."

"Too much, I'd say!" Torden called over his shoulder. "Ya listenin' to 'em, Lad? Pah, best pals they became while ya napped. Like a pair o' hens squawkin'."

"Shut it, dwarf." Scarlett commanded, raising a playful fist into the air. "We outnumber you two-to-one."

"I could handle three o' ya when I'm drunk. Nay, six even! Ain't got a drop o' liquor in me now, I could handle the both of ya with one arm tied behind me back. In fact, there's this story 'bout a great dwarf, known as Bogtin One-Arm, who-"

"Enough," Talon moaned. "I just woke up and all this noise is too much."

"Indeed. Maybe we could all keep to ourselves for a bit, hm?" Glaive, sat snugly at the front of the cart, smacked his palm against its side for emphasis. "Glad to see you up, Talon. Wasn't sure if you were going to make it or not."

Sighing, Talon laid back down, ignoring the warrior's concern. "How far out are we from Brimlux?"

"Few days still." Glaive cracked the reins held loosely in one hand. "Enough time for you to get back on your feet, I'm sure."

Talon hummed softly in answer, the five riding on in silence for several minutes before he spoke again. "How many of Marbleton's people are still alive?"

No one jumped at the prospect of answering, fingers tapping along wooden boards while eyes avoided his. Eventually, Scarlett glanced his way, and couldn't refuse his pleading stare. "They, well... two... Evrich is healthy, though he hasn't said a word since we left Fallkirk. The other is this one girl, Lilyana. Her arm seems to be broken or at least fractured and she's clearly in shock. Don't know if she'll be alright, even with time."

"The others," Glaive jumped in, "were either eaten or crushed. Honestly, it's a miracle that none of *us* died."

"A miracle, huh?" Talon moved his focus back towards the sky, birds flying overhead under the clear blue. "The storm."

Glaive leaned back, stretching his back over the wagon's lip, craning his neck to look over at Talon. "What about it?"

"It was strange," he answered simply.

"That it was," Glaive agreed. "That it was."

Scarlett laid down next to Talon, hands interlocking over her stomach. "Think it was magical? Or maybe divine intervention?"

Talon shrugged, the motion awkward in his current position. "No idea. Wasn't natural, that's for sure."

Selora sniffed, taking the redhead's lead, and lying down beside the two adventurers, cushioning her head with a hand. "I suggest not questioning it. Just be thankful that it happened, because we'd all be dead otherwise."

"Maybe. Just... nevermind." Talon closed his eyes. "Where were you, by the way? You disappeared for a while. Thought you might have died or just run away."

"I fell behind a bit, that's all." The elf explained no further, and Talon didn't ask her to. It was good enough for him.

—•—

The days passed slowly, Talon's wounds largely healed by the fifth evening, when he finally found himself back in Shadow's saddle. Others weren't so quick to rebound, lacking his supernatural healing, Scarlett needing to rest in the wagon often, though she insisted on saddling up when she could. Keeping Ruby close to Shadow when she was able, Talon and Scarlett passed the time with idle chatter. He talked to Amelia a few times when Scarlett needed rest, and on occasion, Rolt would join him as well, his silent companionship calming.

Sometimes when Talon looked at the giant, he saw flashes of a black blade piercing through him, his chest clenching on reflex. He tried to shake the visions off, but they always lingered, fading only when another, usually Scarlett, distracted him. If Rolt noticed his discomfort, he made no signs of it, his demeanour statuesque.

These visions became less frequent and more abstract as the days passed, but the clenching chest and unease never fully dissipated, even as Brimlux came into sight and Talon's problems switched to those of the mundane.

They stood by the northern gate, their small gathering off to the side so as not to obstruct traffic.

"This is goodbye then," Evrich said, his first words in several days. "I do not know if Duke Giles will be back to himself when we return, but regardless, I thank you for helping to rid my city of the corruption that was plaguing it from within. I will make sure it does not happen again."

Talon nodded, an awkward silence following the slight movement.

Clearing her throat and elbowing his side, Scarlett spoke up. "Can't say you really need to thank us. Wasn't ever our intention to help anything. You paid for a job, and it was completed, it's as simple as that."

"I see." Evrich shrugged, his every movement slow, like heavy chains were dragging him down. "Very well then, adventurers. Regardless, I wish you nothing but good fortune, and hope that if our paths ever cross again, that they are under... friendlier circumstances."

Scarlett forced a smile, wrapping an arm around Talon's shoulder. "Don't bet on it. We're pretty good at finding our way into cells."

"Just try not to find yourselves in *my* cells any time soon." Glancing over at Lilyana, Evrich nodded to himself. "Farewell, Scarlett. Talon." Leading their horses away, the two remaining guards from Marbleton departed Brimlux.

"Well, come on then." Scarlett slapped Talon's back, turning on her heel. "After we report to Gale, you're going to buy me dinner and I'm very, *very* hungry."

Though he couldn't see it, he could hear her smiling, the elation in her voice impossible to hide. "Yeah... sure." Turning from the gate, he followed after Scarlett, allowing himself to be swallowed up by the city's bustling streets.

"So you two will be sticking around after all, huh?" Scarlett picked at her shepherd's pie, her fork clinking against the plate as she listlessly stabbed down.

"Aye," Torden slurred, alcohol fresh in his system. "Can't rightly go back ta Shadowfen. Still got me some folks lookin' fer me, I bet. 'Sides, I like the lad 'ere, and gettin' some real work won't hurt either."

Selora nodded along with the dwarf. "I don't really have any other place to stay at the moment, and I can learn a lot more about the outside world from a place like this. Even ignoring that though..." She glanced over at Talon, fidgeting, ignoring the harsh stare from Scarlett. "From my perspective, I'm still in your debt for saving me during our first meeting."

Talon considered dismissing her reasoning altogether, but

settled with a noncommittal waving away. "You do whatever you want. Won't say no if you decide you want to help around here."

"You say that, but this place has gotten pretty crowded since you left." Motioning around with her free hand, Scarlett took a bite of her dessert. "Mostly just kids hoping to make a name for themselves, but still, there's not even a spare room at the guildhall anymore."

"Hmph. Always preferred having my own little hideout anyway. Though I know someone who might prefer me bunking with them." Cutting into the seared trout sitting before him, Talon inclined his head towards Scarlett.

Snorting, she elbowed him in his side. "Shut it. I'll have you know that I kept up the payments for your old shack. You owe me for that too, among other things."

"Hah! She's gotcha by the beard, don't she, lad?" Torden brought his tankard to his lips, ale spilling out and dripping down his chin. Drinking it down in a single draft, he slammed the oversized cup down. "Another drink over 'ere!" He waved down a barmaid, who ignored his shouts to take care of another customer. "Bah! No respect fer ole' Ironfist, I see."

Talon shook his head, unable to hold back the loose smile that spread across his face.

Scarlett placed a hand over his, smiling even wider. "Welcome home."

"Yeah... home."

Gale slumped in his chair, elbow braced against his armrest, head held softly in his hand. In the other, one of a hundred different reports he needed to read through and approve, stacked upon his desk in two neat piles. Sighing, he threw the sheet over to the second pile, a magical gust guiding it perfectly to the top.

"Now *that* is quite the noise for the great master of the guild to be making." Jacques closed the door behind him, another stack of papers cradled in his arm.

Tired eyes looked up from their drooping rest. "If those are more reports for me to look through, I'm going to set you on fire."

Jacques placed a hand over his hand, feigning shock. "Dear me, that'd be quite impressive, for someone who doesn't specialize in pyromancy. But no, thankfully for me, this is the research you wanted me to gather on its... ilk."

"Ah, you do move fast." Waving a hand towards a clear cabinet pushed against his office wall, Gale returned his gaze downwards. "Over there, if you would. I'll look through it later. We have time to spare, I know that much already."

"Less so now, but that is the way of things." The Master of the Vault heaved the stack of parchment where indicated, huffing while he dusted himself down. "So, what do you think, after reading Talon's report?"

"Well, he's either full of shite, or we may have a problem."

"The lightning troubles you, too?" Jacques walked over to Gale's desk, standing straight, arms hidden within his sleeves.

Gale nodded, the movement barely perceptible. "Yes, and I assume for the same reason as you. Having his glorious eyes upon us would be catastrophic, to say the least. We'll have to deal with these kinds of matters in the future with... a subtler touch. And under no circumstances can we allow things to get so out of control again."

"Should I hold off on preparations then?"

"No. This will take time, but the others will begin waking, now that the first seal has been broken. Stay on track. Just... keep a closer eye on the situation."

Jacques bowed. "As you say." Needing no sign to depart, he left the guildmaster's office.

Only when he was truly alone again did Gale allow himself to sigh again, cradling his head in both hands. "How I wish you were still here to council me, my old friend. What would you suggest now, I wonder?"

EPILOGUE

The three guards rode together under the black sky of Marbleton. It was always so dark now, Evrich thought, even two months after the collapse. Filled to burst with cinder that refused to fall, and stacks of smoke that continued to burn, Marbleton stood now as barely more than a ruin inhabited by beggars and thieves. Sigurd, his lieutenant finally back to full strength, and Rickard, recently reinstated into the force, rode on either side of him down the cold, marbled streets.

Through the inner wall, its doors charred black but still standing, bringing into sight the Citadel's ruins. A bleak reminder of the tragedy that befell the city, dried blood permanently staining the inside. Empty streets led them past the manors of government officials and wealthy merchants, places that once held quaint soirees and boisterous parties, now simply sheltering those inside from the reality of the world outside.

The dourest of these estates stood separated from the rest, half-a-dozen guards patrolling its perimeter at all hours. The duke's manor, its exterior patched up and interior cleaned, echoed with the beating of metal footsteps. Clanking armour circled around the ruined yard, the garden chopped down after discovering a body hidden in the bushes, the singular boarded window sticking out like a sore thumb.

The horses whinnied as the trio pulled close to the house, Evrich stopping them with a signal. He slid from his saddle, followed by the pair acting as his right and left hand. "You!" He pointed at the pair flanking the front door.

The younger of the two jumped, gulping hard. The older one simply stood, unflinching.

"Come here and watch our horses. Make sure they don't run." Evrich didn't wait to hand the reins off, marching past the scrambling sentinels as they rushed to get the horses under control. His scowl deep and his brow furrowed, Evrich pushed his way into the manor, making no attempt to stay quiet. Stomping up the steps, and pushing past the young woman standing watch, he entered the duke's room. Crashing in with such force that the door's hinges nearly separated from the wall, the captain's mere presence made the cleric kneeling before the duke's bed jump.

"Ah... captain," the middle-aged priest muttered. "I see you're lacking in your usual manners." He nodded silently towards Sigurd and Rickard, who stood in uncomfortable silence behind their superior.

Evrich bared his teeth, hand tightening into a fist. "I have no time to waste, Father. How is the duke's condition?"

"Hmph." The priest stood up, leaning over the duke's prone body and running a hand across his forehead. "He is stable, but remains catatonic. The affliction upon his mind is beyond my powers to heal, I am sad to say."

Pinching his nose, Evrich growled. "What of the other officials? How many survived?"

The Father's eyes dropped. "Only two. The treasury's keeper, who sustained minor injuries, and an ambassador, who had been absent from Marbleton during the collapse. All others are either missing or dead. Though... with the Prime of Law having been responsible for so much, I must say that it might be a good thing that the corruption was so thoroughly stamped out in one go."

"Those below her were unaware of her treachery," Sigurd

jumped in.

"Perhaps," Evrich nodded. "But we still need people in charge to get things back under control." He walked over to the window, repaired from the adventurers' destructive escape, staring out into Marbleton. Its once pristine architecture gone, replaced by ruins and fire. Glancing over at the duke, diminished in form and usefulness, Evrich grinded his teeth. Stopping Sepulchre had helped nothing, and there was no time to waste. Gripping his sword's pommel, Evrich knew what had to be done.

Someone had to take charge, and there was no room for weakness.

The crypt was damp, as it had always been, water dripping in from high above, sliding down the seven ancient pillars of stone forming a circle around the chamber, moss and prickling vines wrapped around every centimeter. From each pillar, a chain dangled, kept pristine by primordial magic, forged from divine metal found beyond the mortal realm. Held betwixt these chains sat a figure, a collar forged of the divine metal clamped unyielding around their neck. Amidst the humid chamber, withered knees dug into the ground atop a large circle of intricately scrawled lines and runes, their body listless, arms hanging lifeless at their side.

The chamber quaked. A violent, toppling earthquake disturbing the ancient serenity.

The chains rattled a violent tune, red-hot seams of ember spreading across the glimmering links. One of the chains, the first of seven, burst. Tiny shards numbering in the hundreds exploded around the room, slicing skin and cracking stone.

The prisoner screamed, curling in on themself. Bestial and raw, embodying millennia of pain and rage that disturbed dust and moss, boney fingers digging into their groaning stomach.

Hunger.

Dying.

Not dying.

Can't die.

Devour.

Must devour.

Hungry. So hungry!

One seal broken, a raw sense of purpose returned to the indefatigable existence, and with it, a horrible call to action.

Talon muffled his screams as he sat up, a cold sweat soaking through his clothes. Multicolored sheets wrinkled within his iron grip.

The first wavering rays of morning light slipped through the fogging glass of a nearby window. Vision blurry, he stared at foggy ghosts from quickly forgotten dreams. Voices mumbled at the edge of his consciousness, strangers and friends, taunting endlessly his failures, praising his accomplishments only to bring him back down.

He was alone in the little shack he had made his home, the cramped cot shoved against the wall. A long chest sat against the foot of his bed, holding clothes and adventuring gear behind an iron latch. Groggy and disheveled, he tossed the white and red sheets away, the diamond-patterned duvet a homecoming gift from Scarlett. Clambering to his feet, the cold floor sending a shiver up his spine, Talon stumbled outside.

The autumn breeze brushed his cheeks, leaving them flushed and numb. Rubbing his eyes clear, Talon made his way around the small shack to a circular opening. Formed from half-a-dozen other houses, an old well stood vigil in the small yard. The following minute was a mindless one, Talon tipping the bucket over the edge, cranking one way then the next. Fresh water sloshed around as he settled the bucket on the well's sun-bleached edge, crystal clear liquid reflecting the adventurer's face.

The immaculate reflection wavered and rippled, Talon

plunging his hands in before splashing his face, the wanton movement soaking his collar. He shivered, frost escaping from his lips. The water continued to ripple, droplets dripping from his face in an uneven rhythm.

Through the disturbed visage Talon spotted a strange anomaly in his left eye: a sickly, green halo, reaching out with jagged splinters from the edges of his natural blue. The green quickly spread out into the red of his bloodshot eye, splinters wriggling like tentacles. Breathless, Talon pulled away from the reflection, hand shooting up to cover his eye, the cold air unbothered by the mortal.

For what felt like hours but could have only been seconds, he stood still as stone. Grabbing his face, he forced the few steps back to the bucket and its clear reflection. Lips quivering, he bent over the pool, removing the hand from his eye, and stared.

And a pair of perfect sapphires stared back.

Afterword

Well, here we are. After three whole manuscripts, a serious amount of rewrites, and a little over eight years, we've finally reached an end. The culmination of almost twenty years of practice as a writer, starting from the very first fanfiction that I ever wrote, thrown online at the ripe age of seven.

Quite frankly, it was a disaster, as you would expect. Even so, I persevered, improving my writing with terrible first chapters to dozens of deleted stories, and not an insignificant amount of roleplaying on forums that I'm too ashamed of to even look at now.

It was only after several years of this where I improved enough for my writing to not be immediately lambasted by online readers (admittedly, a fairly low bar to cross at the time), and for me to develop the willpower to finish my first real story. I was thirteen at the time, the ending was terrible by any standard, and it barely classified as a novella in terms of length. But I finished it, nonetheless! Take the wins where you can find them, trust me.

I completed several more stories after that, but even so, writing this first volume of *Guild Tales* after all these years has left me feeling green, as though this were my first ever go at writing. Though I suppose, in a way, it is! Never before have I had to so meticulously comb through my chapters, rereading them until the words lost meaning, just to be told by someone else that something didn't work or that I'd used the word 'tome' far too many times (thanks, mom).

I've grown as both a writer and a person throughout my time crafting this story, and I hope to continue growing as I write even more. And, hopefully, this and whatever else I write in the future is better received than my first story.

So, again, here we are. At the end to the first step of what I hope to be a long and exciting journey within the sometimes fantastical, sometimes horrific, world of Gaea (and other planes of existence!). I hope you'll keep an eye on this series, and stick through this journey alongside me.

Acknowledgements

To speak of the accomplishments that I've achieved on my own would end up a pretty short list, and would also be a disservice to the people who've helped me get to where I am.

More than anyone, I have to thank my mother, who has supported my creative endeavours since the beginning, pushing me down the path that has led me to actually finishing the book now in your hands. At a time where I had no idea what I wanted my life to be, she encouraged and pushed me to create. And while I've winded through different iterations of this, she's always supported my decisions, no matter what they were. From the years spent sketching anime characters, to my two-year attempt at making webcomics, to being the first person to read through my book and give me my first dose of much needed critique, her support has never wavered. For raising and supporting me through it all, I can never truly repay her.

I also have to thank my editor, Shaun, for scraping through every paragraph in an attempt to keep my ramblings from being too, eh, rambly. Certainly didn't realize some of my writing faults before he came into the picture. For tight and efficient work, I give you my thanks as well.

And my thanks go out to Rashed as well, for creating a stellar cover and bringing to life the characters I've only been able to imagine for almost a decade now. Was definitely worth waiting the four months for your schedule to clear up so you could take on this personal project of mine. Can't imagine what it would look like without your stellar skills behind the paint strokes.

And to anyone whose hands have found this book, I thank you as well, for giving this story a chance. Even if it doesn't exactly fit your tastes, I hope you can find some small bit of entertainment from these pages.

Until next we meet, thanks.

Glossary

Gaea - the Mortal Plane

Lyth'wa - the Divine Plane

Sol'tel - the Plane of Death

Udrela - the central continent within Gaea, home to The Eternal King, and the Adventurers' Guild

Elysium - Gaea's blue moon

Tartarus - Gaea's blood-red moon

Lei'Vania - the Goddess of Life, and Forger of Souls

Zeichfer - the God of Death, and ruler of Sol'tel

O'deus - the God of Light, and Master of Forges

Solis - the God of Light, its brilliant corpse providing illumination to Gaea and Lyth'wa high beyond the clouds

The Lady of Shadows, aka *Los* - the Goddess of Darkness

Be'luun - the God of War, and Master of Blades

Aggoth - the God of Stone, and Progenitor of Dwarves

Ma'tura - the Goddess of Nature, and Progenitor of Elves

Domitras - the Goddess of Corruption, and Progenitor of the Tennim, better known as Dark Elves

The Eternal King - the immortal ruler of Udrela

Sons of the Eternal - religious order that reveres the Eternal King as the true god and sole ruler of Gaea

About the Author

CONNOR KIMBLEY lives in Houston, Texas, struggling to create while partaking in almost none of his hobbies, of which there are far too many.

www.ingramcontent.com/pod-product-compliance
Lightning Source LLC
Chambersburg PA
CBHW032145190626
46814CB00005BA/1840